love...in the aisles

A Small Town Romance

Heather Van Fleet

Jessica Calla

love...in the aisles

A Small Town Romance

Heather Van Fleet

Jessica Calla

Sunrise Valley Series

Tenacious Books Publishing

Published by Tenacious Books Publishing

Published by Tenacious Books Publishing in 2020
Tenacious@TenaciousBooksPublishing.com

This book is a work of fiction. Names, characters, places, and incidents are either the product of the author's imagination or are used fictitiously.

Library of Congress Cataloging-in-Publication Data
Heather Van Fleet, Jessica Calla. First edition.
Sunrise Valley Series / Heather Van Fleet, Jessica Calla
ISBN 978-1-7338974-5-7 (print)
ASIN B08GQNQHMB (e-book)

Cover Image: © ShutterStock
Cover Design: Anita B. Carroll www.race-point.com
Content Edits: Erin and Deek Rhew
Line Edits: Erin Rhew

Printed in the United States of America

www.TenaciousBooksPublishing.com

To our real-life, ginger-headed Bag Mag:
May you always frazzle your customers to the
point where they continue to write more romance novels inspired solely by your crooked
smile and red hair.

chapter one
Charlotte

My world shouldn't have fallen apart in the middle of a supermarket. But when it came to the mess called my life, I didn't get vacation days.

"Yoo-hoo, Charlotte?" A crotchety voice called out from behind me. "That you, dear?"

I cringed. She only called me *dear* when she wanted something.

"Mommy?" Jake, my four-year-old son, tugged on my sweater sleeve from his seat in the shopping cart. "Ms. Ruby's talking to you."

"Was she? I didn't hear anything." I steered us out of the bread aisle, passing the meat counter where Paul the Butcher stood hovering over something grotesquely bloody.

Paul waved when he saw me and opened his mouth—probably to say good morning—but I shot him a look that said *don't you dare*, then sprinted toward the last aisle in the store. Later, I'd apologize, maybe even offer to slip him some free pie the next time he was at the diner. But if I was going to get out of this place unscathed today, I had to do it incognito. That meant no socializing with the butcher, no Pictionary on the frozen food doors, and most importantly, no conversing with the leader of the GOLs, the town's gossipy old lady crew, Ruby Pearl.

Aka my own personal devil in pearls.

The cart's wheels squeaked to a stop when I parked behind a cardboard cutout in Aisle Thirteen—the forbidden location on Sundays in Sunrise Valley, Georgia.

The liquor aisle.

"Paul?" Ruby harrumphed from where I'd just been, the sound echoing through the air like a screeching clarinet. "You see Charlotte Dawson runnin' round here with her boy? I could've sworn that was her."

A beat passed.

For a moment, I was sure Paul would give away my secret.

"No, ma'am. Afraid not." He cleared his throat. "Now, you need a roast to go with all those carrots in your cart? Or are you planning on making soup for Sunday dinner tonight?"

I looked at my son and breathed a sigh of relief. He stared at me, amusement dancing in his crystal clear eyes. "Are we playing hide-n-seek?"

"Yeah. We are." I nodded. "You okay with that, buddy? It's just for a few minutes."

"I love hide-n-seek." Jake bounced in his seat even more, the plastic beneath him clicking.

I settled a hand on his knee. "Good. But if you want to win, we're gonna have to be super quiet, okay?"

The sweet sight of Jake's wide smile and dimpled cheeks warmed my chest. Looking at him tore me from the here and now and threw me back in time to when I'd first met his father. I'd been a shy girl in Chicago, working the graveyard shift at an all-night diner, when Jonah had walked in. He'd promised to make all my dreams come true, and in a lot of ways, he had.

Jake looked just like Jonah. Even at four years old, my son had his dad's wit and mannerisms—not to mention his dimpled grin, bright blue eyes, and towheaded hair.

Though my husband had passed away almost three years ago, I'd always remember him through the heart and soul of our little man.

A whistle filled the air, distracting me.

It was close—too close for comfort.

I stiffened, praying to every holy entity there was that whoever had just whistled stayed far, far away. The last thing I needed was to be caught in the liquor aisle and deemed the town drunk, especially with Jake here. It was one thing for the people in Sunrise Valley to hate me, but it was a whole other thing to have them look at my son like he was some sort of case that belonged to the state instead of with me. I'd lived through that as a child, and the last thing I wanted was a repeat performance with my son.

"Look, Mommy." Jake pointed at something behind me. "That man found us."

Footsteps skidded to a stop in the aisle, and all whistling ceased. I shut my eyes, thinking the worst. Was it a friend of Jonah's? The store manager, Adler? Despite the size of our town, the options were endless.

"Hey, uh," the masculine voice called out. This voice was very much *not* deep Southern, like I'd grown used to in this town. "Sorry to be the bearer of bad news, but we can't sell alcohol before twelve thirty in this county."

"Oh God." I squeezed my eyes shut and clung to the shopping cart handle like it could save me from this moment. *Hello, worst nightmare? Meet me, your victim.*

"Miss?" The voice grew closer, more tentative. "Are you okay?"

I opened my eyes and took another deep breath. Jake huddled closer to my chest. Unlike me, he was all about conversing with strangers—something I normally would've chided him about.

Jake looked over my shoulder. "We're playing hide-n-seek."

I turned on my heels, ready to do damage control—laugh it off, play it off, whatever it took to get rid of this man and continue hiding until Ruby gave up and left the store.

But then I saw the man's face.

I blinked—several times. My heart jumped into my throat, choking me. When I tried to speak again, the words wouldn't come out. Instead, I stared at this stranger, whose freckles spanned the bridge of his nose and cheeks and whose red, shaggy hair, just short enough to look like it was meant to be styled that way, fell over one of his golden-green eyes.

"Uh," I mumbled, gulping down sounds I couldn't fully form into words.

"Miss?" His smile faded, and soft concern filled his eyes, which furthered my mortification.

"I... I..." *Breathe, Charlotte. Just breathe.* "Hide-n-seek." *Classy all the way.*

His lips twitched. "That so?"

I cringed and nodded, shoulders slumping. Southern grace was most definitely *not* my specialty.

The stranger shot a look toward Jake, who was now wrist deep inside a bag of something or other in his lap. Plastic crinkled. What felt like a bouncy ball slid to the floor and bumped the toe of my shoe. I looked down, widening my eyes when I spotted a purple grape, then another, and another slide out from between my Keds.

Lovely.

"Who are we hiding from exactly?" the man asked.

I looked him over. Based on his denim shirt, paired with a bright green vest that said Adler's Market in the top right corner, I deduced that he was an employee. A very *tall* employee who had me tipping my head back just so I could look him in the eyes. And an employee I'd never seen before. I definitely would have noticed him.

I opened my mouth to excuse us—now was not the time to have fantasies about men in grocery stores—but my son, and his four-year-old tongue, had other plans.

Again.

"We're hiding from Ruby." Jake grinned with bits of grape in between his teeth.

"Ruby Pearl?" The stranger lifted his ginger-colored brows as he glanced back to me. "The elderly lady with..." He pointed to his neck.

"The pearls, yes." I cleared my throat.

He folded his arms. "Nice woman."

I almost said otherwise—the truth sat on my tongue eager to pounce—but I thought better of it. I didn't know this man, but it was obvious he knew the head honcho GOL. The last thing I needed was to go off about how *not-so-nice* she really was, only to have it get back to her somehow.

Even though Ruby had been Jonah's great aunt—the non-blood kind, thank goodness—and technically part of our family, she'd hated me from the start. Undoubtedly, she had a list stashed away of all the reasons why I'd never been right for Jonah and why I didn't belong in this town—in her domain.

I sighed, frustrated. Because of Ruby, I avoided coming to the market on Sundays. If I hadn't been desperate for Jake's fruit roll ups, we wouldn't be here today, hiding from that awful woman and her terrible mothballs-meets-oranges perfume that made me gag.

"We need to go." I turned back to Jake. My cheeks had gotten so warm I wanted to stick my head into the nearby cooler. Instead, I chose the saner route.

Needing something to do with my hands, I shoved the bag of grapes behind Jake and pushed the cart away from the man. Jake whined until I promised to give him one of those sugary fruit roll ups he loved so much if, and only *if*, he played the quiet game for the rest of our outing.

"Hey," the man called.

I stiffened, not knowing what to say. Maybe I'd be better off running away. I did that *so* well, according to my sister.

"I'm sorry," I whispered, more to myself than the grocery man. "I have to go."

I was Cinderella, leaving behind grapes instead of a glass slipper.

Not that the guy was my Prince Charming or anything.

Leaving the aisle the same way I'd gone down it, I prayed Ruby had left. I kept my head bowed the entire time and repeated the prayer like a chant. The stranger didn't try to stop me again. For that, I was thankful.

Totally not disappointed at all.

I took a deep breath and tiptoed past a few more aisles. Jake grabbed the grapes again and snuck his fingers back into the bag, trying—and failing—to keep it a secret. I didn't mind.

There was only one more stop before I could make a clean getaway, and that was Jake's fruit roll up aisle— the primary reason I was sacrificing my sanity to come to Adler's on a Sunday in the first place. I grabbed two boxes, tossed them into the cart, and took off toward the checkout. Just when I thought I was going to make it out free and clear, I heard the unmistakable sound of wedged heels clunking behind me.

Dang it. And I'd been *so* close too.

"Don't you run away from me, Charlotte."

"Not running, Ruby. Just in a hurry," I grumbled.

Jake looked up at me again, questions swimming in his baby blues. I crossed my eyes and made a silly face, hoping the distraction was enough to curb the nervous energy I was no doubt radiating.

"Oh my. I know what the issue is here." Ruby slipped up beside me, without making a sound. She was incredibly agile for an old lady. "You've gone and taken up the bottle, haven't you?"

"*What?*" I skidded to a stop, both offended and caught off guard. Though I knew I hadn't put anything alcoholic in my cart, I glanced down, just to be sure. I hated that this woman had me questioning my sanity.

Once I'd confirmed it was free of any scandalous materials, I took a deep breath, centered myself, and continued toward the checkout, determined not to let Ruby Pearl get the best of me today.

"I thought I saw you runnin' from the booze aisle." Ruby tsked and shook her head—always so judgmental. "Just so you're aware, I heard from my dear friend Betty—who'd heard from Edna's grandson, Carl—that you'd gone out last night."

Of course, this was about Carl—the local sheriff, Jonah's best friend, and an all-around hero in this small town. He was a good guy, for the most part, but we'd never really been friends. For one, he tended to gossip more than his grandmother, Edna. And I'm pretty sure he hated me for reasons I couldn't help—reasons that had everything to do with his little sister, Annabelle.

I clenched my jaw. Every time I thought of Annabelle, I got all twisted up inside. Not because I was jealous but because of what she stood for in my life—an irrevocable, unavoidable mistake that was in no way my fault.

Jonah and Annabelle had been childhood sweethearts right up until he'd enrolled into the military a week after his high school graduation. They'd been the golden couple—the cheerleader and the quarterback—the one couple in Sunrise Valley everyone had admired and rooted for.

But then I'd come along—the lowly *northerner* waitress—and stolen the town hero's heart…along with the ring that should've been on Annabelle's finger.

The icing on the crap cake of their failed romance was that Annabelle had run away from Sunrise Valley, and she'd only returned twice—once for their ten-year high school reunion and again for Jonah's funeral.

Since then, the residents of this town hadn't exactly welcomed me with open arms. To them, I'd broken up their dreams with my homewrecker ways. Funny thing was, *Jonah* had been the actual homewrecker, not me.

Irony was messy like that.

"Yes. I was out for Laila's birthday." I headed straight for the checkout without looking back at Ruby. "She just turned twenty-one." Not that it was any of *her* business.

"You think that's okay? Goin' out late at night, leaving that baby boy of yours alone?"

I narrowed my eyes, keeping my stride. "I think it's totally acceptable to hire a babysitter—in the form of my mother-in-law, *your* niece—so I can go out for a night to celebrate my baby sister's birthday."

"In Atlanta though? Really?"

I yanked my cart to a stop and swiveled to face her. "How do you know we went to Atlanta?"

"Carl told Edna he'd seen a strange vehicle coming into town 'round three a.m. Then he followed it to your place, imagine that." She placed a hand on her hip. "Said some man was driving y'all on home."

"That *man* was our rideshare driver." Ruby was so stuck in her old-timey ways, she probably didn't even know what a rideshare was. "Now, tell me how Carl knew we were in Atlanta."

"Carl pulled the man over on his way outta town. Had a busted tail light. He's the one who told him."

"Well, *Carl* obviously has nothing better to do with his time then, does he?" I gritted my teeth and inhaled through my nose.

Deep breath in, deep breath out.

Ruby brushed some hair off her forehead and harrumphed. "Now that your Jonah is gone, bless his soul, Carl's the only good man left in this town. You're lucky he's still willing to keep watch over you and that sister of yours."

Willing was a stretch. If anything, Carl was looking for a reason to run me off like the GOLs were, if only to get Annabelle back to town.

"My *sister* and I don't need anyone in our business watching over us—especially not you, Carl, or anyone else in this town."

Ms. Ruby gasped and clutched her pearls. She wore six strands of them, all of which had come from her six different—and now deceased—husbands. She likely killed them all with her incessant nagging.

"Well, the townspeople might start calling you out on your behavior, if they haven't already. Going out with the likes of that girl." She shook her head as if a true tragedy had occurred.

"'That girl' is my *sister*." I seethed.

"Don't matter. It's only been three years since Jonah passed. Show some respect, Charlotte."

"And what would you have me to do, Ms. Ruby? Marry Carl?"

"Oh, absolutely not." She curled her nose and waved me away. "That boy is way too good for the likes of you."

For the love of God, this woman was going to give me an ulcer. Or possibly poison me in my sleep. "I'm still grieving. Dating is the last thing on my mind."

While that wasn't necessarily true, I wanted to throw Ruby off. No one but me needed to know the truth, that thinking about Jonah didn't hurt as much as it used to. I still missed him, but I mostly missed having a father for Jake.

When the doctors initially diagnosed Jonah with Stage 4 sarcomatoid carcinoma, only giving him a few months to live, I'd worried for Jake. Jonah had done the responsible thing and gotten us financially stable, and while I'd appreciated it, I was still bitter that he hadn't chosen to spend that time with his son instead.

"Well, what's Jake gonna think, hm? You bringin' strange men back to your place at all hours of the night like that. Got to be confusing for that poor little boy."

Sweet Jesus, Mary, and Joseph. The only male I'd had in my bed over the last three years wore footed pajamas year-round and slept with a dog puppet tucked under his chin.

17

With a strength I didn't know I possessed, I managed to ignore her nonsense and walk away. I kept my head held high until I reached the checkout. Six or so people stood in line ahead of me, their carts piled with enough food to serve armies. I looked down at our measly lot of groceries—bread, juice, cheese, fruit roll ups, and a now half-eaten bag of grapes. This small town store seriously needed an express lane.

"You hear me, Charlotte?"

I squeezed my eyes shut. There was no point in trying to explain the unexplainable to Ruby Pearl. She'd just twist everything around and spread her dirty little lies like wildfire to anyone who wanted to listen. No way I would let my pride get beaten down by an old woman who'd had more husbands than I had pairs of shoes.

"Loud and clear, Ruby." I grabbed a gossip magazine, feigning disinterest in her, then ruffled Jake's feathered hair. Finally, mercifully, the devil in pearls walk away.

I shook my head. This town... Baby Jesus himself could attest, if it weren't for my mother-in-law, Paula; Laila's undying love for her new photography business; and the house I owned—the first thing I'd ever considered mine—I would've moved a long time ago. Not back to Chicago though. No way would I go down that road again. But maybe somewhere up north, with less gossipy seniors.

With a sigh, I flipped through the magazine pages, accepting defeat like always, but then a headline caught my attention:

LEFT AT THE ALTAR! WHERE IS HOLLYWOOD'S MOST ADORED MAN?

His name was Tate, but I wasn't sure if that was his first or last. I'd never heard of him before, but apparently everyone else had. According to the article, he'd recently gone into hiding after his fiancée left him on their wedding day.

I skimmed most of the words, taking in the photographs instead. The Tate guy was tall and muscular, with dark brown hair that needed a cut. His light blue eyes though... They looked empty. Lost even. The man was handsome, yes, but obviously unhappy. All the pictures in the article were of him and the ex—a classically beautiful woman with short blonde hair and razor-sharp blue eyes.

The *beep, beep, beep* of the checkout brought me back to life. So did Jake's burp and giggle.

"You're gonna get a bellyache from eating all those grapes." I frowned.

Mouth still full, he grinned knowingly, the sticky, purple juice dripping all over his chin and onto his Spiderman t-shirt.

"Did you find everything okay today, Charlotte?" Becca Park—my only friend in this town, a friend I'd never *actually* talked to outside of the market and the diner I waitressed at—smiled at me.

"I did; thanks for asking." I smiled back and studied her short blonde curls. She was really pretty, a cheerleader type, and she had a kind heart. I could easily see myself painting her back in the day...back when I actually found joy in holding a paintbrush.

"Anyone ever tell you that you look like Marilyn Monroe?" I asked.

She blushed, her cheeks turning an adorable shade of pink, as she scanned my items. "Actually, no. But that's a real sweet compliment. Thank you."

Before I could reply, Jake started bouncing in his seat. "Mama, I need to go potty."

I put my hand on his knee. "Soon, baby. I—"

"So, who won?"

My heart skipped at the voice. Because I was a glutton for punishment, I lifted my head and found the freckle-faced stranger from the liquor aisle now bagging my groceries. He glanced at me and his golden-green eyes locked with mine. Then he grinned, his full, red lips lifting higher on one side in a crooked smile. He seemed confident, not arrogant—something that was hard to find in a man these days.

Not that I cared. Or had time to look for a man at all.

"She found us." Jake nodded as he answered for me. "Mommy doesn't like to lose. It makes her cranky."

The man chuckled. He lowered his voice and said, "Well, between you and me, little dude, she's not very good at hiding."

Jake giggled.

I did not.

Instead, I looked away, yanked my card out of the chip reader, and then shoved it back into my purse, trying to keep my hands from shaking. What in the heck was wrong with me?

"Don't forget your receipt," Becca said, handing it over.

"Oh...right." I smiled and reached for it.

"You okay, Char?" She glanced between me and the guy, something twinkling in her eyes.

"Yeah," I said. "It's just that I'm..."

A muscled forearm caught my eye. Grocery man's forearm. Or should I say the *bag man's* forearm. He'd pushed up his denim sleeve, revealing a light dusting of red hair across corded muscles. A few freckles covered his arm too, and I had the strangest urge to use my paintbrush to play connect the dots with them.

"Mommy, I gotta go." Jake bounced up and down in the seat.

I blinked and looked up, meeting the bag man's eyes again. "You and your little man need help out today?" he asked.

"No!" Because... Wait. Why was I yelling?

"Maaamaaa! Stop talking to Freckles."

Freckles? Oh God. Only my son would give the hot bag man a nickname.

"Right. Potty." I nodded and stared at the floor. The floor was safe. Becca was safe. Bag Man was *not* safe.

"Th...thank you, Becca." I barely looked at her before refocusing on Jake. "You ready?"

A throat cleared, this time from my right. I glanced that way and froze at the sight of Ruby. She lifted her painted on brows in question as she stared between me and Bag Man. I could only imagine what was going through her head.

"Maaamaaa." More t-shirt tugging ensued.

Right. My son. The bathroom.

"So, you need help outside then?" Bag Man's gaze flitted to Ruby and then me.

"No!" I yelled the word—again—as I gathered my purse and put it over my arm.

Bag Man nodded slowly, watching me with an amused expression. Our eyes connected and held once more, his from beneath a set of thick lashes that would have undoubtedly sent my sister, Laila, into Swoonville, population one. Maybe two, if I were invited to stay.

I licked my lips. He watched the movement, losing his grin. The heat in my cheeks went from warm to flaming, and I found it difficult to function—at least to function consciously. With another deep breath, I guided my body away like it was being controlled by a robot.

A very awkward, unsteady, robot.

"Excuse me," I said, clipping past him and hitting him in the thigh with the corner of my cart.

Bag Man grunted. I cringed, maybe even apologized too. He chuckled as I began to walk away. At the simple sound of his laughter, my fingers began to sweat and my knees knocked together so badly that I didn't even see the metal stand stacked high with DVDs.

Didn't. Even. Spot. It.

The handle of the cart dug into my stomach as I crashed directly into the center of the DVD stand. The videos tumbled to the ground beneath us like they'd just landed inside the Seventh Circle of Hell: Checkout Edition. The metal frame followed right after, creating a domino effect as it smashed into the bookshelf behind it.

"Uh-oh!" Jake pointed to the disaster on the floor.

And he wasn't talking about my idiocy—I couldn't get off that easily in the luck department today. I looked down, finding his shorts soaked and his legs equally as wet.

Pee. A waterfall of it puddled over my shoes, landing on the collection of DVDs scattered beneath us.

Kill. Me. Now.

chapter two

Ian

Icouldn't help but talk to the curly-haired, beautiful brunette. What a breath of fresh air. Small-town Georgia, free-spirited, fresh air. Clearly *not* Southern, fresh air. There was nothing wrong with Georgia women, but in the few weeks I'd been there, I'd learned to spot outsiders almost as well as Ruby Pearl herself.

These people were exactly the opposite of my ex, Brittany, with her fake tan and platinum white hair. I'd heard Brittany had gotten hair extensions for the wedding. Of course, I hadn't seen them since she'd taken off hours before the ceremony. She was a Beverly Hills woman to the core—spawned from her award-winning director daddy, who'd introduced us, and her socialite mama, who'd tried to pick me up more than once.

Disgusted that all my thoughts somehow led back to my ex, I squeezed the mop over the bucket of the brunette's son's pee, chuckling at how my life had changed in the matter of a few months. Since coming to Georgia, I'd washed the dye out of my hair, let it go back to red, and stopped covering up my freckles. I'd even taken out my blue Hollywood contact lenses and sported my natural hazel eye color. It felt like I'd been hiding out forever, avoiding the reporter who'd caught me boarding the flight from Los Angeles to Atlanta three weeks ago. I kept waiting for someone to discover me. Even being undercover at Adler's Market felt like being in a fishbowl.

Apparently, I was still noticeable, at least to the brunette. Couldn't say I'd ever caused a woman to crash a shopping cart though.

Freckles. Her kid had called me that. I smiled to myself.

"Hey Becca." I called over my shoulder as I pushed the mop back and forth. "Who was the woman who knocked over our DVD display?" I hadn't been able to shake the stupid grin off my face since she left.

Becca handed a receipt to an old lady—the millionth senior of the day—and waved goodbye. "You take care now, ya hear, Mrs. Billings? Not too heavy on that aspirin. It's bad for your liver."

After Mrs. Billings grunted something in response and shuffled away, Becca turned her attention to me. "What's that, Red?"

I scoffed at the nickname she'd given me when I met her on the first day of my fake job. Becca was continually snarky with me, but I enjoyed her company as a coworker and Sunrise Valley expert. Still I kept her at a distance so she wouldn't look too hard at me and discover my true identity. Even Becca, who was young and seemed pretty "with it" regarding the ways of the modern world, hadn't recognized me yet, so I felt confident that my secret was safe at my stepfather's store.

No one would ever guess that "Ian Cleary"—a nobody from New York University with a business degree who'd decide to apprentice at Adler's Market, of all places—was really Ian Tate, the brown-haired, blue-eyed star of the political thriller *Murder in the White House* and last year's Academy Award winner for Best Actor. I had to give my mom props for creating such a boring, but inconspicuous, pseudonym and backstory for me.

I'd even discreetly removed the *Murder in the White House* DVD from the rack that the brunette beauty had smashed into with her cart.

I hadn't been near a mop in ten years or so, but I picked up the technique of squeezing it out in the bucket after a couple of tries. Leaning on the handle, I glanced up at Becca. "The mom with the cart driving skills. Who is she?"

"Oh, that's Charlotte Dawson. She's a sweetie. Her husband was the town hero."

The word "husband" was a complete buzzkill. "Was?"

"He was our fire chief. Worked every day, except the day little Jake—the kid whose pee you're cleaning—was born. Jonah died though, God rest his soul." She looked around the store and leaned over the back end of the bagging table.

She cupped both hands around her mouth and whispered, "Cancer."

Screw cancer. Took my father at a way too young age. My heart broke thinking of that little kid growing up without a dad, like I had. My stepdad, Adler, hadn't come along until I'd already left for Broadway. "That sucks."

"Since Jonah died, the old ladies in town are always on Charlotte's case, even when she just smiles. Like she's not allowed to be happy or something. She's not even thirty. What's she supposed to do?" Becca rolled her eyes. "She has to move on, you know?"

"Makes sense to me." My mother had moved on after my dad. I'm glad she did. She deserved every bit of happiness she could find, and Adler McDowell and this small town always put a smile on her face. I'd kind of hoped that Sunrise Valley would work its magic on me, like it had for Mom.

I was tired of being the runaway bride's ex. Tired of the partying. Tired of feeling like I was on a treadmill, churning out movies and mingling my way through Hollywood. I felt like a cliché. Moving on sounded a heck of a lot better. Since there was no way I could do that in California, here I was in Sunrise Valley, pushing a mop over a puddle of kid pee.

"Why you askin' about Charlotte?" Becca grinned a half-smile.

I looked down at the now clean floor. "Just curious. Don't see many ladies who look like her in this town."

"You mean hot? Because I take offense—"

"I mean brunette." I lifted the mop and plopped it back into the bucket. "All you blondes are beautiful. But I haven't seen a brunette since I got here."

It wasn't a lie. In this town, every woman under the age of forty seemed like a carbon copy of another. Blonde, blue eyes, sun-kissed skin. Kind of like California in a way.

"Well, she's a northerner, which is another issue for some folks. And you should know we haven't seen a ginger since you showed up either." Becca winked and then turned to her next customer—which was, not so shockingly, another old lady.

The lady looked me over and smiled. "In my day, we drowned red-haired babies. Thought they were the devil."

Becca gasped, but I took it with a grain of salt. Old ladies were old ladies, never really knowing when to keep their mouths closed. I smiled my Hollywood grin at her. "Good thing it's not the old days anymore, or I'd be toast."

The woman smiled wide, her dentures gleaming as bright white as her hair. "That's for sure. And your Aunt Mary would kick our butts from here to Kalamazoo if we laid a finger on you anyway."

I laughed and squeezed out the mop for the last time. Sunrise Valley was full of characters. From what I'd come to learn over the last three weeks, there was more drama in this little town than in Hollywood—and that was saying a lot. After waving goodbye, I stuck the mop in the bucket and pushed it back toward the custodial closet.

"Hey, Red?" Becca hollered from behind.

I turned. "Yep?"

"Charlotte usually shops every Tuesday, and she works at the diner down the road." She smiled knowingly as she lifted a bag into the lady's cart. "In case you're taking notes."

"Not taking notes." I turned back toward the closet.

Still, I repeated in my mind... *Charlotte Dawson, works at the diner down the road, shops every Tuesday*. Even though I knew I shouldn't be scoping out the widow of Sunrise Valley's town hero, I repeated the phrase until my shift ended.

With both hands in the pockets of my khakis, I walked back to Mom and Adler's house, my temporary sanctuary out of the spotlight. The crickets echoed through the night as I followed the path cut by the moon. I couldn't help but think about Charlotte Dawson and chuckle to myself at the image of her crashing her cart into the DVD rack.

I picked up my pace and shook my head to clear it of the cute brunette. Now was not the time for me to be thinking about women. Especially women with children, who were settled in Sunrise Valley, Georgia. Now was the time for me to regroup and relax.

Hopefully, this stint hidden away from the spotlight would give me a sense of who I really was, and what I wanted to be, because God knew that somewhere along the road to stardom, I'd lost my way. I'd spent so much time trying to make it, yet once I had, I wasn't sure I wanted it. The Academy Award was major, but after that, the thrill of performing had faded. Acting had suddenly become work and jobs instead of hopes and dreams. Then, I started dreading going to sets and dealing with directors and producers—people only using me to get ahead. As soon as my breakup with Brittany happened, I knew it was time to get out of Cali for a bit.

I heard the squeak of the old wooden rocking chairs before I could see the house. Mom and Adler sat on the front porch, like they did every night—the picture of Southern wedded bliss, sipping sweet tea and shooing away the bugs.

I took the porch stairs two at a time and kissed Mom on the cheek. "Seeing you like this makes me forget you were born and raised in New Jersey."

Adler let out a laugh as he reached out and gave Mom's arm a playful pinch. "I turned her Southern the minute she married me. How's the store holding up, son?"

I sat on the top step and rested my elbows on my knees. "Still standing. Well, barely. Some nice lady tried to plow through the DVD display, but we were able to put it all back together."

"Mrs. Beaufort?" Mom asked. "The woman can't see. I don't know why she refuses to wear her glasses."

"No, not Mrs. Beaufort." I glanced sideways at my mother, practicing my acting skills to hide my true interest in Charlotte. If my mother knew what I was thinking, she'd go overboard, like she always did. And all I wanted was some intel. "Charlotte...something? Dawson maybe?" *Charlotte Dawson, works at the diner down the road, shops every Tuesday.*

My mom grimaced. "Really? She's klutzy but usually a bit more put together than that. Poor thing, widowed so young. I heard she's been partying with her sister lately. Maybe being a single mother is taking its toll on her. I know she has some help with her little boy, but I just hope it's enough."

I stood and leaned on the porch rail, folding my arms. "The kid looked fine. He was shoving grapes in his face and doing things that kids do, I guess."

Like peeing on the floor.

Mom went back to rocking, but I wasn't ready to change the topic yet. "What's the deal with her husband?"

Adler placed his empty glass on the porch next to him. "Jonah Dawson was the best kid to walk these streets. Worked for me while he was in middle school to help his mama pay the bills. Joined the army the day after high school graduation. Came back with a Bronze Star Medal and was appointed fire chief within a year. The poor guy had plans to run for mayor, and then we lost him."

Mom cupped her hands around her lips, just like Becca had. "Cancer," she whispered. Why did everyone whisper that word? "Just like your father."

"I heard." I rubbed the stubble covering my chin as my mind ran through my recently gained knowledge of Sunrise Valley. "Isn't the stadium at the high school named the Jonah Dawson Stadium?"

Adler rocked and swatted bugs. "They dedicated it to him earlier in the year."

Dude was like a superhero. "Poor Charlotte." My sympathy was genuine, even though I couldn't help but think of her curly, dark hair and the way she'd blushed when she'd crashed into the DVD stand.

"She shops every Tuesday," Adler said. "I'll make sure to put you on the schedule."

"Adler McDowell!" Mom poked him in the arm. "Ian's still nursing his broken heart after what that witch Brittany—"

"Mom." I grinned. "Brittany's not a witch. She's just confused. Where's your Southern politeness now?"

"Well, you can take the girl out of Jersey, but you can't take the Jersey out of the girl. If I ever see that woman again, I'm going to kick her in the shins and give her a good talking to. You don't do that to my boy and get away with it. I don't care how many movies her daddy directed."

I shrugged. "I'm over it, Mom. Really."

I didn't want her to worry. The guilty feeling started to creep up my gut. My presence in her little town was risky for her reputation. It was nice that she'd let me come stay with her, interrupting the peace she and Adler had established.

They'd even lied about my identity. Everyone in town knew that Mary had a son when she'd married Adler, but in an effort to keep my celebrity status out of the town and away from the gossips, Mom had told them I was "overseas." To her, Los Angeles was basically overseas from Sunrise Valley, so nobody questioned her story. I hated thinking about how this town would react if they found out the truth—that the "northerner" had been lying about her famous son all along.

But the truth was, I needed to be around Mom and Adler. I didn't have anyone else. Worse, I wasn't sure if I was over Brittney. Not because I still loved her but because she was all I had known for five years. Stuff like that didn't just up and go away with the snap of two fingers. Being left by someone I thought I loved for so long had shattered my heart into pieces and putting it back together was no easy feat.

Which had me wondering...did Charlotte Dawson feel the same way about Jonah?

chapter three

Charlotte

R ise and shine, buttercup." Laila yanked the bed covers off me and tossed them on the floor like she used
to do when we were kids.

I loved her. God, did I ever. But to wake me up before six
a.m. on a Monday—one of my only days off—meant war.

"Go away." I groaned and rolled over, burying my face
into the pillow.

I felt the weight of the bed shift as she took a seat and
started plucking at the elastic of my knee-high socks.
"What's with these?"

"My feet get cold at night." I yanked them away.

Laila giggled. "You know it's, like, ninety degrees
outside, right?"

I rolled my eyes, too tired to explain—yet again—that I
had the body temperature of an icicle from the thighs on
down. "What do you want?"

She bounced a little. And bouncing reminded me of Jake.

More specifically, Jake and the grocery cart.

Jake, and the grocery cart, and the pee, and the *nightmare* that had been yesterday's trip to Adler's. For a blissful
moment in time, I thought it had all been a fever dream.

"Today's the day. You gotta get up. Get ready." She lowered her voice—likely because she'd just noticed Jake, who slept like a burrito in a blanket beside me.

I lifted my head, just enough to get words out. "We have four hours 'til they come over."

"So? I neeeeed you." She grabbed my hand and squeezed.

"What do you *need* me for?"

The house was clean. I'd stayed up late last night to help make it that way. Then, when the buyers came later, Jake and I had planned on going to the park, then having lunch with his grandma after. Laila would have the whole house to herself.

"Support." She scoffed and waved her hands around, looking like a human windmill.

"Fine. Let me get up."

"Thank you, thank you, *thank you*."

I rolled my eyes, sat up, and grabbed my robe off the bedpost before following her out into the hall. Though Laila was twenty-one, and a phenomenal photographer who ran a successful studio out of the basement, she tended to struggle emotionally sometimes. I think we both did. She needed people around constantly, while I preferred things to stay small and intimate. She was an extrovert to my introverted ways, and though I didn't necessarily understand it, I always managed to do what needed to be done to keep her happy. It'd been that way since I was eleven and she was three—one of the first of many times that our mom had checked out in favor of booze and gambling.

In the kitchen, I grabbed the biscuits Jake loved from the fridge, popping them open against the sink edge. Laila pushed herself up to sit on the counter beside me and grabbed the coffee filters and a couple of plates.

"Did Jake keep you up again last night?" She tapped the back of her heels against the cupboard doors like Jake always did whenever I propped him up there to watch me cook.

I yawned into my shoulder, then nodded as I prepped the coffee.

"It wasn't my music was it?"

"Nope," I lied, not wanting to upset her.

Laila currently had a broken heart the size of Kentucky, thanks to her creepy, musician ex. She could do a lot better, and she probably knew that deep down too. But I wasn't the type to say, "I told you so."

Instead, I turned a blind eye—or ear in this case—and let her jam out to early 90s heavy metal at all hours of the night. I just prayed it didn't last forever. My sister's heartbreak was a prime example of why I stayed emotionally distant when it came to men.

"Good." She nodded and stared down at her fingers.

I touched her wrist. "Are you sure you're doing okay?"

She whipped her head up and scowled. "Why wouldn't I be?"

"Because of you-know-who." I filled the coffee pot with water.

"There are a lot of good things going on in my life right now, Char. Including today's buyer. I refuse to think about *him* anymore than I have to, and I'd appreciate you not bringing it up anymore."

"Fine, fine." I held my hands up. "But you know I'm here for you, right?"

She grabbed my hand and wrapped her pinkie finger around mine. "Always."

The thing about my sister and me was that we were incredibly resilient. We kind of had to be after growing up the way we did. Always hungry, never knowing if or when we'd eat again, never knowing if we'd have a roof over our head or a bed to sleep in every night.

Maybe that's why I'd fallen so fast and hard for Jonah when he'd shown up at that Chicago diner all those years ago. He'd been an escape. A handsome escape, with a Bronze Star on his chest. Someone I could be proud of. A chance to find real happiness when I'd never known it was possible.

"You're right." I shook off my thoughts and smiled. "We should be celebrating."

I laid the biscuits on the cookie sheet, then popped them in the oven. Laila jumped off the counter, hip checking me on her way to grab the sugar from the pantry. Our kitchen wasn't huge, but it did the job we needed it to, especially since there were only three of us.

"Sooo, enough about me." Laila said. "Let's talk about tomorrow."

"What's tomorrow?" I frowned as I poured two cups of coffee. I brought them to the table, sat down, and pushed one toward Laila, who was already seated across from me.

"*Tomorrow* is Tuesday."

"And what happens on Tuesdays?" I arched a brow, playing stupid. I really shouldn't have told her what had happened yesterday at Adler's.

Then again, if I hadn't, Jake would have.

"The market, silly. You always go to Adler's on Tuesdays before you go to work."

I cleared my throat, needing to think about how I wanted to word this—mostly so Laila wouldn't get the wrong idea. She was already pushing me to ask Bag Man out, especially since I'd mentioned—mistakenly—how attractive he was.

Who would've thought I'd have a thing for gingers? Gingers who reminded me of certain kilted Scotsmen from TV.

"*Actually*..." I paused, stirring sugar into my coffee. "I think I might go to Atlanta from now on to do our shopping. At least for a few months."

"And why would you do that? Atlanta's an hour away."

I ran my finger across the crack on the table. "You're the one who's always telling me I need to branch out more."

"Socially, you dumb-dumb. Not to chain stores to do your grocery shopping." She stood, grabbed the carafe of coffee, and brought it to the table, already done with her first cup before I could even take a sip of mine. "Besides, we both know you wouldn't do that to Adler McDowell. Not after everything he did for you."

I winced. Guilt forced my stomach to drop. After Jonah died, Adler had taken up sending groceries and meals to our house. He and his wife—they were two of the best things about this town.

"I'm not trying to make you feel bad, Char, but my guess is your bag man either won't be working at all tomorrow, seeing as how you've never mentioned him or saw him before yesterday, or won't remember you."

"But what if he does?" I slumped lower in my chair.

"Then more power to you for being memorable."

I pursed my lips. "Memorable" was most definitely not the word I'd use for my humiliation.

Just the thought of facing that man again did something to my belly that went well beyond a simple swoop. I settled a hand over my stomach, willing the enthusiastic, flip-flopping summersaults to slow their roll.

"It's just that I'm..." *Mortified, humiliated, ready to rely on Instacart for the rest of my grocery buying life if need be.*

"You're embarrassed. I get it. But why not use that to your advantage?"

"Huh?"

She grinned. "I say you work that embarrassment. Tell him straight up that he was so handsome you got distracted. Men live to have their ego sated."

"No. Not happening." I rubbed both hands over my face and sighed. "I'm not a flirt. Never have been."

"No, you're not. But I could teach you how."

I glared at her. She shrugged.

"Seriously." She pointed the end of the sugar-scooping spoon at me. "Stop being the sad, twenty-nine-year-old widow who's been out of the dating game for way too long." She dumped three clumps into her coffee. "It's time to regroup. Start...*dating* again."

"I'm not going to *date* the bag man." Even as I said the words, I knew they were a lie. Because if that man so much as breathed the word "date" in my direction, I'd likely become the loose harlot those GOLs made me and my sister out to be.

Laila cocked her head to one side. "Are you looking down on someone's career choices Ms. I'll-Never-Stop-Being-A-Waitress-For-As-Long-As-I-Live?"

"You know what I meant." I shot her a glare. "I don't care about his job. It's just that if I dated anyone in Sunrise Valley, it would get...*messy*."

To the GOLs, Jonah would always be an impossible act to follow. Therefore, any man I might decide to date one day would be treated as unfairly as I had been when I first showed up in Sunrise Valley. Even after Jonah and I had gotten married and had Jake, I'd still been nothing more than a speck of dirt on their shoes, especially after what I'd supposedly done to Annabelle. If I said any of that out loud to Laila though, she'd likely beat me over the head with one of her biscuits and call me a chicken, accusing me of letting those old women rule my life.

Which I didn't.

Or I tried not to, at least.

"Is that why you dated the trucker then?" My sister leaned back in her seat. "Because he doesn't live around here?"

"I dated him because he was kind." I clenched my jaw as I took another drink.

"Liar."

"I'm not lying." I totally was.

She smirked. "It was the mullet, wasn't it? *That's* why you broke off your man-ban for him. I mean, I get it. Those things *are* impossible to resist."

I rolled my eyes but snickered under my breath at the same time.

Laila dropped her head back dramatically and sang, "Business in the front and party—"

"Would you stop it?" I laughed harder.

"That's a good question." She tapped a finger against her forehead. "Let me just *mullet* over."

"He wasn't that bad."

"Yeah. He was Joe Dirt meets Peter Pan."

She had a point. So maybe Marshall hadn't been the best man to get my feet wet with when it came to re-upping my dating game. But he'd come into the diner every Thursday night for the Turkey Special for months, and after the fifteenth time of him asking me if I had a boyfriend, I'd finally broken down and told him no.

He'd been charming. Tried to *woo* me with tiny elf figurines he'd found at various truck stops he'd visited during his time on the road. His hair had been bad—and he'd still watched cartoons—but he'd made me laugh. Something I hadn't done in a long time.

Marshall had also been an enigma to me, which was exactly why I hadn't let our fling—if that's what I could even bring myself to call it—go on for longer than it did. It was safe, non-serious, easy companionship. We'd lasted six weeks and two days. And we'd only ever kissed one time. I'd hardly call that a relationship.

"You remember why he didn't cut his hair?" I tapped my fingers along the side of my cup.

"Because it was his daddy's dyin' wish for that long hair to live on in his legacy.'" She snort-laughed. "He looked like a serial killer."

"But he had a nice family up north in Kingston and talked about his mom all the time."

"And that didn't scream creepy at all, did it?" She folded her arms again, lips twitching at the same time.

"St-ah-p, would you?"

"You remember those awful jokes he used to tell us?" Laila continued to snicker, most definitely *not* stopping.

"Yup." I remembered all too well.

In the beginning, when my sister learned I'd taken up talking to a trucker at the diner, she'd come and sit with me on the nights he'd show. Jake was always with his grandma on Thursdays, so Laila had claimed boredom. But I knew better. She'd stayed with me at work because she'd been worried he'd off me after one of my shifts. After all, he *had* looked a little like a serial killer, not that I'd ever admit that to Laila.

Laila did her best Marshall impersonation, slow words with a strong twang. "What do you call a belt made of watches, Char-lotte?"

I giggled. "A *waist* of time."

She snapped her fingers a couple of times, then stroked a pretend beard like Marshall used to. "How does a train eat?"

This time, I tossed my head back and groaned as I answered. "It goes chew, chew."

"Boy, he was something." She leaned back in her chair.

After that, we sighed in unison, quiet and thoughtful in the moment. Pre-Jake, pre-real life, pre-sunshine, just Laila and me enjoying each other's company not only as sisters but as friends. In a way, I almost wished life didn't have to keep changing. Jake could stay little and innocent, and Laila could live with us forever. But that was selfish of me. And if there was one thing I wanted out of life, it was for my baby sister to find her way...without me.

Laila broke the silence first. She set her coffee down and put her hand over the top of mine. "You've given up so much for Jake and me. It's time to do something for yourself."

"And *you* gave up just as much in life when you turned down that scholarship to Cal Arts so you could move here and help me with Jake after Jonah died."

She rolled her eyes and piled her long, brown hair on top of her head in a messy bun. "Please. You let me stay here rent free, and you let me take over your basement and turn it into a studio. I have plenty of time for art school. Now is *your* time. If anyone deserves praise, it's you."

"Maybe I've lived a good enough life already." I sighed.

"Buuut, you're lonely and..." She widened her eyes, shook a finger at me, and stood. "Hold that thought."

Laila raced out of the kitchen. Her feet paddled like little motorboats as she headed down the stairs toward her basement room. Taking the spare moment, I got up to check on the biscuits, finding them just the perfect shade of golden brown. I pulled them out of the oven and set them on top of the counter.

Golden brown.

It was a color I wouldn't normally find fascinating. A little plain, but when paired with red hair, freckles, and...

"Oh, who am I freaking kidding?"

I dropped my face into my hands, a goofy grin on my lips. Though the thought forced my cheeks to heat, I secretly couldn't wait to go back to the market. Not that I'd ever admit it out loud to anybody.

What would it hurt to get another peek at all those freckles? If he was there, then maybe I could hide in the frozen food aisle and watch him work his charm. I could see how he interacted with the other customers and maybe figure out if he was a good guy or just someone who knew how to play people.

Not that he'd even be there, of course. Never once had I seen him work on Tuesdays before. And I would, in no way, move my shopping days to Sundays to spy on him when that meant facing the GOLs.

If he wasn't there tomorrow, so be it. That would be the end of my bag man fantasy once and for all.

But if he *was* there...

"Okay, I think this will be perfect for you to wear."

I spun around, widening my eyes at the *thing* in my sister's hands. "Bloomers?"

I squinted, thinking I needed to get some glasses. No way I would wear that out in public. It'd barely cover my butt.

"It's a skirt, you dummy."

"And why would I wear a skirt?"

Laila huffed. "If you wear this to shop in tomorrow, maybe even shave your legs while you're at it, then—"

"I shave my legs." On occasion, when it was necessary.

"You have the most incredible legs, Charlotte." She pouted, showing her sisterly jealousy. "It's time you flaunt them."

I laughed and ran my palm over the skirt's laces, which crisscrossed at the side. It was soft to the touch, light pink, and something a girl ten years younger than me would wear. In fact, I was pretty sure Laila had worn it on her birthday.

"I've got short, pudgy baby legs. That thing wouldn't fit." I shook my head and leaned back against the counter.

"Hardly." Laila rolled her eyes. "You don't do that *Hot Legs* workout four times a week and get pudge."

My face heated. Sure, Laila was always telling me how pretty I was, but it'd been a long time since an actual *man* had taken notice of me. Marshall had barely paid attention to my body. Not even Jonah had taken a lot of time appraising my appearance during the latter years of our marriage. Once he became the fire chief, and after Jake was born, his compliments felt more like an afterthought on his part. That's probably why the spark between us had faded so quickly.

I had never felt truly beautiful in my life. I had stretch marks on my belly that had never quite disappeared, and the surgical mark from my C-section was hideous and still bright pink.

"Just do me a favor and wear the skirt tomorrow, please?" Laila shoved it into my hands.

I held it to my waist and frowned. "I have a feeling I'm gonna regret this."

She leaned her shoulder against mine. I could almost hear the smirk in her voice as she said, "Trust me when I say, you'll be thanking me later."

chapter four

Ian

L ooking good, Red," Becca said from her perch behind the register. She snapped her gum and twisted
a blonde curl around her finger as she looked me up and
down. "Got a hot date?"

Adler, counting out the cash drawer behind her, turned
and nodded. "Looks like you did something different with
your hair there."

I sighed and touched my hair. It needed a cut. Made me
miss my barber in Cali even more. "It's called gel. Don't
you have gel here, or are you all just naturally beautiful?"

"So, you're not all gussied up for our Tuesday shoppers
then?" Adler grinned. "You know, those petite brunettes?"

"Ha-ha." Not that I'd admit it to anyone, but that was
exactly why I'd taken extra time getting ready that morning. *Charlotte Dawson, works at the diner down the road,
shops every Tuesday.* "I don't know what you're talking
about. You hardly have any customers here under the age
of seventy."

As I puttered around the register, trying to look busy until Becca and Adler lost interest, I noticed my picture—well, *Ian Tate's* picture—on one of the Hollywood rag mags. Today's headline read:

WHO IS TATE'S LATEST DATE?

I grabbed the stack, grimacing at the cover photo which showcased my long since faded fake tan and discreetly moved it to the bottom of the rack, behind some dusty old cooking magazines. I hadn't been seen with a woman besides Brittany in five years, so whoever they thought I was *dating* had likely been photoshopped in beside me.

Becca gasped and turned to Adler. "You mean Red's got the hots for Charlotte?"

Adler laughed again as he shut the cash drawer.

I gave him a dirty look. "I don't have the *hots* for anyone."

"Why not?" Becca asked. "Married?"

I wiggled my bare ring finger at her. "You know I'm not."

"Gay?"

"Nope. I just want to be on my own for a while." I looked at Adler, lifting my brows in a plea for help.

"He's learning the business, Rebecca." Adler patted my shoulder, saving me. "He doesn't have time to woo the lovely ladies of Sunrise Valley."

"But Charlotte's as sweet as pie. I always sit in her section at the diner. She sneaks me free fries." The smile melted off Becca's face, and she scowled at me. "You think you're too good for her?"

"Of course not." If anything, I thought *she* was too good for *me*. "Can't a guy be single down here? Or does everyone have to be attached?"

She frowned. "Those of us who are single don't do it by choice. At least if you have someone, you're not bored out of your mind in this dumb town."

"Bite your tongue, Rebecca Turner." Adler puffed out his chest. "Sunrise Valley is the best town in Georgia. Heck, probably in the entire South. Now, instead of harassing each other, why don't we all get to work?" He pointed at me. "Ian, you restock the produce. Becca, when you have no customers, why don't you stock up on Jake Dawson's fruit roll ups and Mrs. Teddy's cinnamon bread. She'll buy three."

Becca took her phone out of her pocket and swiped over the screen. "Betty Teddy doesn't shop on Tuesdays. It's Pie Day at the diner."

Adler lifted his chin. "She called Paul yesterday and said her son is in town, and she asked for a special order of steaks. She'll be here." He looked from me to Becca as we stared at him. "Well? Go."

When he started waving his arms, I walked through the store to the refrigerated storage room. I stopped and stared at the bright yellow lemons in wooden carts on the shelf as I replayed my memory of Charlotte plowing into the DVD rack.

"What am I doing?" I asked aloud to nobody. I'd won an Academy Award, yet there I was—in a produce stock room, freezing my butt off—waiting for a woman who'd been married to a saint to *maybe* show up. For what reason? To ask her out?

"I'm Ian Tate." I tried to remind myself, but the name sounded foreign on my tongue. "I don't ask women out."

During my rise in Hollywood, pre-Brittany, I couldn't recall ever asking anyone out. Women just appeared around me, and I took advantage. Now, in this strange little town, they relied on etiquette, and manners, and all that. Mom had raised me well, but I knew if I made one false move with the Valley's famous widow, I'd be the town gossip for the foreseeable future.

Mom was already on shaky ground being from the Northeast. She'd only garnered favor from the locals because she was married to Adler, a beloved Sunrise Valley native, and she had shown deference to the old ladies who ran the town, asking them advice and for recipes, all while morphing into one of them. She was even starting to get the accent. Last thing I needed was anyone poking around, discussing my manners, and stumbling upon my true identity.

I cleared my throat and looked around the stockroom. Empty. As far as I knew, nobody worked at the store on weekday mornings besides Becca. I was still learning the place and hadn't even met all the staff. When he'd taken me on, Adler had said he could use me mostly on weekends for the "big crowd," but it seemed to me like the deliveries, and the more interesting customers, showed up on weekdays.

"Char-lotte." Her name rolled off my tongue like a song as I practiced the greeting. "Charlotte," I said again. Should I call her Ms. Dawson?

I sang her name as I walked through the stockroom. "Char-lotte Daw-son." When I stopped and looked up, I was facing a shelf of fruit. I cleared my thoughts and tried to plan a dialogue again. This time, I focused on a pineapple, pretending it was her. "Good day, Charlotte. I was wondering if you'd like to accompany me to..."

To where? Even Becca had said there was nothing to do in this town.

I squinted at the pineapple, then placed a hand on each side of it. Mustering up my acting skills, I moved closer. "I think you are incredibly beautiful, Charlotte. I'd really love to take you out sometime."

The heavy door slammed behind me.

Of course it did.

"If you two want to be alone, that can be arranged." Paul, the butcher, with his bloody apron and big belly, laughed at me. "I didn't know you were into produce. The melons look pretty ripe too, in case you're interested."

I tilted my head, waiting for him to finish making fun of me. "I was practicing."

"Practicing talking? To a pineapple?"

"What's wrong with pineapples?"

"Nothing. It's just...not normal to call a pineapple beautiful and ask it out."

I turned my back to him and fumbled the pineapples into a line on the shelf. "You're not supposed to embarrass me. That's not the Southern way, according to the good ladies of Sunrise Valley."

"Well, I ain't Southern. I'm Texan. Big difference." His accent intensified. "And you're a weird dude."

"Thanks."

"It's the red hair. Although I did hear that pineapples are really into redheads—"

"Are you done yet?" I acted more annoyed than I felt. The whole scene was ridiculous.

"If you want to ask Charlotte Dawson out, just be a man and do it. What's the worse she'll say? No? You never heard no before?" He chuckled. I rolled my eyes, which only egged him on. "I bet she'd be more receptive than that there pineapple. She shops on Tuesdays." Paul looked down at his watch. "Usually she's in by now."

"She is?" My gut tightened, in a good way. I couldn't wait to talk to her, to see her, to get that feeling I used to get when I talked to women before I became a celebrity.

Without waiting for Paul's answer, I pushed past him and opened the door leading back to the store.

"Hey, Red." Paul's loud voice boomed inside the cavernous stockroom.

I turned to answer him as a pineapple flew at my chest. Luckily, my survival instincts kicked in, and I caught it in one swift move.

Paul pointed at it. "You forgot your girl."

I flung it back at him, aiming for his head. "Shut it, Tex."

His laughter followed me as I sulked out of the storage room and back into the store.

After two hours, I'd done about three hundred laps around Adler's Market. I'd restocked the produce, checked out the cinnamon bread supply for Mrs. Teddy and the fruit roll ups for Jake, listened to Becca recount every minute of her old cheerleading days, and declined five calls from my agent.

I wasn't ready to talk to him yet. Hollywood was so far removed from my mind, especially when all I could think about was Charlotte Dawson. Charlotte Dawson and her sparkling brown eyes, wild curls, and pink cheeks.

"Mind out of the gutter, Tate." I mumbled the warning to myself as I pushed a new shipment of canned goods to Aisle Four. Stocking the cans was not on Adler's agenda, but I needed to stay busy, seeing as how I'd done all my necessary stock boy duties before noon.

I scanned the storefront as I went along, hoping she'd magically appear and ask for fruit roll ups or something. We'd meet in the water and soda aisle, bond over a shared love of Diet Dr. Pepper. Then I'd follow her as she pushed her cart through the cereal aisle, where we'd talk breakfast foods—granola bars vs. Pop-Tarts. Then she'd tell me what cereal she fed her boy, which would lead to me asking if I could cook for them.

At that last thought, I froze in place, a hand over my stupid grin.

"What is my problem?" I needed to lay low and forget about this woman—not fantasize about what it might be like to date her, let alone be a part of her son's life.

Pushing all serious thoughts from my mind, I busied myself in the canned food aisle, lining up the baked beans, the corn, and then the canned yams. It was nearly impossible to make room for the new stuff when the shelves were already fully stocked. No Sunrise Valley senior would be caught dead buying these canned items anyway, so I didn't know why Adler stocked them. Maybe the younger generation had embraced the idea of canned goods. Maybe Charlotte liked them since she was probably busy, a single working mom with the kid...

I groaned. God, I couldn't get my mind off her. I was becoming obsessed.

Who am I?

In an attempt to stop thinking about Charlotte Dawson, I whistled along to Sinatra playing on the speakers. Adler had insisted on choosing musical themes for the store, and I loved when he chose Rat Pack day. I did a little step-ball-change, a move I learned in my first role as a background dancer on Broadway, and then spun.

It wasn't until the second verse that I saw her, watching me shuffle to the sounds of Frank with a tiny smile on her gorgeous face. I froze. She was a lot prettier than that pineapple I'd asked out a few hours before.

I let my gaze travel quickly down her physique—from her short, pink leather skirt to her cowboy boots and back up to her dark hair, which was curled and hit just below her shoulders.

Like an idiot, I grinned, sure that animated hearts were flowing from my eyes. Then I waved, and she waved back.

She pulled her bottom lip between her teeth in an adorable, nervous way.

I opened my mouth to say something, but it came out
garbled and not at all in the smooth, Hollywood hunk way
I'd hoped.

"Hiyo...hurrrgle."

When I felt my face burn, I knew that Ian Tate, world
famous actor, didn't exist in Sunrise Valley. I'd become
Red. Ian Cleary. A bumbling idiot, smitten with a local
sweetheart and her heart-shaped face.

Man, was I in trouble.

chapter five

Charlotte

There was a fine line between being flirty and making an idiot of myself. At least that's what Laila had told me before I'd walked out of the house fifteen minutes ago.

"Don't talk about Jake."

"Don't talk about the weather."

"And for the love of God, Charlotte, don't go on one of your waitress tangents, m'kay? Nobody wants to hear about the time you found cockroaches in a fryer back in Chicago or how you suffered through fifteen hours of labor before having a C-section."

Whatever. I thought those stories were both...*informative*.

The problem now was, I had zero clue what to talk about. We hadn't gotten that far into Flirt 101. Probably because we'd spent so much time talking about Style 101.

Bag Man blinked at me, a shy smile on his lips, as we stood a good six feet apart. "You're really here." He was adorably flustered, and that made me feel, like, a zillion-and-a-half-times better.

Unless, of course, he was bumbling because he didn't want to see me.

Oh God. What if I'd read the signs wrong? What if his charming smile on Sunday hadn't meant to be charming but customer service friendly instead?

My stomach rolled at the thought, and I turned to face the cans on the shelf. Peas. I needed peas. Four cans of them. Granted, nobody liked peas in my family... Still, I set each of them into my basket like they were a lifeline, or quite possibly grenades, praying he didn't notice how badly my hands were shaking.

"Charlotte, right?" he asked.

"Huh?" I whipped my head to the right.

"That's your name..."

I nodded. Once. Him knowing my name could be a good thing...or a bad one.

Dark lashes framed his golden-green eyes, distracting me again. They batted against his freckled cheeks like they were rustling in the wind.

Not that eyelashes could rustle in the wind.

But if anyone's *could* rustle, it'd be this guy's.

"Oh, um, yup. Charlotte." I laughed awkwardly. "That's me."

"It's nice to officially meet you."

I nodded, cursing the words that had gotten stuck in my throat again. Instead of speaking, I stared at his freckled cheeks like a moron. The longer I looked though, the pinker they seemed to get. And the pinker they got, the more his freckles popped off his skin.

Inspiration, in the form of a portrait, hit me right then—two colors, gray and red. Bag Man's profile, the dark night lit by gray stars...the freckles exploding off his cheeks like fire light.

I blinked, resurfacing to the here and now. "It's, um, it's nice to meet you too."

He smiled.

I didn't. Not because I didn't want to. I just couldn't. I was too stunned by the fact that I'd been inspired to paint something for the first time in years.

Maybe my sister was right. Maybe it *was* time to put myself out there again.

"You playing any games today?" He stuck his hands into the pockets of his khakis. Instead of a denim button up, he wore a white Polo today. The green Adler's vest only made the colors in his eyes look lighter.

I shook my head. "Um, excuse me?"

"Never mind." He chuckled, then ran a hand down the front of his face. "Do you need help hiding from anyone, or finding anything?"

My sanity, perhaps. "I was just..." I pointed to a can of generic-brand corn this time, picked it up, and then settled it back on the shelf. "Deciding on some things."

More nerves kicked in, to the point where I started to bounce up and down on the toes of my boots. Sweat coated my hands too, which caused the basket I was holding to grow slippery.

"You really do come in on Tuesdays then?"

I stiffened. He was still talking to me. Still seemed inter-ested, despite me spewing nonsensical sentence fragments at him. "Um, yes?"

"Sorry. That sounded stalker-like." He cringed, then looked to the floor, nothing like the confident man he'd been on Sunday. For some reason, I liked this version of Mr. Bag Man even more.

"It's just..." He scrubbed a hand over his mouth, a shak-ing hand at that, then let it fall to his side. "Becca told me you always do your shopping on Tuesdays. I didn't see you all day, so I thought she was messing with me. Yet...here you are."

Becca, Becca, Becca. Always running that mouth of hers. I'm not sure if I loved her for it or not.

I looked at his name tag for a moment and blinked a few times. Ian. His name was Ian. It...fit.

"Becca's kind of nosy." I bit my lower lip again, feeling suddenly like a fourteen-year-old crushing on the untouch-able, senior quarterback. "Don't get me wrong. I love her, but she tends to run her mouth a little."

"Does she?" He laughed. "I hadn't noticed."

I snort-laughed and then immediately smashed my lips together, praying he hadn't heard the sound. He glanced at my mouth and then lifted his gaze to meet mine. The corners of his lips twitched, and I saw the humor in his eyes.

Great. Now I'd be known as Miss Snorts-A-Lot.

"Becca means well, I think." He folded his arms, calm and relaxed.

"She does. You're right." I nodded, reminding myself that I had to be careful. I didn't know this man. Didn't know his connection to the town—or to the people in it, most of all. Therefore, I needed to tread a little lighter with my snarky, Chicago tongue.

"So..." Ian stuffed both hands into his khakis again and leaned against a shelf, crossing his legs at the ankle.

"So..." I got lost in the angles of his face. That jawline, his lips—full and pink. Those heavy lips drew me right in, no second thoughts. No regrets. Paintable lips.

In a way, Ian looked familiar to me. I couldn't pinpoint why I thought that though. I may not have grown up here like Jonah did, but I knew ninety-nine percent of the people who lived in Sunrise Valley. It wasn't hard, seeing as how we had a population of practically ten.

Hating the quiet between us, I cleared my throat and spoke up again. "No Jake talk," my sister's voice all but screamed in my ear. "Work your embarrassment."

Okay. I could do this.

"I'm not here to purposely knock anything over, by the way. In case you were wondering."

"Hmm," he said. The noise sent a scattering of goosebumps over my arms. "I've got an empty mop bucket up front in the janitor's closet with your name on it, just in case." Then he winked.

Oh God...that Cupid's arrow stabbed me in the heart and made me bleed with swoon.

Channel your Laila. Channel her flirt. Keep going.

I squared my shoulders, set my basket down on the floor, and said the first thing I could think of. "Well, I'll be sure to keep the pee in the potty, just for you."

Horror slammed into me the second the words left my mouth.

No, no, nooo.

Apparently, the verbal filtration system in my brain had taken a permeant hiatus. Either that or I'd spent far too much time with a four-year-old.

I held up a hand and shook my head. "I mean, I won't be peeing all the over the ground like my boy did." And there went Laila's rule number one, right out the window.

He lifted his brows and widened his eyes.

"I only use the restroom." I continued to horrify myself by trying to clarify. "It's not as though I'm suffering from incontinence or anything. Least not like I did after I had Jake. Stuff happens down there post childbirth, even after having a C-section, and..."

Aaand there went Laila's rule number two.

I'm sure the words "Charlotte Dawson" and "humiliated" sat side by side in *Webster's Dictionary*. I wanted to crawl in a hole.

Ian's lips twitched, like he was trying desperately not to laugh. "Is that right?"

"I'm such an idiot." I covered my forehead with one hand. "I'm sorry. It's just that I tend to ramble when I'm nervous, and you make me, well..."

"It's all good, Charlotte." He took a small step closer, tentatively, like he didn't want to spook me.

"Is it?" The scent of his aftershave filled my nose. My head spun a little, the good kind of spinning that made me wish I could bury my face in his shirt for the rest of eternity.

Maybe not *eternity*, but, like, a few minutes at least so I could remember what it was like to be close to a man who wasn't Jonah. Or a trucker who smelled like fast food and oil.

"Yes, because..." He searched my face. "Because you make me a little nervous too."

I pressed my free hand to my chest. Beneath my fingers, my heart thudded harder than it ever had before. For the first time in years, I was struck by the sudden urge to touch a man. An urge that would lead to me forgetting all of my responsibilities, for once, in order to choose recklessness over reason.

Just liked I'd done with Jonah.

No. *No, no, no.*

I couldn't be reckless. Not when I had a son to take care of. A life to live. Not when I still had a world to explore on my own without having Jonah to rely on. And not when I could finally stop worrying about how I'd feed my little sister or keep my mom out of jail like I had back in Chicago.

I glanced toward the front of the store, looking for a quick escape. The sun was setting lower in the sky, proof that I'd been there too long already. I'd done enough stalking and ogling for one day.

"Um, I have to go." I bent over to grab my basket, but something clung to my skirt. Something sharp and pokey dug into my hip bone. I tried to move my hips to get it undone but couldn't. I was stuck. Slowly, I reached down to feel the very shelf Ian had been leaning against had grabbed hold of the laces on my sister's dreaded pink skirt.

Stupid pink skirt. Stupid Laila. Stupid reckless emotions.

I tugged and tugged, trying to break the laces free from the shelving, and...

Riiip.

No. No, no, no, no, no.

"You okay?" Ian touched my shoulder.

He'd come even closer. Too close. Warm and nice and firm. A man's body. He smelled delicious too. Like pine and Christmas nights.

He also sounded so...so *nice*. Concerned. A complete gentleman. But there was no way I could answer him. Not when he was seconds away from the show of a lifetime in the form of my almost naked butt.

"I, um, ha-ha, you see..." My throat burned while I swallowed down the rest of my reply. I gripped the seam of the skirt and then tried to turn the other way, hoping it'd come loose, and...

Riiip.

"Sweet Jesus," I said under my breath.

It was even louder this time; the rip heard round the world. Ian had to have heard it. Had to have felt it or seen it even. This close to me, his hand on my shoulder...

A voice echoed from behind me. Holding the last bits of my skirt—and my dignity—together, I glanced over my shoulder to the back of the store, toward the butcher counter. More importantly, I found Betty standing at the butcher counter.

Oh God. Of all the old ladies...

Betty Teddy, Ruby Pearl's oldest and closest friend, stood in front of the butcher counter, inspecting steaks like they contained the secrets of the universe. Thankfully, her back was to me, and she'd begun chatting with Paul. But I couldn't figure out for the life of me why that old woman needed to buy meat on a freaking Tuesday.

It was Pie Day at the diner. And the GOLs *never* came in on Tuesdays. *Ever.*

Panic rose in my chest and pushed my heart into full blown heart attack mode. *Please, Lord, let me leave here without Betty Teddy seeing me.* If I made it out of here with my skirt not tangled around my ankles, I'd never ask God for a single thing again.

"Hey, you're stuck." Ian reached forward. He placed his hand over mine and...

Riiip.

The laces came undone first, and then the last of the fabric ripped in half and fell to my knees. I squealed, loudly, and bent down to pull it up. But then the entire thing split in half. My backside was completely bare now, save for my underwear.

If Betty heard me, she'd turn around to find out just how improper I supposedly was. I couldn't bear to glance back at the butcher counter. I couldn't stand discovering if she'd seen me. Yet Ian stood on the other side, and I couldn't bear running past him. That idea scared me even more.

"I...I gotta..." I couldn't look at his face, so I stared at his neck instead.

Such a nice neck. A man's neck. A man's neck I would never get to see again because I was never leaving my house again after this incident. For real this time.

As fast as my shaking hands would let me, I bent over, grabbed the back of the stupid, ridiculous skirt—sans the leather laces—and held it over my goods. Then I ran toward the front of the store. I ran until the wind brushed the tears off my cheeks.

"Hey, wait!" I heard him call from behind.

But I didn't stop. Not when there were likely eyes all around. Not when I was ready to die a million deaths. Not when it was entirely possible that my backside would be bare in a matter of seconds if I lost my grip on the torn skirt. The Cinderella in me was back and looking for her way out again. But instead of leaving a trail of grapes, this time, I'd left leather skirt laces.

God, help me. I was such a mess.

chapter six
Ian

Mom wasn't happy with Adler's Market's choice of beef Thursday night, so she insisted we eat out. I would have preferred a run and a shower because I'd gained a solid ten pounds since arriving in Georgia. But what Mom wanted, Mom got without question from me and Adler—her menfolk.

I was able to turn on the charm—and maybe whine just a bit—to convince them to walk. If I'd be stuffing my face with yet another delicious Southern meal instead of working out, at least I'd burn some calories walking to our destination.

The night was warm. Mid-November weather in Georgia was similar to mid-November in Cali—comfortable enough for my jeans and short-sleeved t-shirt but also warm enough for the bugs. Yet, somehow, autumn in the South didn't feel as stifling as in Cali, or even in Jersey and New York. Everything in Georgia felt kind of...perfect.

On the way to dinner, my agent, Jerry Finkus, called again. This time, unlike the other thousands of times he'd tried to contact me in the past three weeks, he followed up with a text and a voicemail.

"I better take this." I held up my phone, and my parents nodded. "I'll catch up."

They walked together in front of me, holding hands and chatting as if they hadn't talked to each other in years. I couldn't imagine a life as simple and complete as the one my mother had made with Adler.

I lingered behind and took a deep breath before dialing Jerry. He answered on the first ring.

"Fink!" I drew out the word. He hated his nickname. "What's up?"

"I know I'm not supposed to bother you," he said, his voice shaking. Fink had a reputation for being nervous with clients but a bulldog with movie execs. "But you need to know something before you read it online. I mean, if you have online there."

I hadn't checked social media in almost a month. "We do, but I'm off the grid. What's going on?"

"Brittany."

I tightened my grip around the phone at the mention of my ex. "Is she okay?"

"She's engaged again. At least, she's wearing a huge rock. She was photographed at Fusion dancing with someone."

I paused, trying to make sense of his words. "Engaged? To whom?" It wasn't that I wanted Brittany anymore, but I thought the woman would mourn our relationship for at least a minute. We were together for five years, for Christ's sake. "Please tell me it wasn't that jerk from Dubai—"

"It doesn't matter who, does it?" Fink's fast breaths echoed through the phone, tipping me off that it certainly *did* matter who it was.

"Who, Fink?" I drew out the syllables.

He paused, and I knew then that it was bad.

He coughed. "Russ."

I held the phone away from my face and looked at it, sure I'd heard wrong. "Russ? *My* Russ?"

Russ and I had been friends since Broadway. We'd started off as two bright-eyed Jersey guys who had discovered each other during an audition. A few months later, we'd become roomies in New York before making the trek to Los Angeles together. He had started distancing himself from me after the wedding was called off—breaking our plans, texting less. Now I knew why.

"I'm sorry," Fink said. "I didn't want you to see it in online and not know."

Ahead of me, Mom and Adler stopped moving and faced each other, hand in hand, the moon behind them. The picture of love. I thought I'd had that with Brittany. How could I have been so wrong? Now, I had not only lost her but I'd lost her to Russ, one of my best friends.

Fighting the urge to scream or throw the phone into the street, I thanked Fink and hung up, grateful to be out of LA before the paparazzi went wild with the story of Brittany and Russ. The thought of the two of them together made my stomach clench. Had they been together while Brittany and I were engaged? I cycled through our memories, hoping that I wasn't a fool, a fool so blinded in love that I hadn't seen what was right in front of my face.

But all I could remember were pieces of things. I remembered proposing, but I couldn't remember what day of the week I'd done it. I remembered being nervous when I met her mother. Maybe, a little? Had Brittany and I ever spent a weekend lounging around, watching movies? The more I racked my brain for answers, the less I could recall about our relationship.

While Mom could tell me things about Adler from years ago—little details like the name of the restaurant and what he had ordered off the menu when they celebrated their first anniversary in Bermuda—I couldn't remember anything about Brittany and me, never mind about Brittany, Russ, and my interactions.

Who knew? Maybe Russ and Brittany had been having an affair right under my nose. Maybe I'd been too self-absorbed and wrapped up in nonsense to even notice.

When Mom waved to me, I jogged to catch up, deciding to let Fink's news go for now. I tried to convince myself that I didn't care—that I didn't need Brittany or Russ—but that was a lie. Though my feelings for Brittany had faded, the betrayal of what the two of them had done stung worse than the day she'd left me on the altar.

But that was why I had come to Georgia. To dull the sting, figure out who I was, and get a do-over. A do-over for a new me, a revived career, and someday, hopefully, a do-over for my love life.

On the outer border of Sunrise Valley, a structure that resembled a silver bullet, with a long blue stripe running the length of it, came into view. As the moon reflected on the silver siding, one thought popped into my mind. *Charlotte Dawson, works at the diner down the road, shops every Tuesday.*

Could this be *the* diner "down the road?" Sunrise Valley couldn't have only one diner, could it? If so, was she here? Tonight?

At the thought of seeing the crash-and-burn-cart-driving, leather-and-cowboy-boots-wearing, Chicago-girl-playing-Southern beauty, my palms started to sweat. I wiped them on my jeans. All thoughts of my time with Brittany flew away in the Georgia breeze.

I hadn't seen Charlotte Dawson since she'd hurried out of the canned food aisle, holding her skirt around her hips and leaving those leather laces behind, like Cinderella. When she'd left her cart of canned goods behind too, I'd smiled, amazed at the effect I seemed to have on her as plain, grocery bag man, Ian "Red" Cleary. She didn't recognize me as a movie star, yet she seemed as awkwardly attracted to me as I was to her, which made me feel almost normal again. Like a real person making real connections.

After I'd watched her run to her car, I'd paid for her order, packed it up in a bag, and offered to drive it to her house. Adler had tsked when he'd written down her address.

"Of course you should deliver these. Hospitality *is* the Southern way," he'd said. "And if she offers you tea, you say yes."

As an inside joke that only I'd understand, I'd even snuck a pineapple into her bag. But when I'd delivered the goods, I'd lost my nerve to see her again, leaving them on the porch instead. I'd rung the doorbell and run, like a coward.

Now, I froze in place, feet planted to the soil like the peach tree in Adler and Mom's yard, and ran a hand through my hair. "Mom, wait!"

I looked around, afraid I'd given away my secret, but the streets were empty. I had to remember to call her Aunt Mary in public.

"What's wrong, baby?" She turned to me.

"Is this the only diner in town?"

"Sure is," Adler said. "Minka's has been around since I was a kid. Sarge, Minka's grandson, runs it now, but Thursday night is still the Turkey Special. Full dinner, like Thanksgiving every week."

"Sarge?" I snorted. "I know a German Shepard named Sarge."

Mom smacked my arm. "His real name is Bo, but everyone calls him Sarge."

"Army?"

"Nope."

I waited, but no explanation followed. Deciding I wasn't in the mood for another Sunrise Valley history lesson, I took a few steps forward and peeked through the windows.

71

The place was packed. No wonder nobody was out and about tonight. They were obviously all at the diner.

I glanced from one end of the silver bullet to the other. Thankfully, there was no sign of Charlotte Dawson. Despite the many women I may have charmed in my lifetime, for whatever reason, I felt like puking at the thought of her pretty face. In a good way. Maybe.

Willing my feet to move, I took a deep breath and mentally recited my Academy Award speech, reminding myself I was a movie star. *Come on, Tate. Where are you when I need you?*

As we stepped into Minka's, the crowd turned and looked our way, then went back to talking. Some shouted hellos to Adler and Mom. Becca sat at the long counter. She twisted in her stool to wave at us before twisting back to her ice cream sundae. Ruby Pearl and her friend, Rose something or other, sat in the first booth next to the door, grinning at us over the rims of their steaming mugs.

Adler took Mom's hand and led us to an empty booth. I scooted into one side and they took the other. When I picked up one of the menus wedged between the wall and the napkin holder, Mom gasped and pulled it away.

"Ian! Put that down. You'll upset Sarge if he sees you looking. You'll have the turkey, like everyone else."

I glared at my mother as she returned the menu to its place. "Are you serious? We don't get to pick? I thought I'd have something lighter. I haven't even been here a month, and I've already gained ten pounds. My agent's going to have a conniption."

"You needed the weight. California made you skinny." She kept her voice low. "And you'll be back there, to the Land of Fruits and Nuts, soon enough."

Adler chuckled. "They eat like birds over there on the West Coast."

I shook my head and then glanced around. Sure enough, everyone had a steaming hot plate of turkey in front of them. Every. Single. Person.

That's when I spotted her over Mom and Adler's shoulders, about four booths away. Her black pants and button-down white shirt fit perfectly, accenting every one of her curves. She balanced a tray on one hand while pulling a straw out of her pocket with the other.

"We don't have sugar-free cornbread, Mr. Wilford," I heard her say.

I loved the melody of her voice.

She jutted a hip as she listened to the older man. Her dark hair was tied up in a curly twist-thing on top of her head, loose strands falling over her eye. As I watched her, she shifted her bottom lip and puffed out a breath, blowing the tendrils from her face.

"Well, Sarge said he'd look up a recipe for you and try to make some next week." She shook her head and the hair fell over her pink cheek again. "For now, I brought you this sugar-free ice cream. You're not going into diabetic shock on my watch."

I grinned, admiring the way she worked her magic with the diner's patrons. She was different with these people than she'd been with me.

Mom had mentioned that Charlotte was from Chicago, but she seemed to have acquired some sort of hybrid Chicago-Southern accent. As much as I hated to admit it, that voice did something to me. I had never, not once in the five years I'd been with Brittany, felt my blood pump faster at the sound of her voice. Well, not until she called and apologized for running off on our wedding day, but that wasn't in a good way. I wondered if she'd call and apologize for hooking up with Russ too.

Charlotte winked at Mr. Wilford, then turned and strutted away. All thoughts of my ex disappeared as my body tightened and my skin warmed at the sight of her. The nerves I'd felt earlier were replaced with a need.

I *needed* to talk to this lady. *Needed* to touch her too. I didn't care if her husband was a town hero or God himself.

"… and then we're going to take one of those moon flights and live on the moon."

Adler's voice pierced through my thoughts, and I directed my attention to him. "What are you talking about?"

"You weren't listening." Mom reached across the table and patted my hand. "Just trying to get your attention."

Behind them, Charlotte walked toward us. She caught my eye and stopped dead in her tracks, that pink in her cheeks returning.

I grinned and mouthed, "Hey."

She stared at me with wide eyes before lowering her chin. That was it. No words, no smile, no nothing. I made her nervous. I hoped it wasn't anything I was doing wrong, or some sort of vibe I'd given off unconsciously.

Mom spun to see the object of my attention and turned back to me, straightening her shoulders and sitting tall.

"I'll set you up," she said, nodding her head like she'd reached an important conclusion.

"Huh?" I tore my focus from Charlotte.

Adler chuckled. "Don't doubt your moth...*aunt*. She setup Lucy from the craft store with that lawyer guy, Kenny, so she can setup anyone. If you want it to happen, she's your best bet for a matchmaker. Better than any of that online stuff you kids do."

As Charlotte walked closer, I shushed my stepfather and whispered to my mother. "No setups. Don't say—"

Then suddenly, Charlotte was next to us, her gaze on everyone but me. That pink hue spilling over her cheeks and down her neck was even brighter up close.

"Good evening, Mister and Missus McDowell."

"Good evening to you also, Charlotte. How's that beautiful boy of yours?" Mom sat up straight and smiled widely.

"He's fine; thank you for asking."

Mom cleared her throat and caught my eye. "I heard you've met my nephew, Ian. He's staying with us for a few months, learning the grocery business from Adler."

"May not take him that long at the rate he's learning," Adler said, smiling with pride.

I gave him a quick look of thanks, a sort of sideways wink. I hated that they had to lie to their neighbors because my life had become a mess and I'd needed refuge.

Charlotte puffed out her bottom lip and blew a loose strand of hair from her face like she had before. "Nice to see you again, Ian."

I worked to steady my voice. "And you as well, Ms. Dawson."

"Charlotte." She whispered her own name. "Just Charlotte."

"Charlotte." I loved the way it rolled over my tongue. Just like when I'd practiced in the stock room. I cringed inwardly at the thought.

She took a heavy breath, then pushed her shoulders back as she spoke. "I, um, know how Mister and Missus McDowell prefer their turkey specials, but not you." She blinked down at me, fidgeting with the notepad in her hand. "So, tell me, Ian. How do you like it?"

The second the words left her mouth, she widened her eyes and fumbled with her pen, nearly dropping it. I'm sure I was the only one at the table who caught the unintentional innuendo. Mom and Adler were pressed close, lost in each other, like always.

Less than a second later, she cleared her throat, finally meeting my gaze. "How about I, uh, just bring you some turkey with *pineapple* on the side, hmm? I heard from Paul that you like pineapple, a whole lot."

My jaw dropped. "That son of a..." I'd kill that guy the next time I worked.

Embarrassed that she knew about my being caught in the act with the produce, I pulled the menu from its spot behind our napkin holder and opened it over my face.

"Actually, instead of turkey, I think I'll have the Caesar salad." I spoke loud enough to announce it to everyone within hearing distance.

When I put the menu down again, my mother gasped and hid her face in her hands. Adler looked around nervously. The diner seemed quieter.

"What?" I smirked.

"Shhh." Charlotte yanked the menu out of my hand and set it on the table in front of me. "If Sarge hears you say that, he'll come out waving his shotgun."

"He has a shotgun? In the kitchen?" I looked past her to the open kitchen window, where a handful of turkey dinners waited to be taken to their final destinations.

"Doesn't matter what you order. I'm still going to bring you turkey." She shifted her weight from one foot to the other.

I loved the bit of sassiness that seemed to have overcome her shyness. I tried to play on it. "But you don't know how I like it."

She twisted her lips, and a dimple dented her cheek before she answered. God, did I love dimples.

"Well, let's see." She cleared her throat, eyeing my mom and Adler and then me again. "I'm, uh, guessing you keep yourself in good shape. You're, like, one of those guys that wants to eat healthy." She fumbled her notebook, then caught it midair. "My guess is, you'd probably order the no-gravy-baked-not-mashed-hold-the-cornbread special."

I opened my mouth to agree, but she held up a hand to stop me.

"But you're also a secret eater. You have to be because your aunt here..." She glanced at Mom, who raised an eyebrow at me. "...makes the best peach cobbler in the county."

Mom beamed. Then Charlotte leaned over the table, her shoulder inches from my nose. I took a deep inhale and got a whiff of her lemon-scented shampoo as she whispered to Mom.

"But please don't tell anyone I said that." She dropped her voice even lower. "The ladies of Sunrise Valley would have my head if they heard me say that someone from *Jersey* makes the best cobbler in town."

I wished I could keep her close—savoring that moment, and that scent—but she straightened and lifted her notepad again.

"If that busybody Ruby or any of her friends give you a hard time, you let me know." Mom pointed toward Charlotte. "I'll put them right in their place. How dare they give a sweet, hardworking mom like you a hard time?"

"I appreciate that, ma'am." Charlotte lost her smile.

"Since you like my wife's cobbler that much, you'll have to join us for some this weekend." Adler glanced my way, and I raised my eyebrows at him.

Mom nodded at Charlotte. "Yes, that sounds great. We'd love to have you over. Jake and Laila too."

Charlotte took a step back and looked at me with panic in her eyes. Her control seemed to falter as red patches spread over her neck. She was about ready to bolt out again, like she'd done at the grocery store.

What was it with this lady? I hated that she seemed freaked out by me. One minute, things almost felt flirty. The next, she put up a wall, hiding behind her shyness.

"I...I mean, thank you for the invite." She ran her hand over her hair, pulling the loose strands behind her ear, only for them to pop out again. "How about I check my schedule and get back to you?"

"I'd love to see you," I added, in case there was any doubt in her mind. I hoped she wouldn't put up that wall again.

"That's nice of you." She scribbled onto her notepad, avoiding my gaze, while Mom asked her about yams. When a shrill bell rang out from the kitchen, we all jumped.

"I better get back to serving. Again, thank you for your kindness." She ripped the paper off her notepad, placed it on the table in front of me, and turned to leave.

As she walked away, I unfolded the tiny paper, my heart pounding as I read the note.

Thanks for delivering my groceries. Your family's dinner is on me tonight.

I held the note up for Mom and Adler to read. Mom clutched her chest and pouted, letting out a sigh that sounded like, "Aw."

Adler chuckled.

"What's so funny?" I asked.

"She likes you too," Mom said. "Like I said, I can set you up..."

Instead of arguing with her, I shook my head and folded up the note, sliding it into my back pocket.

chapter seven
Charlotte

Ibit down on the tip of my pencil, then zoned out completely. The plate full of cornbread in front of me no longer looked as appealing as it had five minutes ago, mostly because my nerves were fraught and my head was spinning with both confusion and exhaustion.

Thursdays were always insane. Nothing hit a person's stomach better than Sarge's turkey dinner, which is why it was always so busy. But it wasn't the fact that I'd been on my feet and waited on a half dozen more tables than usual that had me so quiet and worn. It was the fact that I'd seen Ian again instead.

Flirted with Ian really. Had a million more *fantasies* about Ian. He was officially consuming my thoughts and ruling my head, even when he wasn't batting those pretty eyes my way.

I sat on a chair, leaned forward onto the diner counter, and covered my face, sighing. The pencil slid from my hands onto the floor. I didn't have a single ounce of motivation to pick it up.

Mateo, the twenty-one-year-old busboy-waiter who worked here with me most nights, settled onto a stool at my side. I knew it was him without even looking up. He smelled like spicy cologne and fried foods.

"You want me to stay and finish your shift?" he asked

"Nah." I waved him away and slowly lifted my head. "I'm just tired. I'll make it." Not to mention mortified and emotionally drained by the fact that my head was at war with my heart, all thanks to a certain new guy in Sunrise Valley.

"You sure?" Always the perceptive one, he tipped his head to one side, studying me. Thick chestnut-colored glasses, matching his dark eyes, slid down the bridge of his nose. "Because you look like you're seconds from passing out." He paused, considering me for another moment. "I think you work too hard."

"I'm fine." I patted his shoulder and forced a smile. It was time to buck up. "If anyone works too hard, it's you. Which is why *you* should leave a little early tonight." I bumped him in the ribs with my elbow. "Maybe *finally* ask Becca for her number? Huh? *Huh*?" I winked, knowing he had it bad for that girl.

According to Mateo, Becca was way out of his league, which annoyed me to no end because he was so adorable. Becca was super sweet too, nothing like the girl he said she used to be in high school. He just needed to grab the bull by the horns and make things happen.

Not that I was one to talk when it came to dating and relationships.

Mateo would never act on his feelings unless encouraged though. Something about his family and Becca's family being too different and hating each other over something. Even still, he was a play it safe kind of guy, not one for taking risks. I could totally—sadly—relate.

He flushed, his cheeks growing even darker, which proved my point, just as the food bell rang across from us. Like every other night, I knew I'd be hearing that thing in my dreams the second my head hit the pillow.

"Order up." Sarge pushed the plates my way, giving me a nod.

I stared up at my boss and smiled. Everyone else in this town tended to steer clear of Sarge, other than to visit his restaurant and eat his delicious food. With his mysterious past, that dark beard, his shiny bald head, and a sleeve of tattoos, he was the black sheep of this town. We had that in common, at least.

He'd asked me out once, but I'd turned him down on the spot. Not because he wasn't attractive—if anything, he was incredibly handsome. It was more because I didn't like the idea of dating someone I worked with. Nor did I like the idea of *dating* at all.

Sarge had a soft side to him, so I knew he'd make someone very happy one day. Any guy who would drop everything in one state and move to another to care for his ailing mom and her diner would always get an A in my book.

"Thanks, Sarge."

He grunted—his version of a "you're welcome." He was a man of few words, but a better chef than anyone I knew. Since he'd taken over the diner six months ago, business had begun to thrive. Sarge made the best stuffing and cornbread for miles, and the turkey he prepped every Thursday was to-die-for delicious.

I threw on my waitress smile and loaded up my tray. I was determined to get through the rest of my shift without passing out into a pile of cornbread.

"You sure you're okay?" Mateo followed close behind. He was the protective little brother I'd never had. "Because Ruby and Rose ate you alive out there tonight."

"You noticed that?" I winced at the thought and piled two glasses of water onto the tray as well.

"Everyone in the diner noticed. Why do you let them treat you like that?" He eyed the few people still left.

Because fighting back is too hard. Because I have to live here for the foreseeable future and don't want to deal with the backlash. My excuses were endless.

"They weren't all that bad." I forced a smile.

"Ruby pushed her plate off the table in front of you like a kid, then claimed it was your fault." He shook his head. "I swear, that lady belongs in preschool."

I winced and wondered if Ian had seen that. Everyone knew the GOLs were out to get me. They had their reasons, but that didn't mean they were right.

Living here and interacting with the GOLs was hard because of who I was. Because of who Jonah had been. Maybe someday they would get past their dislike of me. For now, I'd deal with it.

"The next time one of them comes in to get their car serviced, I'm gonna cut a wire or something." Mateo grumbled as he untied his apron and set it on a nearby stool. His disdain for the GOLs was as bad as mine—though I knew he had his reasons too.

"You're not going to risk your father's company's reputation for my sake." I winked, then pushed through the swinging doors behind the counter. "You're a sweetie, Mateo," I called over my shoulder. "But don't ruin your future over a bunch of crabby old biddies."

He grumbled something, and even though I didn't hear it, I smiled. Mateo was fiercely protective. Quiet. A boy with the weight of the world on his shoulders but never the type to shove his own problems off onto anyone else.

As I went to deliver my final meal, Mateo hung close behind as he bussed the neighboring tables. I was thankful the diner was finally clearing out for the night. And despite the setbacks, all in all, the evening had been a good one tips wise.

"Here you go, Edna. Turkey, light gravy, extra buttered corn, add extra stuffing, and two extra slices of cornbread." I set her plate on the table.

She stared down her nose and didn't even bother to thank me. At least she wasn't as bad as the rest of her friends who'd been in earlier—which surprised me since Jonah's ex, Annabelle, was her granddaughter. A lot of that had to do with the fact that her husband was still alive, thriving, and sweet as the pie. The single GOLs were a lot more hateful than the married ones.

"And all the fixings for you, Larry." I set his plate in front of him. Unlike his wife, Larry didn't need his order repeated back.

"What's this?" Edna huffed at my back when I started to walk away.

"What's what?"

She screwed up her nose and used a fork to push through the mashed potatoes on her plate. "I asked for creamed corn, not extra buttered."

"You know Sarge doesn't do creamed corn on Thursdays. That's why I always add extra butter for you." I sighed, biting my tongue.

What I really wanted to do was pick up the corn and throw it into her perm, but...manners. The Southern way. Yada, yada, yada.

Slowly, she lifted her gaze from her plate, eyes turning into slits as she focused on my face. "He *always* makes exceptions for me."

I inhaled a slow breath, gathering what little patience I had left. "He does make exceptions for you. On every day *but* Thursdays."

Mr. Larry reached across the table and held his wife's hand. "Dear, just eat your corn how it is."

"You just pipe down, Larry. This hussy here is—"

"Do you happen to know the definition of hussy, ma'am?" A dark voice echoed from behind me, laced with anger and disbelief. Tiny shivers danced their way up and down my arms—shivers that made my knees lock.

Ian was back.

"Because I can tell you right now, from what I've seen since moving to this town, Charlotte here is one of the most respectful and admirable women I've ever met. The word 'hussy' should never be used to describe her."

"Oh. It's you." Edna curled her lip, glancing around me to Ian. "Mary and Adler's..." She waved a hand in front of her face. "Something or another. I told my grandson, Carl, he needs to be looking into you, boy. Can't trust out-of-towners any more than you can throw 'em, even if they are who they say they are."

My chest rose and fell. Nothing about this situation could end well...which was why I had to stop things before they began.

"Ian, hey! Fancy seeing you here." I turned and nudged him backward, setting my tray on a nearby table before taking hold of his arm. "Let's get you a piece of pie to go, okay?"

His eyes raged like a fire, the flecks of gold shining brighter than his red hair. His nostrils flared too, but he nodded just once, eyes softening when they finally met mine.

With my arm tucked through his, I walked him toward the back of the diner, then into the hall that separated the two restrooms. Not thinking twice about my actions, I pressed both hands to his chest, holding him against the wall.

Would he listen? Or would he rage and fight back against me like one of mom's old boyfriends used to? I didn't know this man—didn't know if he was a lover or a fighter just yet. But something told me if I let him go, I'd regret it. I just wasn't sure in what way.

The diner grew eerily silent to our left, other than Edna raising a hoot. Mateo's voice bellowed through the quiet after a while, telling her to calm down or leave. I'm pretty sure Sarge was grunting out something too—though he spoke so low I couldn't make out what he said. I didn't have time to worry about them though. Not when I had Ian here before me, his body trembling, his breathing rough and ragged.

"Is that..." He stared at me, jaw clenching. "Do you deal with that kind of *treatment* all the time?"

"It's nothing." I let my hands fall away. My palms still tingled from touching him. "Just go home, okay? Before Edna calls her grandson. He's the town sheriff, and even though you did nothing wrong, he'll probably still find a reason to take you in."

Ian took a step to his left and rubbed a hand over his mouth. "Can't you tell them all to get lost or something? You don't deserve to be treated like that." He looked me over again, his anger lessening, making way for the one emotion I hated more than any other...pity.

"Edna..." I looked at my shoes, the black leather now stained with a layer of grease. Kind of like me in a way. "She knew my husband from when he was in diapers. Her grandson was his best friend, and..."

Did I want to admit the truth? How they all thought I was this huge homewrecker when I'd really been left in the dark about everything until the day I arrived. No. Not one bit. But at the same time, I was a firm believer in honesty, no matter the situation. It was why this was so hard to talk about to anyone, let alone a virtual stranger—even if he was a hottie.

I took a deep breath, deciding to give the quick, abridged version. "Edna's granddaughter and my husband used to be this huge thing. Edna thinks I broke them up and ran the girl out of town." I looked at my feet again. It wasn't the full story, but it was enough.

"Did you break them up?"

"No." I scrunched up my nose. "Of course not. I didn't even know he'd been with someone before we met."

"Then tell her to knock it off."

If only it were that easy. "I'm not rude. I can't just tell an old lady off, no matter how snotty they are with me. There are these...*Southern* rules about being nice to old people, no matter what." Granted I wasn't Southern born, but still, if I wanted to continue my life here in this town, I had to deal with the backlash that came from being a homewrecker. Even if only a handful of people knew the real truth.

Ian shook his head, his eyebrows furrowing the longer he stared at me. "So what? You hide from them in the supermarket, then take their crap lying down at your place of work so as not to ruffle feathers?"

I winced. He made it sound worse than it was. "I do what works for me and my family, so it's really not any of your business."

"You're right. I'm sorry for butting in like I did. But can you answer me one more thing? Please?"

I folded my arms. "What's that?"

He sighed, shoulders slumping in what could only have been disappointment. "Is this what it was like for you when your husband was alive?"

I blinked, thinking I'd heard him wrong. "What exactly do you mean by that?"

"Nothing bad." He knifed a hand through his hair. "It's just that I heard he was the town hero, so you'd think they would treat you better than they do, that's all."

I pressed my lips together into a flat line and looked away, unsure of how to answer him. There was so much Ian didn't know about me and Jonah. How we'd rushed into a relationship after only knowing each other for two weeks. How he'd moved me down to Sunrise Valley, Georgia, no questions asked, and given me things I didn't think I would ever be able to have in life. Peace and stability, someone to love me and take care of me for once, instead of the other way around.

Up until he found solace in Annabelle's arms, just weeks after finding out I was pregnant with Jake.

She'd come back to town for their high school reunion, and since I'd been too sick from my pregnancy to go, Jonah had decided to find a temporary replacement for me. It had only happened that one night, but it had changed things for me and Jonah forever.

Eventually he'd come clean about the whole thing, but only because he'd been caught. I'm pretty sure he would've kept going had I not found them together. I'd packed my bags, ready to move home, even if it meant dealing with a drugged-up mom. But he'd begged for my forgiveness, told me he loved me and wanted things to work between us, especially with a new baby coming. And because I didn't know what I'd actually do if I had to go back to Chicago, I'd forgiven him.

Things had been strained after that. Our intimacy had grown null and void, though that was my choice, not his.

Jonah had tried to fix things in the ways he could. Like the time he'd paid for Laila to get her first apartment on the day she'd turned eighteen, getting her away from our mom and the woman's fifty million creepy exes. He'd even asked his friends in Chicago to help her move and watch out for her and had gotten her hooked up with a good job at the Art Institute. And though his generosity had softened the blow of his unfaithfulness, I still hadn't been able let it go.

After Jake was born, I'd considered separating, but Jonah wouldn't have it. He'd told me divorce wasn't okay for someone looking to be the mayor, not in Georgia. And because I didn't have anything or really anyone else, I'd stayed put. An already despised woman would've been hated even more for divorcing the town hero—even though he was the one who'd been wrong.

So, for the sake of our son and Jonah's reputation, along with his career, we'd agreed that it would be mutually beneficial if we stuck through things, even if it wasn't ideal.

But then he'd gotten sick... and everything had changed again.

Despite all we'd gone through, Jonah and I made peace with each other during those last few months. And though my love for him had never surpassed what we'd gone through, I would always be thankful for Jake. He was our shared little piece of heavenly perfection.

"Charlotte," Ian whispered, bringing me back to the present. "Please talk to me."

"Why?" I sniffled and looked up at him again. This town frustrated the crap out of me, and now having Ian here, unknowingly forcing me to second guess myself, just made things worse.

Yes, I wanted to stand up for myself, more than anything else. But I couldn't. It would only make things more miserable than they already were. So, I would always be Charlotte, Jonah Dawson's widowed wife—the troubled runaway who'd "gotten lucky" to find a man like that.

"I'm sorry. Can we, I don't know, start over?" He moved closer, not touching me but enough that I could feel the heat of him. His voice was shaky, his words softer.

I licked my dry lips. "Start over, as in, you didn't see my near naked backside or witness my crazed cart driving skills?"

My palms began to sweat when he settled a hand beneath my elbow. His grin was so wide, so coy too, that my heart couldn't help but speed up again at the sight. I'm pretty sure I had developed a condition called Ianitus. Symptoms being shortness of breath, belly flips, and a pain in my heart caused by Cupid's arrow.

"Those two incidents have been the highlight of my life, just so you know." He kept his voice low as he trailed his fingers down my forearm. He took my hand in his and squeezed.

I parted my lips as a tingle of electricity shot up my spine. He dropped his hand right then, as if he knew his touch made me burn.

"Then it's obvious you've led quite the lonely life." I smiled, teasing him though not at all sure where it was coming from.

Something flashed in his eyes. A distance threatened to spoil our moment. Thankfully, it disappeared as quickly as it had come.

"I *did* ask out a pineapple this week." He chuckled. "I never realized how boring my life was until I came to Sunrise Valley."

Despite my mood, I found myself grinning. "Well, if you think Sunrise Valley is the place to find all of life's answers, then I'm pretty sure you've taken a wrong turn." I shoved his chest, not too hard, but enough that it could be counted as flirty.

Laila would be so proud.

Before I could pull my hand back, he grabbed it, holding it over his racing heart. He curled his fingers protectively over mine. I looked at our joined hands. His fingers were so long while mine were like a tiny child's.

"What I think," he whispered, his forehead barely grazing mine, "is that I took just the right turn because it led me straight to you."

I shut my eyes. "Do you use that kind of cheese on all your ladies?"

"There's only one woman I want to get cheesy with."

His words should have made giggle. But his fingers gripping mine, urging us closer, made me gasp instead. "Ian..." I shook my head a little. "I don't even know you."

"Then I vote that we get to know each other. What do you say?"

I opened my eyes, meeting his again. "I..."

This was too fast. I was feeling too much. Just like Jonah. But with Ian, everything felt so much...more real.

That scared me more than anything I'd ever been scared of. And I'd been through a lot.

Before I could say no, or yes, or a combination of both, a throat cleared from behind me. I jumped in place, moving so fast that my forehead whacked Ian's nose.

Hard.

"Oh God." He bent over at the waist.

"Ian! Are you okay?" I moved closer, but he put a hand between us, palm side out.

"Is she trying to kill ya, Red?" I winced at Becca's laughing voice while struggling to untie my apron with the intention of pressing it against his now bleeding nose.

"Jeez, Becca. Ever heard of privacy?" Ian groaned.

"Not 'round these parts." She laughed again.

He tipped his head back, squeezed his eyes shut, and pinched the bridge of his nose. Becca stepped around me and used something from her purse to staunch the bleeding. I stood there paralyzed, my hand still wrapped around the knot in my apron.

I lost my voice as I watched the two interact like old friends. It made my heart ache with jealousy, but it also brought reality to the forefront of my mind. I'd nearly kissed a man I didn't know. And Becca had been a witness to it all.

This could have been so bad. Gossip-worthy bad.

I slunk down the hallway and into the break room, hands shaking at my sides. Ian didn't call my name or come after me this time—not that I blamed him. I'd likely just broken his nose.

At a table, I breathed in a deep breath, trying to re-group. Yet the space, painted in a pale baby blue, did little to calm my nerves. I knew I needed to get through my shift. I had customers to tend to as well. But I couldn't move. Not yet.

Before I could let my inner turmoil get too out of hand, my phone buzzed in my pants pocket. I reached for it, knowing that it could have been Jonah's mom since she was watching Jake tonight.

Jake. My son.

That's what I needed to focus on in life—keeping food on the table for him and making sure he and Laila both stayed happy. Making a fool of myself over some guy was not in the cards right now.

I lifted my phone from my pocket and slid my finger across the screen to read the text.

You ran before I could ask you a question. I feel like you're turning into Cinderella on me.

I stiffened, knowing who it was, even as I tapped out my reply.

Ian?

Why do you keep running from me? Let's talk about it.

I flinched, trying to figure out how I should reply. There were so many things I wanted to say.

How did you get my number?

Please answer the question, Charlotte.

I blew out a breath and touched my lips at the same time. I felt my own smile, and God, I hated how happy it made me just to be texting the guy. Still, I had to stick to my game plan. Keep my distance. So, I typed a million— or maybe just four—different texts out before I settled on the right one.

I can't see you again.
I can't kiss you. Ever.
I want to though. Kiss you, that is. I want to so badly.
But the gossip. This town. The GOLs. Confusing my son.

I'll go first. Becca gave me your number. I would like for you to go out with me on Saturday. Apparently, there's some fall festival thing that can't be missed? I'd love it if a certain brunette would accompany me as my tour guide.

I hadn't scared him away with my hard head—literally. And because of his words, I apparently had no control over my actions and reactions either. Which was why I found myself typing the answer to his questions before I could think about it too much.

Ian held a force over me that I wasn't even aware of. Even still, I was incredibly immature to react so rashly. Still, that didn't mean this would be a date. I let out a long breath.

Pick me up at 7:00?

I bit my thumbnail, watching as the three little dots played out on the phone with his reply. He seemed to take forever, and with every passing second, I was sure he changed his mind.

It's a date. =)

Well, crap.

chapter eight

Ian

In an effort to work off some of extra pounds I'd acquired since hiding out in the South, and to manage my first date jitters, I took a long run through the streets of Sunrise Valley. I'd finally gotten in a good run, my first since coming to Georgia, and I returned home a sweaty mess.

Mom followed me to my room as I pulled my workout shirt over my head and threw it on the floor. "I know you're going to pick that shirt up and put it in the hamper, right?" She tsked.

Ignoring her, I examined the contents of my half-unpacked suitcase. "So, what does one wear to a fall festival, exactly?"

"Nothing you'll find in that mess." She flipped through the few shirts I'd hung in the closet. "Considering it's close to eighty degrees, I'd go with shorts. Layer a t-shirt with a nice button-down, in case it cools off later. Layering is key on a day like today." She pulled a navy V-neck t-shirt off the top shelf of the closet and my brown and navy plaid-patterned button-down from a hanger. "Are you excited for your date?"

Excited was an understatement. I didn't know if it was the Georgia air, the hoopla surrounding the "Fall Fest"—as Adler called it—or just the pretty girl that I'd get to spend time with. It was like everything in Sunrise Valley was make-believe, and I was a character in a movie instead of living in real life. "It's only a night out. I haven't been out with a woman in a long time."

"Charlotte Dawson is a sweetheart and needs a night out as much as you do. That is, a night out that doesn't include her sister."

"What I need right now is a shower." It felt good to be working out again. Hopefully my five-mile run had burned off some of that Thursday turkey and cornbread.

"Don't let me stop you. Oh, hey. I almost forgot." Mom ran out into the hallway. When she returned, she was holding an envelope. "This came for you by courier. Looked like a fancy acting thing, so I signed for it."

I took the envelope and tossed it on the bed. "Thanks, Mom. In case I haven't mentioned it, I really appreciate you and Adler letting me hang out here for a while."

"You never have to thank me, honey. I'm glad you're here. Since you've been in LA, we haven't gotten quality time like this." She smiled and hundreds of memories flooded my mind.

We'd always been a team, especially after Dad died. Mom had thrown herself into being a stage mom, shuttling me back and forth from our suburban New Jersey town to Manhattan for acting and dance classes, auditions, and modeling gigs. Even though I'd been a cranky teen, she'd showered me with love and encouragement to follow my dream. Back then, she'd been so invested in my future—financially, emotionally—that it had felt like *our* future.

Then, when I graduated high school, I'd up and left her to follow my dreams. She had never complained. She'd just given me money to get settled and wished me luck. It hadn't dawned on me that when I'd left, I'd taken her whole life with me too.

If it weren't for the fact that she'd found Adler while visiting an old high school friend in Atlanta, I'd probably have cut my career short to go home to Jersey to be with her. While I could repay her the money she'd spent on me a million times over now, I'd never be able to repay the gift of her blessing.

Apparently, she was still trying to direct my life. She waved me into the guest bathroom. "Now, go shower. You can't keep Charlotte waiting."

I kissed the top of her head and made my way to the bathroom. After a quick, soapy scrub, I wrapped a towel around my waist and headed back to the bedroom.

The letter stared at me from the bed. I picked it up and studied the handwritten address. *Mr. Ian Cleary, ℅ Mary Adler.*

With a NYC postmark.

This couldn't be good.

I tore open the envelope. Inside was a single sheet, but the letterhead made my stomach turn. *A-OK! Magazine.*

I scanned the short, typewritten letter.

Give us an exclusive within the next five days, and we'll forget that we know where you are, "Ian Cleary." Stephanie Wilson, Chief Editor, Entertainment Division.

I squeezed my eyes closed, then opened them to read the letter again. *Not now.* I thought I'd have more time.

How could they have found me already? I'd only been here four weeks. I'd just gotten used to the weather. Just had my first workout. I didn't want the peace in Georgia to be gone forever.

And there was also the matter of Charlotte...our first date.

"Crap." I crumpled the paper and closed my eyes.

A knock startled me.

"Not decent," I yelled, wrapping my towel tighter around my waist.

"Get moving, son." Adler's voice boomed through the closed door. "You're going to be late. I gassed up the pick-up for you."

"Alright, I'm coming. Thanks."

I shoved the ball of paper into the pocket of my suitcase and decided to worry about Stephanie Wilson tomorrow. Tonight, I was going to the Fall Fest with a cute waitress that I couldn't wait to get to know better. But just in case *A-OK! Magazine* was lingering around, I put on a baseball hat and tugged it low over my forehead on the way out the door.

Ten minutes later, I pulled up to the front of Charlotte's home. When I was two steps out of the truck, she bounced down the porch stairs and met me on her front path.

"Hi there." She sang the words. Her hair was in a high ponytail, leaving her neck bare. Her pink lips were shiny with gloss, and her brown eyes shimmered in the light of the setting sun.

I couldn't help my smile. "Hi yourself, sweetness."

Charlotte blushed at the nickname.

"You look beautiful."

She returned my smile. Sweeping my gaze over her, I noticed her tight jeans and cowboy boots. I drank in her sunny yellow tank top with ruffles. Her tanned shoulders were bare, and she had a sweater tied around her waist.

"Layering is key on a day like today," Mom had said.

When Charlotte looked back up, she cringed. "How's your nose? I didn't break it, did I?"

I wiggled it around. "Good as new. Nothing broken. But you do have a hard head, in case anyone asks."

"Ha," she said, fidgeting with her purse. "I believe you're here to take me to the Fall Fest, yes?"

I stood up straighter, almost forgetting that I couldn't stand here on the front path and stare at her all night. We were going on a date. Our first. Would there be more? Thoughts of *A-OK! Magazine* nipped at my brain, but I quickly pushed them aside.

"Yep." I paused. "And you should know, I haven't been on a first date in five years."

Her smile fell a little. I could see that wall forming again, right before my eyes. "So, this *is* a date then."

My stomach dropped. Had I read the situation wrong again? "That depends. Do you *want* it to be a date?"

She pursed her lips. "Do I have a choice?"

"You always have a choice in life, Charlotte." I frowned. "And if you don't want this to be a date, that's fine. We can just hang out, two friends enjoying a night out together."

What was Charlotte's past like to make her think that she didn't have a choice in the matter? Was that her husband's doing? Or was I just that oblivious when it came to women now, post-Brittany?

Eventually, she gave me a slow nod. Like maybe she'd made her mind up. I twisted my hands together behind my back while I waited for her answer. Yeah, I wanted this to be a date. But if she didn't, then so be it. Just spending time with her was enough for me.

"Okay," she said, her lips twitching with a small smile.

"Okay? As in, we're calling this—" I motioned a hand between us. "—a date then?"

"Yes." She squared her shoulders, nodding once. "We can call this a date. But just so you know, this is my first date since...Jonah." She grimaced. "Well, my first *formal* real date, I guess. There was the mullet-headed trucker who told bad jokes, but that's a story for another day."

Sensing her nerves—I was learning that she talked a lot when she was nervous—I reached out to touch her hand. "I guess we're both a little rusty then. Maybe we can flub through this thing together. Someday, maybe, I'll get to kiss you."

"Wh...what?" She bit that bottom lip again. But when I caught her grin, I went with it.

"It's all I can think about whenever I'm with you." I flirted my heart out, leading man style. "Just so you know what you're up against."

As much as I was trying to frazzle her, I wasn't entirely joking. I just hoped I wasn't pushing it too far. It was better to put it up front that I was interested in her—even though I wasn't sure what that meant yet.

Charlotte's blush crawled down her neck, but before I could let her off the hook, she sucked in a breath, stood on her tiptoes, and took my face between her hands. "Then I guess we better get it out of the way, huh?" Her fingertips lightly stroked my cheeks before she leaned forward and... kissed me on the cheek.

Her lips left an imprint when she pulled away. "You... you kissed me." I reached up and touched the warm spot, realizing that she'd turned the tables and totally frazzled me.

"I did." She smiled and batted her long eyelashes against her cheeks.

Was it possible she was flirting back? Because I think I liked that side of her.

I upped my game. "Not on the lips though."

She laughed. "Down in these parts, good girls don't kiss on the lips on a first date."

"Think I can change your mind on that?" I stuck both hands in my pockets so I didn't drag her forward and kiss her the way I was dying to.

"Maybe. Someday." She grinned wider as her cheeks became redder. "We better go. Miss Cindy's caramel apples are calling my name. Do you hear them?" She tilted her chin and cupped her ear, pretending to listen.

Man, she was cute. "Don't want to disappoint the caramel apples."

"There may be pineapples there too. You know, just in case I end up boring you to death." She giggled at her own joke.

I'd never live down my affair with the pineapple. "You could never bore me, Charlotte. In fact, you keep me on my toes. I like that about you."

"Thank you. It's...nice to know that someone finds me interesting in this town."

"I think you'd be interesting anywhere. Now get in the truck before I trick you into kissing me again."

She scoffed. "You know, *I* actually tricked *you* into letting me kiss you. You and that freckled face of yours."

"Anytime you want to kiss my freckles, I'm here for it." I grinned down at her as I opened the passenger side door, a smooth move that Adler had taught me by example. My mother hadn't opened a car door for herself in a decade since being married to him. I half-hoped Charlotte would grab me again and plant one right on my lips this time. She didn't though.

After shutting the door behind her, I ran around the back of the truck, taking deep breaths. This was already the most fun I'd had on a date, and we hadn't even gotten to our destination yet.

I slid into the driver's seat and turned the key. "To the caramel apples." I bellowed the words in my imitation Adler voice.

She laughed again, and I liked being the reason for it.

As we made our way down the road, thoughts of *A-OK! Magazine* and that letter they'd sent busted through my mind again, despite my best efforts. This could all be over in less than a week—she and I, whatever we were doing. I'd be outed and forced back to California, and she'd likely dump me before I even got to kiss her pretty lips.

"You okay there?" Her voice softened with concern.

I reached across the console and pushed the strap of her shirt up and over her bare shoulder. She shivered at my touch, and I held my palm there once I was done, not wanting to break the connection.

"I'm good." It was the truth too. There was no place else I wanted to be.

But the clock was ticking on my peaceful time in Sunrise Valley. Sooner or later, I'd have to leave the town and the sweet lady sitting next to me.

My heart cracked at the thought.

Sunrise Valley had a population of a thousand or so residents, and every single one of them was at the corner of Main and Noble Street for the Fall Fest. I recognized most people as supermarket customers, but I couldn't remember their names, only faces. Charlotte filled me in on each person's story as they said hi.

"Oh, here comes crazy Mr. Marlin," she whispered as we weaved toward the caramel apple stand, our hands brushing. "When Jake was two, he pulled up the crocuses on Mr. Marlin's front path to give to me, and the man never forgave him. Or me. Even though I replanted new ones the next day."

She steered me onto a different path to avoid him, her hand now tucked through the crook of my arm. The caramel apple booth had a short line. We took our place.

In an attempt to get to know her, I started asking questions. "How is Jake? What does he like to do?"

I had no idea what made a four-year-old happy. I hadn't been around kids since I'd been one.

She hesitated for a second, a small smile touching her lips. "He's an angel. Loves puppies and has been begging me for one since he turned four in May. There's no way I can do it now, not with my schedule and our tiny yard, but I'm hoping someday we can move into a home with a big, fenced in yard so I can get him one." Her eyes grew a little sad as we stepped ahead in the line. "Oh, and he adores all things Star Wars and is really into superheroes these days too. May take him to the multiplex in Carmel when the new Superman movie opens. Did you hear about it?"

"Yep." I'd auditioned for the role. I rubbed a hand over the back of my neck and quickly changed the topic off of Hollywood. "Where is the little guy tonight?"

"He's home with my sister. I wasn't sure if he was invited."

"Of course he was. I'm sorry. I should have asked you to bring him along." I handed the man in the booth three dollars for two salted caramel apples on sticks.

"No worries." Charlotte thanked me when I handed her one. "I would have found a reason not to bring him anyway. It's nice to have some adult time." She glanced at me sideways as we started into the crowd again. "Alone except for every person in Sunrise Valley, I guess."

I chuckled. "Funny. I only see one beautiful lady here. Are there other people?" I spun in a circle, pretending not to see anyone else.

Her smile lit up my world, and I found myself staring at it again. Her cheeks were as pink as her lips. She looked down at her feet, and we took a couple of steps in silence.

"Tell me about New York," she said.

"New York?" Then it hit me. I was supposed to have attended NYU. "Oh, New York. It's a blast."

"Yeah? What was your favorite part about it?"

I lifted a shoulder. "The anonymity, mostly. I liked seeing different people every day." That wasn't entirely a lie. "Everyone's different, but they're also all in it together. There's a sense of community, like we're all a team, even if we are all technically strangers...if that makes sense."

"So, it's kind of like here." She pressed her lips together. "Well, in theory anyway. As infuriating as Sunrise Valley can be, we are a team of sorts. It's like family. I can say whatever I want about my family, but if you say something bad about them, you're toast."

"It's nicer here than in the city." I stopped, glanced at her again, and noticing her strap had fallen off her shoulder. I pointed to it. "Your shirt."

"What?" She frowned. "Oh, yeah. It does that a lot."

She lifted her fingers to move it back up, but I shook my head. "Let me."

Loving the excuse to brush my fingers over her skin, I reached for the fabric, slowly tugging it back into place.

Her breath caught when my knuckles glided along her skin. Slowly, I slid my hand back down her arm, grazing a few chill bumps along the way. She shivered, and when I lifted my head to look at her, she stared at me with questions and curiosity. I didn't want to say anything for fear of breaking the connection.

Charlotte solved that problem for me though, slamming her walls right back into place as she stepped away from my touch.

"Thank you." She stared at her caramel apple, not bothering to take a bite. She was really good at changing the subject. "Do you miss it? Big city life, I mean."

"A little, I guess." I frowned and curled my hand into a fist at my side. It still burned from where I'd touched her. "Sunrise Valley is growing on me though."

Continuing down the street again, we passed a few craft booths and a pumpkin carving station. We just made small talk for ten minutes or so as we ate our caramel apples and watched kids run the length of the square.

"So," she said, tossing our apple cores and sticks into a nearby garbage can. "When are you going back? To New York, I mean. Your cousins mentioned you were here temporarily..."

Good question. I wasn't sure how to answer. "I'm hoping I'll know when the time is right. At the moment, I'm perfectly happy in Sunrise Valley." I wanted to add, "Because of you," but I was worried I'd scare her off.

She looked up at me with her big doe eyes. "What made you run away?"

I debated how to answer the question, then went with honesty. "My heart got broken. Thought if I took some time away, I'd be able to heal it."

"How's that working out for you?"

I stopped moving and took her hand in mine, surprised that she didn't pull it away. People formed a traffic pattern around us and watched, but I didn't care. All I wanted to do was lose myself in this woman, this night. "It's working great so far."

A nervous twitch flashed across her face, and her gaze flittered to the nosy bystanders. I thought maybe I'd gone too far. But then she pointed at my chest. "You know what else heals a broken heart?"

I shook my head.

"Warm apple cider."

"Really? I'm sure nobody's ever drowned their sorrows in cider." I rolled my eyes, and she playfully nudged me in the ribs.

"Not just any cider. Warm *apple* cider. Follow me."

Her curly ponytail swung as she strolled through the crowd, ignoring people who called out hellos. When she stopped and spun, she caught me staring. She didn't call me out on it though. She just pressed those pink lips together and smiled back.

It was my new life goal to knock her walls down.

Finally, she stopped moving and pointed to the booth in front of us. "Warm apple cider. Cures broken hearts."

"I don't see that on the sign." I laughed.

"It's in fine print. Trust me." She winked, then held up two fingers to the man behind the booth.

He gave her a thumbs-up. "You got it, Charlotte."

Holding onto our cups and each other's hands, we headed toward the back of the booths. I loved the way her tiny fingers felt in mine. Delicate but strong.

We walked for a couple of minutes to a quieter section of the square, only to end up at a circle of haystacks surrounding a fire pit.

"Sometimes I bring Jake here to play. He climbs that tree there." She pointed to a huge old willow a few yards away. "Then he jumps off and I catch him, and then we roll around in the piles of leaves below it. He loves it." She plopped down on top of the haystack, lounging with her face to the sky.

I wanted to join her more than anything in the world right then. But I couldn't. Not yet. Not when the simple sight of her—her hair falling from her ponytail and framing her face, her bright eyes tinged with just a touch of nostalgia—stole every last breath I had left in my lungs.

It was a moment I knew I wouldn't forget.

Watching as she took her first sip, I shook my head. I was getting too far into this. So far that I'd never be able to claw my way out if the paparazzi descended and turned this little town into a media circus. No way would I let that happen. I'd leave before it did.

But in the end, my pull to her was stronger than my fear of being found out, so I sat on the stack of hay beside her. Instead of looking up at the stars, I looked at her. "What's your favorite thing about this town?"

After handing me her cup, she pulled the sweater from her waist and slid her arms into it. Tucking her knees close to her chest, she smiled at me. "I like how things feel safe here. I like how people grow roots in Sunrise Valley too. Like it's our own little world. Of course, that's the worst part about it too."

When she reached for her cup, her fingers grazed mine.

Small electric shivers traveled through my whole body at her touch. "Did you ever think of leaving?"

"Yep. All the time actually." Charlotte took another sip of her cider. "But I'm too crazy to leave. Just crazy enough to stay though. Jonah left me the house, and I'm debt free for the first time in my life."

"And family? What about them?"

"My mom and I no longer speak. She's...got problems."

"I'm sorry." I touched her arm for a moment.

"It's okay. Really. I've made peace with that time in my life."

I could relate to making peace with the bad parts of life. She made it sound a lot easier than it was.

"So, the bottom line is, I'm a Sunrise Valley Lifer now. Here, I can try to make a life for me and Jake. Keep an eye on Laila, who is in love with this area for some reason." She shrugged again. "You know what they say... Bloom where you're planted. I'm planted here now."

I touched her chin. "You're the prettiest bloom in this garden, that's for sure." Even in the dark night, I could see the blush crawl over her cheeks. "So as much as this place gets in your business, you secretly like it here."

"Shh." She grinned and bumped her shoulder against mine. "Don't tell."

Then I decided to do something I'd wanted to do from the first time I laid eyes on Charlotte Dawson. I couldn't resist the urge anymore. Not when she was shushing me, with a finger over my lips. Staring at me with those dancing brown eyes. I put down my cup and reached up to touch her face. My hand was warm, but she shivered when my fingers touched her cheek.

I wanted to kiss this woman more than I'd ever wanted to kiss anyone. So, I moved closer, shut my eyes, and didn't open them until she gasped.

I was suddenly aware of my jeans. Warmth overtook me. I pulled away and looked down. Charlotte's cup of cider had dumped all over in my lap.

"Fuhhh." I was careful not to let the entire curse word escape as the warm cider spilled onto my crotch, soaking into the denim.

Her eyes grew three sizes. "Oh, Ian. I am so sorry."

I stood and jumped up and down, stupidly hoping maybe the cider that had soaked through would drip out. In a flash, Charlotte was on her knees in front of me, using her sweater to dab at the zipper of my jeans.

Mortified but amused, I reached down to stop her. "Please don't do that. It's okay."

"I know how to fix this. I need some club soda. This cider will stain if we don't get it cleaned up."

I nudged her shoulders to stand her up. "Really, Charlotte. It's okay."

"I'm so sorry. I'm such a klutz." She looked down at my pants again.

"Could you, you know, not worry about any of this?" I waved my hands below my waist, then did a little dance to loosen things up down there. "Forget it even?"

We stared at each other awkwardly until she spurted out a laugh. "I'm so s—"

"Don't say you're sorry. I'm not sorry. Not at all." Happy for the cover of the dark sky, I took her hand in mine. "Come on. We're on a date. We should do something date-y."

"Date-y?" She squinted and then widened her eyes in excitement. "Wait. I know the perfect thing. Follow me."

She pulled me behind her, walking in and out of the crowd. "What's the plan?"

I almost rammed into her back when she stopped short. Spinning, she yanked me closer, taking both of my hands in hers. "We are going to go on a hayride. I've always wanted to do that."

Sure enough, a big red pickup truck was parked a few yards away, with a rackety-looking trailer hitched to it. A hayride sounded awful, especially with a wet lap, so I focused on the silver lining. Making a memory with Charlotte. "Let's do it."

We climbed a short ladder to get on the wooden trailer. Side by side, we sat on piles of dirty hay, her leg pressing to mine, the scent of her lemony shampoo doing things to my chest. We waited five minutes for the ride to fill up, but I didn't mind.

I was feeling things for Charlotte. All of her—from her clumsy charm, to the soft skin of her shoulder, to her musical laugh. All I could think about as we sat there waiting for the hayride to start, soaked in cider with hay sticking to me, was our near kiss. A few days ago, I'd had no idea that the perfect woman lived in Sunrise Valley, Georgia, and, by a miracle, our paths had crossed at just the right time.

Well, almost the right time. I'd have to tell her the truth about myself before the press did, and I hoped that what we might be starting wouldn't crumble into bits because of who I really was.

chapter nine
Charlotte

Ian settled his warm hand along my back, the perfect comfort on this chilly night—a comfort I needed more than anything right then. Two minutes into our ride, all good things about our "date" had come to a crashing halt—and it had everything to do with the sudden infestation of GOLs now riding in the back of the tractor.

Ruby, Edna, *and* Betty were all there, huddled together and staring like a group of gossipy teenagers. I had never in my life felt more like a wild animal in a cage—on display, just waiting for ridicule...or worse.

Tears burned the corner of my eyes. Their gossipy whispers floated in the air, barely contained behind their wrinkled hands.

This was my favorite time of the year—that time before Thanksgiving, just six weeks before Christmas, yet they'd already turned it into a nightmare for me. Any other time, I'd be living for this night and enjoying the town's decorations—the wreaths and orange strings of lights hanging from every window and the leftover pumpkins from Halloween that still stood in the storefront doors. Fall leaves drifted beneath the surface of the water in the giant fountain in the town's center. Their vibrant colors glinted and shined in the glow of the moon.

But all I'd seen were sneering, wrinkly glares from eyes filled with a hate I didn't deserve.

"Charlotte?" Ian nudged my shoulder with his.

"Hmm?"

"Why'd you get quiet on me? What's up?"

I sniffled, nonchalantly wiping my eyes on my shoulder. "Nothing's up. I'm okay. Just...allergies. The hay and I don't get along well."

He frowned. "You want to get off? I can ask the drive—"

"It's fine." I refused to let those nasty women ruin this for me. *For us.*

"You're not fine." He touched my chin and tipped my head back. Our eyes met. All I wanted was to get lost in his soft gaze, escape inside the protection he openly offered.

Taking a deep breath, I forced an even wider smile. "I am. Trust me." My throat burned with the lie.

He frowned and opened his mouth to say something but snapped it shut a moment later. After a brief pause, he said, "You'll tell me though, right? If you want off."

"You're sweet." I stroked a finger along his wrist, slowly tugging his hand down and holding it on my lap. "But I promise. I'm okay."

Since there was no point in giving those women any more ammunition for their gossip, I turned away from them, hiding Ian's hand in mine.

I leaned my head back against the wood and gazed at the sky. Even over the tractor noise and the kids giggling and squealing around us, I could still hear the low murmurs of the GOLs. Ian seemed oblivious, thankfully. He didn't need to be brought down because of me. That thought made my mind wander even more. Maybe dates with handsome men, who had soft souls and sweet words, weren't even worth it. The GOLs managed to ruin most good things in my life.

From the corner of my eye, I caught Ruby staring at me. With my lips pressed into a firm line, I finally met her gaze with a glare of my own. Her answering look reminded me of a cat, predatorial. Her green eyes shined even in the black of night. She gripped her cup with white, fluffy mittens and huddled closer to her friends.

I should've looked away. Should've ignored them. But my blood began to boil hotter than ever. So, I continued to glare at them, even when all three pairs of eyes zeroed in on me at the same time. If they wanted to have a stare down, so be it.

"What are they all looking at?" Ian moved forward, glancing toward the women in the back.

I stiffened, then winced, unsure of what to say.

He sighed, likely catching on, and God, did I hate myself for letting them get the better of me, especially since Ian had noticed.

"You know I don't care what they think about you, right? They're just some old ladies with too much time on their hands."

Life would be so much easier if I stopped caring what other people thought of me and my choices.

"It's fine." I was annoying myself with that two-worded lie now.

He squeezed my hand and lowered his mouth to my ear. I shivered from his closeness, his warm breath. I closed my eyes as his words washed over me. "It's not fine. I've seen how they treat you, and it's not *fine*, Charlotte."

"I know." I exhaled a shaky breath. "Would you believe me if I said they're a lot better than they used to be?"

"No." He huffed and leaned in closer, our joined hands now on display over his thigh. "What's their problem with you anyway? I get that you're not originally from this town, but neither am I."

I tipped my head to the side, smiling a little. "You're a lot cuter than I am."

He ran a finger down my chin. "Doubtful."

My face warmed at his touch, but from his words most of all. He didn't have to say much to make me feel like I'd won the lottery in the date department. A woman could easily fall for this man, and if I wasn't careful, I'd be doing just that.

"Tell me what happened," he said. "Was there some big scandal that turned them all against you?"

I winced, weirdly wishing there were. "No scandal. Just me, showing up one day out of the blue on the arm of the most eligible bachelor in town, with a ring on my finger." I shrugged. "Jonah's family founded Sunrise Valley, so his last name, Dawson, is legendary among the townspeople. Ruby's his great aunt."

"Jesus," he said.

"What sucks the most is that even when I try to make things right, it usually blows up in my face. So now, I just try to stay out of their way."

"Nobody should stay out of your way. You're too good."

I wished everyone thought of me the way Ian did. "Guess even old ladies need enemies."

"Yeah right."

"They also think I tried to kill them once." I snort-laughed, surprised I could find it in me to make light of the memory.

"What?" Ian jerked his head back. "You're serious?"

"Dead serious." I sighed, recalling that fateful, lovely, God-help-me-I-hate-my-life day.

"It started back before Jonah was fire chief." I licked my lips and then lowered my voice even more. "I was young and didn't cook much of anything, other than boiling Ramen and boxed mac and cheese. Growing up, Mom was either drinking at the bar, sleeping away a hangover, or working, so she didn't teach me much of anything cooking wise, other than how to order takeout or make a PB and J with spoiled jelly and moldy bread."

Ian stroked his thumb over the top of mine. "I hate that you had to live the way you did."

"It's okay, I swear. That part of my life shaped me into who I am now."

He nodded thoughtfully. But he kept his expression even, so I had trouble figuring out what he was thinking.

"Anyways," I said. "For the first Sunrise Valley get-together after Jonah and I got married, I made this casserole thing I found in an old cookbook at the library in town."

I lowered my voice a bit more to avoid being heard. "I wanted to fit in so badly, to be worthy." I shook my head, hating how I'd spent so much time trying to make them like me when, in the end, they never would.

"You don't give yourself enough credit," Ian said. "You're perfect just the way you are."

My cheeks heated again, and I looked at my lap.

"So, what happened?" Ian asked. "With the party and the casserole."

I bit my bottom lip and snuck a quick look at Ruby and her minions. Thankfully, they were deep in conversation and no longer eying me.

"Vomiting happened." I winced. "Apparently, I'd undercooked the chicken in my casserole and gave the whole town—well, anyone who'd eaten my casserole at the party, including my own husband—food poisoning." I shook my head. "Of course, the GOLs accused me of sabotaging them."

"You're kidding?"

"Nope." I popped the P sound, laughing under my breath. "They all said I was jealous of them. Can you believe that? A bunch of old women. I mean, what did I have to be jealous of?"

Ian ran a hand through his shaggy hair. "So, you, what, cooked a bad batch of chicken casserole and they all want to take you down for it?"

"No. Yes." I shook my head again. "The whole home-wrecker thing, paired with the bad chicken and being an outsider, just doesn't sit well with them."

Since that incident, I had avoided the GOLs at all costs. It was bad enough I'd heard their secret whispers along the street over the years. Now there I was, in plain day—or night, with a new guy, and all their eyes were on me once more.

"Back at home in Cal..." Ian fidgeted in his seat and let go of my hands, rubbing his own up and down both thighs. "New York, I mean, I used to go to this gym. The majority of the guys that showed their faces were a bunch of muscle heads who insisted on cleansing and juicing, things like that. It was a nightmare trying to get through my routines without being judged."

I folded my legs up to my chest and wrapped my arms around my shins, laying my head on my knees as I watched him talk.

"That holistic thing wouldn't fly here in Sunrise." I shivered at the slight chill in the air—not even the sweater draped around my shoulders could curb it. "The people in this town love their greasy fried food too much."

Ian untied the sweatshirt wrapped around his waist and tucked it over my shoulders, but he kept his arm wrapped around me when he finished. The action was so sweet I didn't want to move for fear I'd wake up and find out this was all a dream.

"Which is why a guy with abs like this has got to be careful." He patted his tummy, the move drawing my gaze to his hands. When I didn't look up right away, he cleared his throat. Our eyes met, and a knowing grin spread across his lips.

"What I'm trying to say is, I didn't care what anyone thought of me," he said. "I did my routines and ate the way I wanted. Didn't jump on those fad diets. Just kept living how I was meant to live."

"But you did at first though, right?"

"What's that?"

"Care what they thought of you? The gym-goers."

"Sure. But after a while, nothing mattered. Not their opinions of me, not their judgment either. It takes time to learn to stand up for yourself and what you believe in, but anyone can do it." The moon highlighted the strong angles of his cheekbones, making my stomach do that flip flop thing again. "Including you."

Ian lifted a finger to trace a line across my cheek, just as the ride came to a stop. I found myself leaning into the small touch, forgetting where we were. The affect this man had on me was intoxicating.

"Ian?"

"Hmmm?" He moved in a little closer, his cheek brushing against mine, his chin on my shoulder. He smelled like soap and that same pine scented aftershave. I inhaled, savoring it. I knew I should move, but I suddenly didn't care for once.

"Thank you for tonight," I whispered in his ear, though I wanted to say more.

Thank you for making me feel like I matter. For making me feel like I deserve something beyond the life I've come to accept.

"It was my pleasure." He nuzzled his nose against my cheek, and my breath caught in surprise. Before I could beg him to sweep me away to his truck, beg him to kiss me in a way I'd been terrified of before tonight, he pulled back, giving me a small smile as he reached for my hand. I took it, again not thinking of the consequences as we stood and made our way off the tractor. In fact, I was pretty much oblivious to everything except for Ian.

Until I wasn't.

"You know...I do reckon the Fall Fest was Jonah Dawson's favorite event growing up," a voice grumbled from behind me.

I stiffened, arm outstretched, my hand still in Ian's. He was a pace ahead of me, but he turned back when I stopped moving. He raised an eyebrow, questioning my sudden change.

My chest squeezed. There was no need to look and see who was talking. I knew exactly who it was. In fact, I'd been hearing that voice far too much over the past week.

Ruby.

"Oh my. That man was such a good fella," Edna cooed. "So handsome. Dying so young like that was a real shame. It's also a shame his memories aren't being honored the way they should be."

I died a little bit inside from that terrible, hateful sentiment.

Ian growled under his breath when he realized they were talking about me. He gripped my hand tighter. I wanted to run, God did I ever, but it was like my feet were cemented to the ground.

I would not cry. I refused to cry, dang it. Not again.

"Tell me not to go over there." He tucked a strand of hair behind my ear before leaning forward to kiss my forehead. "Tell me to stay here with you."

I opened my mouth, ready to speak.

"Well, at least he left himself a nice legacy in Jake," Betty Teddy said. "Can't say the same for the rest of his family though."

"Hey!" Ian moved around me, his body hard and stiff, his voice even more so. His words were even. Calm.

"Ian." I gripped the front of his shirt. Déjà vu hit as I remembered Thursday night at Minka's. He was making a habit out of coming to my rescue. It was time I stopped him.

His eyes met mine. "Do you trust me?"

I nodded once.

Ian moved me around to face the GOLs head-on. He held me close to his side, like we were a unified force.

"Ladies." He looked from one to the next. "When Jonah Dawson looks down from heaven, I'm sure it breaks his heart to listen to you talk to his widow like this."

Ruby gasped. Her hands flew to her pearls. "Well! I never!" Her trusty sidekicks, though, bowed their heads. They weren't actually ashamed, were they? My heart skipped at the thought. The good kind of skip, for once.

Ian looked to the sky. "Forgive them, Jonah and Jesus. We pay them no mind." Then he grabbed my hand and tugged me toward the parking lot.

I glanced over my shoulder and found the ladies how I knew they would be—huddled together, shaking their heads, and eyeing us.

"Wow." I ran to keep up with Ian's pace. "You really are learning how to deal with them, huh?"

"Aunt Mary's taught me a thing or two." He grinned. Then under his breath, he said, "I still can't believe you have to put up with that crap."

Instead of responding, I just cringed. Someday I'd stand up to those women myself.

It just wasn't going to be tonight.

chapter ten

Ian

Three days had passed since Saturday, and I didn't want to be away from Charlotte for another minute. When I'd seen her at the store earlier that day, she had been all business. Her fake Southern politeness had overshadowed the cute, flirty woman I'd seen at the Fall Fest, before the senior squad shot her down. Although I had caught her dancing in the aisles to Sammy Davis, Jr. and gotten her to admit that she liked shopping on Tuesdays because Adler tended to play the oldies then.

After she'd thanked me for bagging her groceries, we'd shared a smile. I'd understood its meaning. *Don't give up on me*, it had said.

And I wasn't planning to.

In fact, Mom had provided me with a peach cobbler, and an excuse to visit Charlotte. Considering the fact that every time we were in each other's company, noses got smashed, skirts got ripped, or jeans got spilled on, I thought maybe I should dress in armor for the visit. But with the autumn rain falling in droves, I'd probably rust anyway. Since Adler had the truck—and there was no such thing as public transit in Sunrise Valley—instead of armor, I wore a raincoat and headed off toward what the old ladies at the market called "the other side of town."

Since it rarely rained in California, we didn't need these heat-trapping, dumb raincoats. I felt like I was baking in the thing, but Mom insisted that no true gentleman would be seen without a jacket on a day like today. So, armed with Mary McDowell's famous peach cobbler, I skipped through the puddles and hoped that maybe I looked like Gene Kelly in *Singin' in the Rain*. Then I wondered if Charlotte had ever seen it. I made a mental note to ask.

When I'd dropped her off Saturday night after the Fall Fest, the air had felt heavier between us. I hated that the people of this town—this town where she'd decided to raise her son—were so blind to her attributes. Instead of seeing the hardworking, sweet, and sassy gem she was, they only saw her as the widow of a man they'd felt was too good for her.

How could Jonah let the town think that? How had he not paraded her around like the prize that she was, convincing all the old ladies that he was humbled by her partnership? Why hadn't he bragged that she was the wind beneath his wings and the power source that let him shine? Let the man rest in peace, and strike me down for saying it, but I wasn't impressed with Jonah Dawson. Not at all.

As I crossed Main Street to get to Charlotte's side of town, a dark car pulled up alongside me.

Like an idiot, I'd ducked under a tree and waited until it passed, cursing under my breath the entire time. I thought for sure it was *A-OK! Magazine* until it drove away, leaving me behind without incident. Stephanie Wilson had given me five days to contact her about the exclusive. That meant I had two more days to decide what to do. Fink was no help. He said he'd support whatever decision I made. But I didn't think I had a choice. The last thing I wanted was the paparazzi invading Sunrise Valley. Like Charlotte had said, this town was its own little world. I'd hate to be the cause of an invasion by dreaded outsiders.

Still, I cringed thinking about doing the exclusive.

It was bad enough that I had to go back to Los Angeles after the holidays and face my life, face Russ and Brittany, and start prepping for *Murder in the White House 2*. But knowing it meant that I'd be leaving Charlotte, Mom, and Adler hit me like a knife to the gut.

I wasn't sure if I was ready for any of it. Or if I ever would be again.

As I approached Charlotte's little house, with the traditional big porch and swing, I decided to worry about the magazine, and my life as Ian Tate, tomorrow. Tonight, I had a peach cobbler to deliver and a sweet woman to woo.

I took the porch steps two at a time and was about to ring the bell when a large hand wrapped around my arm, stopping me. I turned to find Carl—or rather *Sheriff* Carl—staring down at me like I was a criminal he'd just caught in the act of committing another crime.

He nodded toward the front walk, indicating for me to follow. His police car was parked across the street, a few doors down. *Sneaky fellow*. When we reached it, he boxed me between the car and his body. His gold badge tinged as raindrops bounced off of it.

"Can I help you, Sheriff?" I asked politely. I didn't want to get into it with him in the middle of Charlotte's street while holding, of all things, a peach cobbler

He crossed his arms and puffed out his chest.

I sighed. *Here we go...*

"Just thought you should know that I know who you are."

Crap. "And who might that be?"

I squeezed my eyes shut, hoping that I was having a bad dream and that Carl the Sheriff wasn't standing in front of me, about to call me out on my identity.

Carl chuckled. "*Murder in the White House* was one of my favorite movies. But that don't mean that I like you being here." He looked down his nose at me.

Double crap. I had no response, so I gulped and took some deep breaths. This was bad.

"Listen, *Tate*. I found out about you, and about Mary being your mom. Luckily, I tracked down your agent— some Finkus guy—who told me you're only here until the New Year."

"That's true," I said, nodding. "I don't want any trouble—"

"The last thing I need is the paparazzi parading into this town, *my town*, especially when I'm down two men at the station."

"Nobody knows I'm here," I lied, my voice shaking. Stephanie Wilson at *A-OK! Magazine* knew, but Carl didn't need that tidbit of information. "Like my agent said, I'm only here temporarily. Just needed a break, that's all. I'm sure you can understand."

"Does Charlotte Dawson know that?" Carl asked. "Because that doesn't seem nice to lead her on and then leave her."

Sadly, Carl wasn't wrong, not that it was any of his business. "Charlotte and I are going to be having a talk soon. Just...please let me be the one to tell her, okay?"

Carl scoffed and looked to the sky. "This rain wasn't expected. It's going to drench the decorations the Sunrise Valley Rotary Club just put up at the town square." He looked down at me, glaring sideways. "Maybe if someone made a donation to their holiday decorating fund, it could make the town a whole lot prettier come December."

Refraining from rolling my eyes, I fake smiled at Carl. "I'd be happy to make that donation." I pointed a finger at his barrel of a chest. "You'll let me talk to Charlotte? And you'll keep my identity a secret?"

"As long as you don't give me a reason to not to," Carl said.

I held my free hand out for him to shake. He laughed and pulled open the driver's side door of his car.

Jerk.

The car window slid down, and Carl looked out at me. "Don't make me regret my decision, Mr. *Cleary*."

Once the sheriff drove away, I walked back to Charlotte's house. I had to tell her, and soon. Despite Carl's assurance that he'd keep my secret, Sunrise Valley was not the kind of place where secrets lived long. Shaking off our interaction, I ran up Charlotte's stairs and rang the bell.

Screams blared out from inside—kid screams. The door flung open, and I was greeted by a tall brunette, panting, covered in something that looked and smelled like whipped cream. Her blue eyes widened at the sight of me, through the fluffy white dessert topping.

"Oh my. May I help you?" She all but purred the words as she checked me out.

Jake, dressed in nothing but SpongeBob SquarePants underwear, peeked from behind the woman. His hair was matted with whipped cream too.

"Freckles!" he screamed, pointing at me. Then he started running in circles.

"Hey, Jake."

He didn't even slow as he grabbed a play sword off the ground. Spinning, he swung it around, battling foes only he could see.

I looked at the woman. "I'm Ian."

"*The* Ian? My sister's Ian?"

I grinned, liking the idea of being Charlotte's Ian. "You must be Laila." I thought about reaching out to shake her hand, but I held up the cobbler instead. "I brought Aunt Mary's cobbler."

Laila winked, causing whipped cream to drip from her eyelashes to her cheek. "Then you're welcome here. Please, come in." She smiled politely but then turned toward the miniature banshee boy yelling and tearing up the house.

"Jake!" she yelled. "Okay, fine, you won. You are the whipped cream king of the world. Now upstairs. To the bath!"

131

She turned back to me, wiping streaks of whipped cream off of her face. "Sorry about the chaos. We were having an epic war."

"I won!" Jake tossed his sword and ran up the stairs.

Laila blatantly checked me out. I was afraid she'd recognize me, until she said, "Why don't you come in and make yourself at home."

I entered the tiny living room. Dots of whipped cream covered the worn hardwood floors. The place was small but cozy—filled with toys, color, and warmth. Homey.

I saw pieces of Charlotte everywhere, from the sweater she'd worn at the Fall Fest, hanging on a hook near the doorway, to her Minka's Diner white button-down, folded on the top of a pile of laundry in a basket near the staircase.

"So you're Ian." Laila sang the words dreamily. "Char's in the kitchen, the lucky lady."

Snickering, she followed Jake up the stairs. Once Laila disappeared, I wandered through a doorway that I assumed led to the kitchen.

And then I saw her.

Charlotte—with a pair of headphones over her ears, folding laundry at the kitchen table. Her back was to me, and she was dancing.

She moved her hips like she'd never hear music again. My instincts told me to walk up behind her, maybe wrap both arms around her waist. Dance with her even. But I didn't want to scare her or seem like a creep.

Standing there, I thought about how much fun it would be to take her hair out of the clip that held it up and let it spring out, all those tiny curls tickling her neck. In the end, I propped myself against the doorframe and decided to stay quiet and enjoy the show.

Charlotte

I stood at the kitchen table folding up my last load of laundry while the hypnotizing voice of an up-and-coming country singer I still didn't know the name of seduced me through my earbuds. He was crooning about Georgia mud and watching someone fall in love—a song that was infectious to my hips, which were currently moving faster than they had in years. I danced so hard, in fact, that a thin layer of sweat broke out along my temples, making the homemade face mask Laila had mixed up for my sudden stress outbreak drip down my cheeks. No matter, I was in the zone, getting right with the world and putting what little homemaking skills I had to work.

Shaking out another bath towel, I spun around on my toes and belted out the chorus—or what I knew of it—only to find a very large man in the doorframe of my kitchen.

"Holy crap, Ian!" I stumbled backward, dropping my towel to search for any underwear that may have been on display behind me.

"Wh...what are you doing here?" Hands shaking, I yanked a pair of cotton briefs off the table, then stuck them into the waist of my cut offs, covering them with my shirt for good measure. We'd already had one too many embarrassing near butt shots lately.

He pointed to his ears.

"Huh?" I squinted.

"Earphones," he mouthed.

"Oh, yeah." I tugged them off and settled them along the back of my neck. A pile of mud mask gunk fell off my face and onto the floor in the process.

I shut my eyes. This was it. The moment I would begin digging my grave so I could officially die of embarrassment.

He rubbed a finger over his bottom lip. "You've, uh, gotta a little something on your face."

I sucked in a slow breath and blew it out before I could think twice about my next statement. "It's for my pimples."

He quirked a brow.

"Adult acne?" I hesitated. The back of my neck grew warm. "I get it when I'm stressed. Laila makes up this good stuff for my temples and forehead."

"Really?" His lips twitched.

"Uh-huh. Yep." My face grew even hotter beneath the already tingling mask. Another bit of it fell off my chin just then, landing with a *plop* on top of my floor.

My world couldn't get much worse at the moment.

"Well, you look great, even with the gunk." Ian approached, holding a foil-wrapped dish out in front of him. "I texted that I was coming with peach cobbler. Did you not get my message?"

I searched inside my pockets for my phone and pulled it out. I scrolled through, finding his sweet words. I'd added a tiny heart emoji behind his contact name, like a thirteen-year-old girl. *How pathetic am I?*

"Sorry." I winced. "Jake was playing with my phone earlier."

"I thought the Luke Skywalker GIF meant 'yes.'" He jabbed a thumb toward the door. "It's okay. I can go—"

"No!" I yelled the word, which added to my embarrassment. "I mean, you came all the way in the rain. With a cobbler at that."

He grinned and placed the cobbler on the counter next to the pile of Jake's fruit roll ups. "But if you're busy, I really don't mind coming back late—"

"I'm not busy." I ran to the sink and splashed a few big scoops of water onto my face until the slimy residue was gone. "It's just that my house is a mess. *I'm* a mess."

"It's not possible." His footsteps echoed behind me, signaling his approach. From the corner of my eye, I watched him lean against the counter, the epitome of casual—like always.

"What's not possible?" Water dripped off my lashes and onto my cheeks. Instead of staring at him, I stood upright and looked out the window.

"You being a *mess* is not possible."

He reached forward and tucked a loose strand of hair behind my ear. When I turned my head, he pulled back just enough so our gazes locked. Ian's eyes twinkled, like he could see into my soul. And with that recognition, something ran through me, like warm electricity burrowing through my veins, and kickstarted my insides back to life.

Like with Jonah, it was happening again. Too fast. Those suppressed feelings I thought I'd buried were resurfacing, and I was powerless to stop it.

"You're gorgeous, Charlotte," Ian whispered, breaking down the last of my walls.

It didn't matter what my head thought anymore because my heart had always been in full control, from the second this man walked into my life. It had just taken me a hot minute to figure that out.

"Look at me."

I didn't know I'd looked away until I felt his finger on my chin, lifting my head up.

Ian had managed to wiggle his way into my heart already. It was terrifying. I couldn't risk falling for him when he'd inevitably be leaving Sunrise Valley. His aunt and uncle had said his stay was temporary, or so I'd heard through the grapevine. I could already tell Ian was too big for this town. He had too much personality and energy.

He'd leave, and it'd crush me. I couldn't take the heartbreak.

Still, that didn't stop me. "Can-you-kiss-me-please?"

He searched my face. Somewhere along the way, he'd lost the raincoat. He'd pushed up the sleeves of his shirt, revealing taut forearms, and my mind raced with thoughts of how they'd feel wrapped around my waist.

"Kiss you?" He cocked his head to one side.

I nodded slowly, my heart beating like a thousand racehorses had just dashed out the gate. I'd already humiliated myself more times than I could count, so why not jump the gun and go full throttle with the mortification?

But Ian made no move toward kissing me, no move toward me at all. Instead, he studied my face, brows furrowed, like I was an abstract painting he couldn't quite discern.

He ran a hand across his mouth before taking a step back.

My stomach twisted. I blinked.

Lord have mercy. I just banged that one up really, really fast.

"Ha!" I pointed a finger at him, trying to save face. "I was kidding. Seriously." I turned away, squeezed my eyes shut, and started messing with the handle on the sink—even though I had no intention of doing dishes.

Ian leaned over me and shut off the water. "You weren't kidding."

"Uh, yeah." I rolled my eyes to hide the forming tears. "I totally was."

Where in the heck is my chill? Where is my inner Laila, dang it?

As Ian stepped closer, his knees skimmed my thighs. It took all of my willpower not to turn and look at him this time. Not even when he grazed my ear as he whispered.

"If I kiss you, Charlotte..." he murmured, his hot breath fanning over my cheek. "I'm pretty sure I won't be able to stop."

Slowly, I lifted my gaze, turning my head just enough to look at him from over my shoulder. "Yeah?"

He put both hands to my hips, spun me around, and pulled me close. I gasped.

A ghost of a smile touched his lips. "Try me, sweetness. I dare you."

With no second thoughts, I lifted my hands, slid them into his hair, and—

"Jeez, Char! What the heck did you feed that boy of yours for lunch..." Laila, sneakers squealing, skidded to a stop in the kitchen.

I jumped and cleared my throat. "Um, sorry, what?"

She glanced between me and Ian, eyes wide. Seconds later, she smirked.

I hated her smirk.

"Hey, um, yeah... Phew! How about you two just," she waved a hand between us, "pretend I was never here."

She left the room, giggling under her breath. I'd catch some serious crap for this later.

Ian pressed his forehead to mine. He flashed me a wide grin, apparently not embarrassed in the least.

I couldn't say the same for myself.

"I'm sorry." I cringed.

"Don't apologize." He kissed the space between my eyes. "Just know that I'm gonna work extra hard now to make this happen."

I swallowed. "What do you mean *this*?"

"Us. Me and you." Still the picture-perfect image of calm and collected, he winked. To my utter surprise, he grabbed one of my shirts and proceeded to fold my laundry, all while whistling.

"You're really folding my laundry right now?" I frowned. "After dropping that bomb on me?"

"Yep." He popped the P. "I'm in a hurry."

"Oh, you have to go?"

"Nope. I want to hurry so we can start eating the cobbler quicker."

I bit my bottom lip, unable to ignore the flutter in my chest. "You're going to stay for cobbler?"

"If you'll have me." He winked again, then grabbed a towel and attempted to fold it.

Nothing was more attractive than a man who stepped up and at least *tried* to fold laundry.

"Fine. If you're going to stay for cobbler, you might as well stay for family movie night too."

Laila wouldn't mind. If anything, she'd probably volunteer to take Jake duty tonight, to give me and Ian *alone* time. I could already hear her smug voice as she taunted me.

"Movie?" Ian cleared his throat, flustered for the first time this evening. "What, uh, are we watching?"

I bumped his shoulder with my own, wondering if I'd freaked him out with my invitation. He was obviously interested in me, but maybe the idea of family movie time was too much? Or maybe it was too much too soon? Uninviting him would be rude though.

"*The Sound of Music*. I'm more of a classic movie kind of lady. I prefer them to the current ones. That okay with you?"

He blew out a shaky breath and nodded. "Yeah. *The Sound of Music* sounds great actually."

Minutes ago, he'd been Mr. Charming, Says-All-The-Right-Things Ian. But there were times when I caught glimpses of fear in his eyes—like now. It was as though he was terrified of something he'd never admit.

139

Either way, I knew what that was like. We all had our secrets. Who was I to call him out when I wasn't ready to share mine?

Side by side, we finished folding the last pieces of laundry, the music still blaring from my earphones on the table. Like this, I was at ease. Settled.

I just prayed it wasn't temporary.

chapter eleven

Ian

With our bellies full of peach cobbler, we lounged in a line on the couch. I sat between Charlotte and Jake, and Laila sat on the recliner. They all laughed when I sang every song in *The Sound of Music* and recited key dialogue. I told them I'd played Captain von Trapp my senior year of high school—which was true—but I didn't add that I often used "Edelweiss" as an audition piece to showcase the best of my horrible singing voice. Of the few roles I'd gotten in musicals, my dancing had made up for my singing.

I missed musicals. Since my career had taken off in Hollywood, I'd done mostly action roles and drama. I liked the work—and the Academy Award nod was a dream accomplishment—but nothing beat the thrill of being live on stage. Every day, a new performance, a new opportunity to shine or fail. No editing, no retakes, just pure craft.

One by one, my hosts started to doze off. Jake rested his head on my thigh as he snored away, peach stains on his pajama t-shirt. Laila, her head on the armrest of the recliner, was curled into a ball. Charlotte held out the longest.

We whispered about the Baroness, Maria, and the von Trapp kids until finally she too conked out with her head on my shoulder. I thought about waking her, but I kind of liked the way it felt to have her resting on me and her son asleep at my side. It was like I was part of their crazy little family unit. Like I was meant to be there.

Anything was better than remembering who I really was. The guy who starred in those *current* movies that Charlotte apparently—thank God—didn't watch.

Eventually, I shut my eyes and fell asleep too, only to wake up to Charlotte's sleepy, beautiful face hovering over mine.

For a second, I forgot where I was and mumbled, "Come back to bed."

When she giggled, I realized we were on the couch.

Jake and Laila had disappeared. The movie had started over and flickered in the background on mute. I sat up, ready to excuse myself for the night, but she pulled me back down.

"Stay?" she whispered, her sleepy eyes already closing once more.

I hesitated for a second, until she stretched out on the couch and motioned for me to join her. Knowing there was nowhere else I'd rather be, I lay down behind her, wrapped my arms around her waist, and splayed my hand over her stomach. She fit perfectly against me, like we were meant for this.

Out of all the places I'd been in the world, out of everything I'd seen—people, places, wealth, and luxury—I'd never been as satisfied and happy as I was smooshed on the couch beside Charlotte Dawson in Sunrise Valley, Georgia, with a belly full of Mom's peach cobbler and supermarket shifts to look forward to all week.

A moment later, she twisted in my arms so that we faced each other. Her eyes closed, she mumbled, "Thanks for visiting."

I kissed her forehead, lingering as I spoke. "Thanks for letting me stay."

"Sleepy..." she whispered.

"Sleep then. I'll be here when you wake up." I stayed awake until her breathing evened out, and then I succumbed to her warmth and let it soothe me to sleep too.

Charlotte

The crackle of something frying in the kitchen woke me the next morning. Laila must've been stressed because she never made breakfast out of the goodness of her heart.

My stomach rumbled from the incredible smell, and I opened my eyes, blinking against the light pouring into the window. When I blinked again, I grinned as I recalled why I was sleeping on the couch in the first place.

Ian. Our night. Falling asleep in his arms.

Obviously, he'd left while I'd been asleep because the only sign of him was the scent of pine lingering in the air.

Maybe it had been exhaustion talking. Or it could've been that I'd finally let myself act upon my feelings. Either way, when he'd lain back down, with his nose to my neck, I'd felt complete for the first time in months.

Maybe even years.

Humming sounded from the kitchen, followed by the clattering of silverware. Curious, I got me to my feet, and while I stretched, I studied the clock on the wall.

Holy crap. Was it seriously nine o'clock? In the *morning*?

I scratched at my bed head and frowned before glancing toward the stairs. Any minute now, I expected Jake to bound down demanding breakfast. Maybe he was still asleep. That'd be a shocker.

"Good morning."

"Ahhh!" I spun around, whacking my toe against the coffee table. "Ow, ow, ow." I jumped on one foot before collapsing on the offending piece of furniture.

"I'm beginning to think I'm your bad luck charm." Ian cringed, looking as handsome as ever with his ruffled hair and stubbly cheeks.

"No. I'm just a major klutz." I reached down to rub my toe. "You're still here. What are you doing?"

He pulled a plate from behind his back. "Making breakfast."

Steam rose from the pile of food, and I inhaled—bacon, toast, and some scrambled eggs too. It looked delicious.

"You cook?" I grinned despite the throb in my toe.

"My mother wouldn't have it any other way growing up." He winked, set the plate in my hands, and then sat beside me on the coffee table.

I took in his outfit, a brown Henley and a pair of cargo shorts. The same clothes he'd been wearing last night, besides that raincoat, which meant...

"You stayed all night?"

"I did. I thought that wasn't...a problem? I was up before Laila and Jake were. And I didn't want to leave without saying goodbye, so I made them breakfast instead of sneaking out," he said, like he'd done the most natural thing. "He was getting restless and wanting you, so Laila took him with her to run some errands."

"No." I shook my head, dumbstruck that this man had not only cooked breakfast for me but had done the same for my son and my sister. "That's not a problem at all. Thank you for...taking care of them. I must've been more tired than I thought."

As I stared at the eggs on my plate, my belly growled, demanding to be fed. Ian leaned over and kissed the top of my head. Then he stood and made his way over to the fireplace.

Once I was sure my toe wasn't going to fall off, I returned to the couch and dove into my plate, scarfing the food down like I'd never eaten a decent meal in my life. Everything practically melted on my tongue, and it took all of my resistance not to moan out loud. Ian could not only cook but he was dang good at it.

He was quiet as he walked alongside the mantel, studying the photographs. Every so often, he'd graze the frames with his fingertips. Most were of Jake at various stages of his little life—his early smiles, him sitting up for the first time, his Halloween costumes, and him crying on the beach the first time he'd seen it. There were snapshots of Jake and me, as well as ones of Laila and Jake. The final one was of the three of us, taken at a distance on a park bench.

"These are amazing," Ian said, awe filling his words.

"Thanks." I mumbled around a bigger bite, then swallowed before I finished. "I'll be sure to tell Laila. Her talent knows no bounds."

"I'll say." He whistled.

I sat up taller with pride, for my sister and for her accomplishments. "She wants to open her own studio someday. Right now, she runs one out of our basement. I told her she could use it for as long as she needed, but she doesn't want to take over the house completely." I shook my head, thinking about how stubborn she was. "Says she's intent on finding her own way without my help."

Aside from taking pictures for anyone and everyone in town, Laila ran errands for the people of Sunrise—even the nasty GOLs sometimes. From taking groceries to people who couldn't leave their house, to mowing lawns, to babysitting, I knew she hated doing it, mostly because people spread rumors about her doing unmentionable or illegal errands to stay financially afloat. But really though, she just worked extra hard for next to nothing most days. And she'd stopped accepting money from me the second she moved to town.

"She's talented." Ian narrowed his eyes. "In fact, I know people who'd pay big money to have her photograph them."

"You do? Like, friends back home?"

He stiffened and looked away for a moment. "Yeah. For sure."

I smiled and walked toward him. "I told her she'd be much better off moving to Atlanta or something for a start-up business. But she won't leave this town for some reason."

"Would you be okay if she left?" Ian asked.

"Yeah. I mean, she's young still. Needs to spread her baby bird wings and all that. I'd be happy to send her on her way if it meant she'd be getting to follow her dreams."

She'd given up that scholarship to move in with me, and I felt bad enough as it was. The thing was, she'd told me within a week of being in Sunrise Valley that she was meant to move to this town. Something about being here brought her mojo back, and her head was clearer about work more than it ever had been in Chicago. Despite the GOLs and the gossip, she loves this place.

"Do you mean that? You wouldn't miss her being here with you and Jake?" Though Ian kept his face neutral, his eyes swirled with emotion, from sadness to curiosity. This man could write a love language with those hazel eyes of his. He was just that expressive.

"I do." I leaned against the mantel beside him. "Losing Jonah was hard, but it's been three years. I don't need her to be my support system anymore."

"Do you miss him?"

I stiffened. "Jonah?"

He nodded.

I hesitated, unsure how to answer that. Missing Jonah was like missing a memory. I missed when we were happy—more specifically, those first few months we'd had before he'd devoted himself to work...and to Annabelle.

"Yes."

Ian looked away before I could read his reaction.

This was new territory for me. I had never even discussed Jonah with Marshall. He'd never asked, and I'd never offered. But with Ian, I wanted to be upfront about everything—the good and bad parts.

He moved down the mantel, studying the framed family photo of me, Jake, and Jonah a little harder and longer than the other pictures. I had been meaning to take it down for a while and put it in a nice album for Jake. But I kept forgetting.

"Do you think you'll ever get over him?" Ian traced a frame with a picture of just me and Jake in it. The photo had been taken over the summer when we'd been at the beach. I was sitting, Jake between my legs, while we built a sandcastle together. Laila always managed to catch the perfect moments.

"If you're asking me if I'll ever stop loving Jonah, the answer is no. But it's not the kind of love that you're probably thinking. Far from it actually."

I wanted to tell him the truth—about the Jonah everyone had thought they knew versus the Jonah I'd known. How he'd cheated on me with his ex but had insisted on staying married for the sake of appearances. How he'd begged for a good solid year to get me to move past things and how I'd ignored his requests, even when he'd gotten sick.

The only people who knew the truth were Laila and my mother-in-law—who'd never been able to get over her son's betrayal.

"Just to be clear though, Jonah isn't holding me back in life." I let go of a slow breath.

"Hmm." His reply was soft.

Tell him.

I twisted my hands together in front of me, not sure why I was so nervous. Ian had been through a similar circumstance with his ex too. So, it wasn't like he'd look down on me for it. The only thing different was that I'd stayed in a loveless marriage when he hadn't even gotten to the aisle with his ex.

We stopped before a painting of a landscape. It hung on the wall closest to the stairs, next to the front door. It was the last canvas I'd painted, about three years ago, and it held both good and bad memories.

Our shoulders brushed, but neither of us pulled away. The more time I spent with Ian, the more I craved being close to him.

"This is beautiful." His voice filled with awe as he leaned forward to touch the moss of the trees. "Did Laila paint this?"

I smiled, pride warming my chest. "No. I did."

He whipped around to look at me, his eyes wide. "You did?"

"Yes." My cheeks warmed at the admiration in his eyes. It was too much, too kind, so I looked back at the painting.

"Charlotte, this...this is *gorgeous*."

"You should see it in real life."

Jonah had taken me there to fish. I'd been so excited to go and blown away by the beauty of the place. But about ten minutes into our little adventure, he'd revealed his ulterior motive. Some landowners had been interested in building a series of hotels in that very spot. He'd been in contact with them and had said he'd make it happen once he was mayor.

I'd been flabbergasted, calling him insane for even thinking about wreaking havoc on the natural beauty of that space for the sake of a buck. The mossy trees, the green and blue water, and the natural stone path leading to the fishing hole, it had all been picture perfect. Jonah had then proceeded to tell me it would be good for the town also, by bringing in money and tourists. I'd told him that money just made people crazier, like it had with my mother.

He'd followed up with a rudeness I'd never heard come out of his mouth before, "I'm the soon-to-be mayor, and you're barely even a wife anymore. Maybe everyone was right. Maybe I should've stayed with Annabelle."

Of course he'd apologized—profusely—saying he didn't know what was wrong with him, that he'd been feeling different. Irrationally angry about everything one minute and then wanting to sleep all the time the next...

Despite his apology, I'd stopped speaking to him for four days.

Three days later, we'd found out he had cancer.

"So, what you're telling me is you've got skills beyond just dancing in the kitchen, right?" Ian winked.

I poked him in the ribs and laughed. "Maybe."

Ian returned his gaze to my painting. "You say you've been here before, right? Where is it?"

"About a half hour drive from here."

He rubbed his fingers over his chin, nodding at my work again. "Do you still paint?"

I thought about my bedroom closet, the piles of paints and blank canvases stacked in the corner. The easels and dirty smocks too. Laila had told me I needed to start again, that the two of us could do something with our talents. But in order to paint, I needed time. And that wasn't something I had a lot of anymore.

"Not really."

It didn't just need time. I needed inspiration too. However, the lines of Ian's face provided some nice inspiration. His jawline looked like a model's, and his lips were fuller than anyone's I knew. And all those freckles... Of everything, they inspired me to pick up a brush again the most.

For the first time in years, the urge to paint struck me. So much so that my hands began to twitch.

He looked at me once more, a sly grin on his lips. "If you want me to model for you, all you have to do is ask."

"Wh...what?" I stammered. "I... No. I'm..."

Good God. I pressed a hand to my throat and swallowed. "You look really familiar to me is all."

The statement, though a perfect distraction, wasn't a complete lie. Ian had a face that was unique and beautiful

151

all the same. A look that screamed "recognizable" but was still unlike any man I'd ever seen at before.

He pursed his lips for just a second, and something flashed through his gaze. Before I could ask what was wrong, he faced me. "Thank you."

He touched my shoulder with one hand and lifted my chin with the other. With his thumb, he traced a slow line up and down my jaw, dangerously close to my lips. I shivered, losing my focus—my thoughts most of all—as I watched his expression go from playful to a little sad.

"For what?" I breathed.

"Letting me into your home last night. Letting me meet your family and spend time with them. They're great. You don't know how much I need that normalcy right now."

I leaned into his palm as he cupped my cheek. "Are you okay?"

"Yeah." His expression said otherwise.

Taking a deeper breath, I moved in closer. I pressed both palms to his chest and held them there, feeling the steady beat of his heart under my hands. His heart felt connected to mine now. The same rhythmic beats grew faster whenever we were close.

"I've never seen a man look so sad when he's supposed to be happy and thankful," I teased.

He chewed on his bottom lip for a moment. "You don't want to hear about my problems."

"I think I do." I moved one hand up his chest, pressing it to the side of his neck, feeling far braver than I had just a second ago. He swallowed and closed his eyes as I rubbed my thumb up and down against the pulse point of his throat. "In fact, I think I want to know all about you, Ian Cleary."

He dropped his forehead to mine. "There's no going back if I tell you things. Trust me."

When he paused, I thought the worst. He *was* married. Or maybe he had a secret girlfriend, or he was an ex-con on the run... Ridiculous thoughts filled my mind, but I didn't *really* know Ian Cleary.

I took a few moments to collect my thoughts and made a decision. "Okay. I'll tell you my secrets if you tell me yours. How about that?"

He inhaled an unsteady breath. "I didn't just get my heart broken like I said. I was left at the altar by my fiancée eight months ago."

I breathed a little easier at his confession, but I kind of hated myself for it. I hated how his heartbreak eased my own pains and secrets. But I also hated the idea that I might just be a rebound for him.

"I'm so sorry," I whispered, despite my fears. "But...I also know what it's like. To be hurt like that."

He frowned. "You do?"

I nodded, then proceeded to tell him everything. The words poured out of me like the fountain of truth exploding from my soul. Maybe it was. I'd held it in for a long time. For so long, that when I finished, it felt like the weight of the world had been lifted off my shoulders. I could breathe, feel, and think clearly for the first time in a very long time.

"Charlotte..." Ian took one of my hands in his. He brought it to his lips and kissed my knuckles.

"It was a while ago." I bit the inside of my cheek. "I'm fine now. Promise."

"Is that why you ran from me when we first met? Because you were scared that I might do the same thing?"

"Maybe a little?" I paused. "But it's more than that. You're leaving, Ian. I'm not."

He lifted my arms, wrapped them around his neck, and settled his lips against my forehead. "I'm pretty sure I haven't said that I'm leaving."

I swallowed hard, wanting to believe him. "But your aunt and uncle—"

"They don't know what goes on inside my head," he whispered. "And since I just learned that my ex is engaged to my former best friend, I'm not in much of a hurry to rush home any time soon."

I gasped. "Seriously? What a nasty scumbag." At least with Jonah, I hadn't actually known the woman. Granted she had been his one true love and all that garbage.

Ian chuckled. "Did you just say scumbag?"

"No. I said *nasty* scumbag." I rolled my eyes and huffed. "Do you want me to call him or your fiancée? Because I've got insults for miles in this head." I tapped my temple, then cupped his face between my hands. "If there's one thing you don't do in life, it's fall in love with your fiancé's best friend. Or your best friend's fiancée. They're both to blame."

"I promise, I'm fine now. Don't worry about protecting my honor."

I leaned back and gave his chest a little shove. He'd been trying to do the same for me when it came to the GOLs.

Still, I wasn't mad about his need to protect me. I found it kind of honorable, especially since Jonah had never really bothered. Still, I wanted to handle things on my own.

"So, Cinderella..." He grinned. "I have a question for you."

"Cinderella?" I laughed.

"Yes, that's what I dubbed you since you kept running from me but leaving things behind."

"Like strings from a shall-not-be-mentioned skirt?"

"Yep." He winked. "And don't forget the grapes and the pee."

"Oh my God." I groaned and lowered my head, settling it against his chest. "Can we never speak about those two incidents again?"

"If you take me someplace, I won't mention them ever again."

I pulled back enough to look up at his face. In his presence, I felt so tiny, but I loved it all the same. "Where?"

He smiled, eyes lighter and clearer than they'd been just minutes before. I kind of hoped that was my doing.

"There." He pointed at my painting. "Take me there."

My chest squeezed at the thought of going back to that place, a good kind of squeeze. "That depends."

"On?" He lifted his ginger colored brows.

I wanted to touch them and trace my fingers through the lines that formed just above them. So I did. "Is this a date?"

"If you agree, then yeah." He placed a soft kiss on the inside of my wrist. "I'd say so."

I bit my lip, feeling braver. "Well, second dates equal first kisses in my book, just so you know."

He moved even closer, licking his lips at the same time. "Then pack a bag. We've got fish to be caught and kisses to be had."

chapter twelve

Ian

With my sweet beauty in the passenger seat of Adler's pickup truck, talking a mile a minute and occasionally throwing around driving directions, I couldn't help but smile. I was glad the mood had turned lighter after our talks about our pasts. Even though I was glad that we were opening up to each other, I hated that I'd gotten emotional telling her about Brittany. Charlotte's admission about her husband, coupled with the fact that she'd lost him and had a little baby at the time, made it seem absurd for me to complain about my ex, who hadn't even been right for me to begin with.

Some days, it still got to me though.

How could I have been so stupid? Why had I trusted my heart with Brittany when everything felt so different than it did now, with Charlotte?

To top it off, I was lying to Charlotte about who I really was, and I hated it. And now that Carl knew, I hated it even more, especially after Charlotte had trusted me and confided in me about her life. When she'd told me how

Jonah—the town hero and martyr—wasn't quite the saint everyone had thought, I'd almost blurted out that I wasn't who she thought either. That I looked familiar to her because she'd probably passed a billboard in Atlanta with my damn picture on it or seen me on the cover of one of the magazines at Adler's. Now I was going to have to find a way to tell her who I was and why I'd have to leave her soon.

For now, I wanted to enjoy our second date—for both of our sakes. We needed a break from the serious getting-to-know-you talk, to just have fun. Enjoy each other while we had the time to do so.

When she directed me down a dirt road, I figured I'd mess with her a little. "Are you sure this is the right way to the fishing hole?"

I didn't know there was a recreational water source in Sunrise Valley, but when I saw her painting, I knew I wanted to visit. The thought of looking out over water, with Charlotte, made me happy. I missed the coast of California—the beauty of the landscape and the sun setting in the horizon—more than I missed any of the people who lived there.

Charlotte's directions, though, weren't meant for visitors to Sunrise Valley. "At the blind farmer's silo, turn right. Then go to the third giant willow tree and veer left. You'll come to the spot where the mayor passed out on St. Patty's Day, and that's where you catch Old 567—which is really 542—and you'll take that to Wendy Waterford's final resting place and hook a hard right."

I couldn't help but laugh. It felt like we were acting out a scene in a sitcom. She rolled her eyes and insisted that she'd get me to our second date place, where I could kiss her. That was good enough for me.

After the hard right following Wendy Waterford's gravestone, which to me looked like a giant spaceship sticking out of a small grassy knoll, I drove right into a line of trees. "Um, this is a dead end."

"Yep," Charlotte said, unbuckling her seatbelt and smiling at me. "This is it!"

Slinging an arm over the back of her seat, I inched closer, trying out my Hollywood smolder on her. "I think you got us lost, sweetness. Even though there doesn't seem to be anything to do here, I'd be completely on board with the make out session you promised me."

Sadly, she didn't fall for my acting skills. "I don't remember promising that. You have a one-track mind, Mr. Cleary." She planted a peck on my cheek and then opened the door and bounced out of the truck.

"Sure do," I whispered to myself, then followed her lead.

At the back of the cab, she handed me a fishing pole.

I cringed. "As much as I'd love to see your inspiration for the painting, I didn't think you'd actually make me fish. I thought you were trying to scare me with the poles and tackle box."

"What's wrong, Freckles?"

I grinned at her son's nickname for me.

She raised one eyebrow, her eyes twinkling. "Don't know what to do with a fishing pole?"

159

I took a step closer, pausing just a second to inhale her freshly washed lemon hair scent. "I guess I can figure it out."

She blinked up at me, a vision in her jeans and very flimsy V-neck t-shirt. "You've never been fishing?" She reached in the cab for the tackle box she'd packed and frowned when I didn't answer.

I had never been fishing. When I was a kid, Dad had always wanted to take me, but I'd been busy with plays and auditions and had always turned him down. When Mom told me he'd died, one of the first things I'd said was, "He never got to teach me to fish."

Charlotte sighed when I told her the story. "I'm sorry. I know it's not the same, but I'm happy to be your first teacher."

"Aren't you from Chicago? And you're a—"

"Don't you dare say because I'm a girl. I'll have to whack you on the head with this thing if you do." She wiggled the pole in front of me, eyes practically dancing. "My mom wasn't around much, so my sister and I spent a lot of time with our uncle. He'd take us fishing whenever he thought we needed a break."

"A break from what?"

She tilted her head to the side, considering the question. "Life."

"He sounds like a nice guy." I took the tackle box from her and balanced my pole over my shoulder, not wanting to dredge up bad memories for her. "Okay, so maybe you know about fishing—and I certainly don't—but I'm pretty sure you need water to fish. And there isn't any water here."

Laughing, she nodded toward the tree line. "Follow me."

"Would love to. Best view."

She spun around, stopping short, and grinned. "There you go, throwing those one-liners at me."

"They're my specialty."

She rolled her eyes, but a red tint bloomed in her cheeks.

"How'd you get so pretty by the way?"

She led me to the tree line and sighed. "Is it the great outdoors that makes you so flirty? Or are you like this with all the ladies?"

"Can't help myself. You're turning me into a charmer with all your cuteness."

"I think you were a charmer before I even met you." She narrowed her eyes as she stepped onto a path of gravel. "I could stand here all day and let you sweet talk me, but we have fish to catch."

"Right. The fishing in the dirt, without the water." I glanced around at nothing but trees.

"Are you doubting me, Ian Cleary?"

"Never." I winked.

Charlotte spun around and started walking again, talking over her shoulder as we headed down a crumbling, wooden walkway. Around us, the brush grew taller, thicker, the shade of the morning sun blocked by tall willows that sunk under the mud surrounding us on both sides.

She was like my own personal tour guide, explaining the history of this marshy land, the sounds that made me jump, and the movement in the water that she said were probably snakes. With every step I took, mud dirtied my designer shoes. If I was going to be nature hiking in

Georgia, I'd need to make a run somewhere for clothes that were more durable.

A dozen or so yards later, the bridge-like structure ended, turning into a sandy, dirt path. The sky brightened too, as the coverage from the trees opened from above. When we reached a clearing, Charlotte stopped walking.

She flung her pole over her head to point at something in front of her. "Ta-da!"

I took in the small, muddy water hole. Her painting had definitely taken some artistic liberties compared to the actual reality of it all. Swarms of gnats clustered over the murky water. A few feet of rocks separated the brush from the pond, and the trees surrounding it kept out any hope for a breeze.

"Pretty, right?" Charlotte smiled as she looked out over the water.

I rubbed a hand over my mouth, hiding my cringe. It was an unusually warm November day in Georgia, and the pond, covered in a layer of green moss, smelled like dying, wet animals. Obviously, I couldn't agree with her about the water. But watching her face light up at the scenery—her eyes widening, her pink lips smiling, the sweat glistening on her neck as she lifted her hair off her shoulders and into a clip—I knew nothing in my life had ever looked as beautiful as she did.

"It's gorgeous."

She thought I was talking about her pond, of course, since her gaze never left the water.

"People have no idea what's hiding behind that wall of trees. It's a secret paradise. I bring Laila and Jake here when we want to hide from the people in town." She shrugged. "This little pond is, like, our private getaway. Jake loves it."

I nodded slowly, not agreeing in the least. "Paradise. Yep, I can see that."

I knew she sensed my hesitation when she said, "Cast a line and see. If you don't catch something within five minutes, I'll—"

"Kiss me?" I suggested, hopefully.

"I could agree to that." She grinned. "But you'll catch something, so it won't matter anyway."

Dropping the tackle box, I walked to the edge of the water and stood on a rock. "I don't know. I'm a beginner. I may not catch anything." I hoped I didn't, but I figured if Jake could catch a fish here, there was a pretty good chance of me catching one too.

Still, I glanced over my shoulder and teased Charlotte. "Pucker up, buttercup. I have no clue what I'm doing." Studying the rod, I spun the handle and watched the string thing unwind.

Charlotte giggled at my confusion. "Want me to show you?"

"Yes, please. Teach me everything."

She rolled her eyes. Then she lifted her pole and expertly flung it behind her.

"It's all in the wrist," she said. Then, as she went to cast her line out into the pond, she froze, mid-action.

With her arms over her head and the pole pointing behind her, she looked at me under her arm. "No. No, no, *no*."

I dropped my pole and took two steps toward her. "What's wrong?"

"This can't be happening." Her face was bright red. She attempted to move her arms but seemed stuck.

I raised my brows. "Talk to me."

"My hook." She twisted, trying to look over her shoulder. "It's stuck."

"What? Where?" I looked behind her, squinting to find the invisible line.

She tugged her arms again, but the pole wouldn't budge. "The pocket of my jeans. I managed to hook my own butt."

I circled to her rear. "Are you in pain? Can you drop the pole?"

"I'm fine, I think. I don't want to rip my jeans." She groaned. "Why me? Why can't I ever just not be awkward?"

I wanted to grab her face and tell her that I loved her awkwardness, but I figured I should get her unhooked first. So, I dropped to my knees and studied her behind. "Maybe this is karma for when you spilled your cider on my crotch."

She let out a nervous laugh. "Is it bad?"

"Your butt? Nope. It's perfect—"

"Ian!" She groaned, trying to twist my way. "You know what I mean."

I held her hip steady. "Stay still."

With my knees soaking into the moist ground and without touching her, I examined Charlotte's butt for the hook. The fishing line seemed to follow a path over the right side of her backside and then disappeared underneath.

"I know this is going to sound..." I cleared my throat, "...*cheeky*, but can I touch you? I think I can unhook you with little to no damage to the goods."

She half-chuckled, half-groaned.

I lifted my hands, waiting for the go-ahead. "So...I can touch then?"

"Please, yes. This is an emergency. Unhook me. My arms are starting to ache."

I walked behind Charlotte and knelt down. Then I ran my fingers along the fishing line to get to the hook. My knuckles grazed her behind, and I peeked around her body to see her face.

She was breathing heavily, her cheeks flushed.

"Are you okay?" I asked.

"Uh-huh." She exhaled in a long breath. "But I need something from you."

"Anything," I said.

"Stand up." Her voice shook. "Please?"

Crap. I stood, ready for her to smack me or yell at me for crossing a line. I'd only been trying to help, not that I hadn't enjoyed the quick feel.

I braced myself as she spun and met my gaze. "I'm sorry."

She chuckled, throwing the fishing pole over her head. The rip of her jeans preceded the thud of her fishing pole as it landed a few yards behind her.

"But your jeans!" I looked past her. "Your pole!"

"Don't care." She weaved her arms around my neck, moving closer.

Ahh, now this is nice. I loved the way this beautiful, clumsy girl felt with her arms around my neck. I settled into her embrace as our bodies lined up together, and I fell prey to her dark eyes as they mesmerized me and put me further under her spell. "You're going to kiss me now, aren't you?"

"Maybe." She bit her bottom lip. "You did touch my butt. I think that's like second base or something. No point skipping over first."

"It was in your best interest." I smiled, teasing her. "Even though your jeans didn't make it anyway. You sure you're not bleeding or anything? I can check it out." I pretended to look around her back toward her butt again.

"How about I distract you with that kiss instead?" She tickled the back of my neck with her fingers. "A deal's a deal, and you didn't catch anything."

I opened my mouth to answer with some kind of flirty response but ended up staring at her, dumbfounded, studying her sweet, pink lips as she stood on her tiptoes and moved closer to me. She was really going to kiss me.

I gulped, scared, like it was the first time I'd ever been kissed. Like I didn't know how to do it. I was a grown man with plenty of experience in the kissing department, but this woman had me feeling like a teenager who was making out for the very first time.

Then, she did it. Charlotte Dawson kissed me. *Finally.* My head spun as her soft lips coasted across my mouth.

"Charlotte," I whispered against her.

At the sound of her name on my lips, she pulled me closer and ran her fingers through my hair, toying with the ends. Our kiss deepened, and I didn't feel like a teen-ager anymore. With massive effort, I kept my control. I dug deep for a bit of my movie star charm and kissed her like I was seducing her in the bedroom, instead of in the swampy, bug-infested fishing hole.

When we finally separated, I moved my lips to her neck, gently nuzzling her soft skin and salty sweetness. "Whoa," she moaned. "Where'd you learn to kiss like that?"

"Movies," I blurted, innocently injecting a piece of my real life into my fantasy world with her.

She didn't respond.

When I lowered my hands further down her back, inch-ing farther down south, I paid for it.

A shot of pain flared through my arm. "Ah!"

Charlotte pulled away and glanced at me, concerned. "What's wrong?"

I pulled my hand off of her backside and held it up, feel-ing the blood dripping down my finger. "I think I found your hook."

Charlotte mumbled under her breath as she led me back to the truck by my good hand. She swung the tackle box from her wrist and carried the poles.

She stomped along the path. "What was I thinking? How does this even happen?"

Even with the hook jammed through my middle finger, I couldn't help my chuckle. "It's my fault. I shouldn't have been tempting you."

"Nonsense. This is on me. You were only doing what I've wanted you to do since the first time I laid eyes on you in Adler's Market." She bit her bottom lip. "I guess that's what I get for trying to...*seduce you*...with a hook in my butt."

The world spun. Something was making me woozy—either the loss of blood or her talking about seducing me. "You aren't terrible at all. I really don't mind. It's only a little blood. Kiss me again though, just in case."

I tried to stop walking and pull her to me again, but she was on a mission. I was just along for the ride.

"Are you insane?" she asked over her shoulder. "I am a disaster, and you want me to kiss you again?"

"Absolutely."

She pressed her lips together, not saying no but not saying yes either. "When's the last time you had a tetanus shot?"

"Uhh..."

"Exactly." She huffed. "We need to get you to the hospital."

"Wait!" I yelled when she increased her speed.

She stopped moving, finally.

"Come here." I used my demanding voice, usually reserved for directors and Hollywood types.

With an exaggerated, drama-filled huff, she tilted her head, dropped the tackle box, and stood in front of me.

"That's better." I leaned in close, ignoring the stinging in my finger and holding my hand out so it didn't bleed all over us. "Now shut your eyes."

"Ian, we have to get you—"

"Stop." I softened my words with a grin. "Close your eyes."

She pursed her lips but did what I asked. I took the opportunity to kiss them, softly, just once. "That kiss over there by the water—"

She reopened her eyes, and they sparkled in partial sun. "You mean the one where you ended up bleeding—"

"Shh." I scowled, feigning annoyance. "Listen."

She dropped her shoulders and waited.

I leaned close to her ear, nuzzling her hair this time. "That was the best first kiss I've ever had." I nibbled her earlobe and, with another quick peck to her lips, pulled away. "But yeah, I better get this hand looked at."

Even in her worried state, Charlotte curved her lips into a tight, pink grin. This time, when she looked at me, I could have sworn her eyes twinkled. "It was a good kiss, huh?"

I nodded, grinning back. We stood there for a long second, unspoken words flowing between us. This was a huge step. We'd both had our hearts broken, and learning to trust someone else, trust that we deserved love again, was a feat we'd maybe thought was impossible. But...here we were.

Charlotte's eyes filled with tears. For a second, I thought maybe she regretted getting to know me, kissing me, trusting me with her heart. But then, she wrapped her arms around me and hugged me. "I'm so glad you found your way into my life, Ian Cleary."

"Me too, Charlotte Dawson."

With my arms full of Charlotte, nothing else mattered. Not my throbbing finger with the hook poking through it, not our pasts, and not even our futures. Holding her, being with her, was the only place for me.

Then a click sounded from somewhere in front of me and brought me right back to reality. *No.* I knew that sound. I glanced over her shoulder, my gut going tight, but I found nothing.

The paparazzi? All the way out here? That trash magazine, *A-OK*!? Even if I couldn't see them, I knew without a doubt that someone had found me. That realization dragged me out of my fantasy of living a life as Ian Cleary with the beautiful, sweet, and funny Charlotte Dawson.

More questions raced through my mind as Charlotte said something I couldn't make out.

Had they already leaked my whereabouts? Would Charlotte and I beat the paparazzi to town when we got back into the truck? I stiffened, praying that my new world wouldn't come crashing down around me just yet. I needed time to explain to Charlotte... I needed...

"Ian? What's wrong?"

I blinked, thankful she hadn't seemed to notice the camera click, and then shook my head. "Nothing." The hook in my hand reflected a beam of sunlight. "My hand hurts... Um...maybe we should go."

"Of course." She felt my head. "You feel a bit warm too. You know, when Laila was ten, she stepped on a nail..."

Charlotte's story fell into the backdrop as I scanned the trees ahead of us for photographers. Maybe I'd imagined the sound? I tried to convince myself that the click had been one of these giant Georgia bugs.

Whether or not the click was from a camera or a bug, it reminded me that I had to deal with my old life before I could move onto a new one. I'd been so distracted with the wonders of Sunrise Valley, including the woman next to me, that I'd almost forgotten that I had a life back in California.

Even though I acted for a living, I shouldn't have been here, with Charlotte, pretending I was free to be hers. I wouldn't be free until she knew the truth and until I figured out how to make everything work between us.

For that, I'd eventually have to go home to Cali, clean up my life there, and deal with the magazine editor. I'd have to leave Charlotte in order to come back to her. And considering the way she had kissed me under the trees, that thought devastated me.

chapter thirteen

Ian

I'd have never guessed that hooks were so hard to remove from fingers. Although the fishing ordeal had resulted in a perfect kiss from my new sweet lady, it had also resulted in a tetanus shot, a heavy dose of antibiotics, two tiny stitches in my finger to sew up the hole, and major guilt for not being honest with Charlotte from the start about who I really was.

Mom and Adler met us at the emergency room. As we waited for the discharge orders, Adler asked, "How on God's green Earth did you manage to hook your own finger?"

I looked at Charlotte, she looked at me, and then we shared a smile.

"Don't ask," I said. Charlotte held her hand over her mouth, hiding her grin.

Mom glanced between me and Charlotte with that all-knowing mom look, and after a pause, she turned to her husband. "Why don't we let Charlotte and Ian say goodbye, and then you can drive her home, Adler."

Mom led Adler out of the tiny examination room, and I sat up on the table and held out my arms to Charlotte. When she nestled between my thighs, I pulled her closer. "Today was the best date I've ever had." I kissed her forehead, holding her there as I finished. "Best first kiss."

She nodded against my shoulder. "Are you sure you didn't hit your head too? Is that the drugs talking?"

"No." My eyes watered and I swallowed hard, knowing I'd have to leave her soon. "I think you should get home. This could take a while, and I'm sure your sister and Jake need you."

I hated letting her go—knowing that I'd have to walk away from her, even if it was only temporary—to figure out my real life. The thought of losing her crushed something inside me that I hadn't known was there. But I had to deal with the magazine, or whoever had found me, and try to protect my girl, her son, my parents, and the tiny, private town of Sunrise Valley from the craziness of my real life.

And I had to tell Charlotte who I really was.

As soon as the news broke that I was Ian Tate, this place—with its parks and fountains, its plethora of senior citizens, and its murky ponds and apple cider—would be turned upside down. I was already lasering in on the widow of the town's most cherished citizen. If I destroyed the peace that had grown here in the last two hundred years, I'd never be forgiven nor would I be able to forgive myself.

With a light peck on the lips, I bid farewell to my klutzy sweetness and called my parents back inside. "Could you make sure Charlotte gets home safely, Adler?"

He nodded as I tossed him the truck keys. "Of course." He held out a bent elbow to Charlotte. "Ready, ma'am?"

She linked her arm through his and looked over her shoulder at me. "Call me later?"

I smiled and waved.

I didn't call her though. Instead, as soon as I got home from the hospital, I booked a flight to New York for the next morning. But I couldn't get Charlotte out of my mind, so I texted her.

I think the meds are kicking in. So tired. Can I call you tomorrow?

She replied in an instant.

Yes! Go and sleep. I'm sorry for the mishap. But not sorry for the reason.

I smiled at the phone, remembering the kiss, the way she'd tasted, the way her lips had melted into mine.

Best first kiss ever.

Then I packed a bag and wrote three letters—one to Charlotte, one to Mom and Adler, and a curt, professional email to Stephanie Wilson.

The next day, Fink met me at JFK International. He pulled me into a one-armed hug.

"You look horrible," he said. "We'll get you to the stylist ASAP."

I didn't have the energy to argue. Instead, I held up my heavily bandaged middle finger.

Fink grimaced. "Nice accessory."

As we walked through the airport, I imagined Charlotte waking up and finding the note I'd left in her mailbox.

Dear Charlotte,
Something important came up in New York that I have to attend to. I'm so sorry to leave you this way after our awesome date, but if I had to say goodbye to you face-to-face, I'd never be able to leave. I'll be back as soon as I can, I promise. I miss you already.
Love, Ian.

Fink and I spent the night drinking in Manhattan. He couldn't believe that nobody recognized me as Tate, the movie star, despite my shaggy red hair, hazel eyes, and chubbier Georgia physique.

"You completely let yourself go," he said, glancing at my appearance with disapproval. "This isn't about Brittany and Russ, is it?"

I shook my head. I didn't think I'd let myself go. Instead, I thought I'd found my true self.

"I'm back to my roots," I declared with a slur. "Even though I grew up in New Jersey, Georgia is where I feel at home. I like it. A lot."

Charlotte's brown eyes flashed through my mind.

"Who is she?" Fink waved to the bartender over my shoulder.

"Who's who?"

"The girl?" He waited, but I didn't answer. "It's got to be a girl that has you wanting to save that little nowhere town from the big, bad magazine."

"My mom is there." I nodded, answering without answering.

He squinted, studying me. "True, but I know there's more to this story."

I ignored him and took another swig of my beer. I thought I could trust Fink, but I wasn't ready to share my secret romance with the world yet.

"You don't have to tell me. Just remember, you're under contract for *Murder in the White House 2*, so you better get back to California, in tip-top shape, by the New Year." He gave me a once-over before pulling out his phone and vigorously swiping the screen.

"Yeah, yeah," I mumbled. "I know."

Actually, I *had* forgotten. Filming started in two months. Even if I could get myself out of this mess with the magazine, I'd still have to be in LA for *Murder 2*. "Ugh."

Fink looked up from his phone. "What?"

"Nothing."

But it wasn't nothing. It was something. As much as I wanted to explore this new relationship with Charlotte, our worlds didn't mesh. She had a life in Sunrise Valley, and I had a career on the other side of the country.

Stephanie Wilson was a tall, slim, middle-aged blonde, dressed in a perfectly tailored gray pantsuit and black stiletto heels. She marched into the hotel bar like she owned the place, carrying a briefcase in one hand and a cell phone in the other. Her gold earrings reflected what little light shone in the bar. A few steps behind her, a tall, brawny dude with a beard and a head full of long, dark hair followed.

When she saw me, she smiled like a winner. She'd gotten me, and she knew it. Stephanie sat across from me at the cocktail table and laid the black leather briefcase on its surface. Mountain Man stood behind her, arms crossed. With her perfectly manicured thumbs, she clicked open the latches and the briefcase popped. She pulled out a manila envelope and closed it again.

Flashing a million-watt grin, she laid two pictures on the case. One was of me and Charlotte kissing, my hands on her butt right after the hook incident. The second was a picture of us walking back to the truck—Charlotte ahead of me, pulling me, the poles, and the tacklebox behind her.

"Well?" Stephanie asked, folding her hands in front of her and flipping her long hair over her shoulder. "Do you like what Oz, here, has captured?"

Damn it.

I gritted my teeth and glared at Mountain Man Oz, but I addressed Stephanie. "You're holding out on me. These are recent. What do you have from before?" I figured it best to know what I was dealing with.

Stephanie smiled and pulled out a third picture, one of me, Adler, and Mom on the front porch of the house. It had been taken from far away with a zoom lens, but it was clearly us. I was used to this nonsense in California, but to see the pictures of me and Charlotte, of me and my family, pierced me in the gut like a knife through my soul. How could I let this happen to them? I should have known that Hollywood would find a way to follow me. Now, it was too late.

"Is that it?" I asked.

She nodded. "Your decision?"

I didn't think I had one. "I'll do the exclusive. All the juice on me and Brittany, and whatever else you want. In exchange, you and your people stay out of Sunrise Valley." Then I turned to Oz. "The pictures disappear. You leave the girl, her family, and everyone in Sunrise Valley alone. You also keep my location a secret."

Stephanie lifted the pictures, tucked them inside the manila envelope, and clicked open the briefcase. She placed the envelope inside and took out a business card.

After she closed it again, she slid the card across the table to me. "Deal. We'll be here tomorrow at noon." She looked me over as she stood up. "Keep the look. It will add to the story."

I glared at her, hating her for doing her job.

"Nice doing business with you, Tate," she said as she spun and walked away.

Mountain Man shuffled backwards and held my stare, almost like he felt sorry that they'd pulled a fast one on me. Without a word, he turned to follow her out.

I squeezed my eyes shut and willed my heart to stay intact, even though it felt like it could explode into a million pieces at any given second. I hated that I'd have to do the exclusive, but I was grateful they'd given me the opportunity instead of blasting the photos all over social media and their dumb magazine. They'd handed me a life preserver, so I'd take it.

I'd do anything, even rehash my relationship with my ex, if it meant keeping Charlotte, our families, and Sunrise Valley safe.

chapter fourteen
Charlotte

I missed Ian like crazy, and he'd only been gone two days. What would I do if he left town and headed back to New York permanently?

Just like I'd feared before, I was getting too attached, and we hadn't done more than kiss.

He'd left so abruptly that I'd only gotten a simple note—even though it *had* said love at the end. Of course we hadn't exactly established anything between us to make me believe he'd fallen for me, so I refused to look into that four letter word. Instead, I focused on what I did know. Ian didn't technically owe me anything.

"You're quiet tonight, Char. Anything bothering you?" Paula, Jonah's mama, stared at me with motherly concern.

I blinked and looked up from my menu. Since Jonah had passed, Paula and I had made it a tradition to go out for dinner once a month at his favorite restaurant and catch up. Languine's was crazy expensive for our small town, but the food was to die for. And it was the only Italian place in Sunrise Valley.

Sitting there now though—growing lost in my thoughts of Ian—I felt like I was secretly betraying Paula, even though she knew Jonah and I had been done long before he'd passed.

"Sorry, I'm just distracted is all." I reached across the table and grabbed my water glass.

"You have any certain reason as to why that is?" She raised her eyebrows.

I loved Paula. So much. In a way, she'd taken over as my parent in the years since I'd left Chicago. Still, it felt weird talking to her about my current dilemma with Ian.

"Nothing important."

"You don't have to lie to me. I won't be mad."

I bit my bottom lip, still hesitating.

"Is it that new fella in town? Mary and Adler's nephew? Heard from Ruby that he was making quite the wave amongst the citizens."

"That *woman*," I hissed. "She's so—"

"Hold on now." Paula reached over the table and touched my hand. Her smile grew soft. "You know I don't listen to a thing she, or any of her friends, say, don't ya? Never have, never will."

"Yeah, well, everyone else seems to."

"You sure about that?" She pursed her lips. "Because as far as I'm aware, half the people in this town hate those ladies as much as my boy did."

"Jonah didn't hate anyone. Least of all, them."

"That's not true." Paula pulled her hand away and fiddled with her silverware, avoiding my gaze.

"It is and you know it. Those women treated me like dirt, and he always turned a blind eye on it." He'd never once stood up for me against them either. If anything, he'd catered to their needs more than he had my own.

When Paula grew silent, I regretted my words. My stomach started to twist. We rarely fought about anything. In fact, Paula had always taken my side over her son's, especially when she'd learned about his cheating. I think it was Paula's way of trying to make up for her son's mistakes. That didn't necessarily mean she always agreed with me though.

"Look, I'm sorry. I didn't mean to upset you. I just..." I blew out a heavy breath, wishing I could start over.

"Listen, honey. We both know Jonah wasn't perfect. Not like everyone in this town thinks. He made mistakes, the biggest a husband can make in fact." She hesitated. "But he loved you and Jake to pieces. That much I do know."

"I know he did." But he'd had a crap way of showing it, not that I would say that to his mama.

"He'd want you to be happy again. He'd want you to move on and find someone you truly loved. Someone who'd treat you a lot better than he did."

I winced, unsure of how to reply this time.

"You think this Ian fella might be the person to do that, don't you?"

I froze, fingers poised over my fork. Swallowing hard, I peered up at Paula, nervous. Only Laila knew how I felt about Ian, and even that hadn't been by choice. But like my sister, Paula tended to see through me.

"Don't clam up on me now, honey," she said with a wink. "Tell me about him. Tell me he's good for you and Jake."

I chewed on my bottom lip, choosing my words carefully. "He's kind. And handsome. He's generous and amazing with Jake. He's just...*Ian*."

A man who seemed too good to be true. A man who'd stolen my heart in a short period of time and made me feel more than Jonah ever had.

Paula nodded once. "Met him at the market myself. Real charmer, that one. Familiar looking too, but with all that red hair and freckles..." She scrunched her nose.

"He's more than hair, ya know." I mentally tallied all the things that had drawn me to Ian since the moment we met—physically and beyond. His forearm muscles, that soft smile, those twinkling eyes. He was also charming and sweet, protective and good. I trusted him with my whole heart, and, well...that was hard for me to do.

"Ahhh." Paula pointed the end of her spoon my way, her blue eyes dancing. "I see."

Our food arrived before I could ask her what she meant. Pasta steamed up from our plates, making my stomach grumble.

"Laila approves," I said. "And you know how protective she can be."

Paula kept silent as she listened. I couldn't get a good read on her, and that frustrated me. Did she not trust him, like the GOLs? That thought bugged the heck out of me, to the point where I couldn't stop the waterfall of Ian compliments from spilling out.

"And any man who can sing along to every song in *The Sound of Music* is a keeper in my book." I took an stab at my food and slurped it in, giving no thought to manners. "I also find him very attractive, thank you very much. I happen to like his red hair and all those freckles." I heaved in frustration. I hadn't been this worked up in a long time. "I don't really care what anyone thinks about Ian Cleary because he's kind to me."

The fact that he didn't run screaming every time I did or said something wacky helped as well.

Eyes wide, Paula stared back at me like I'd grown a second head. "Wow, honey. I've been waiting a long time for this day. I'm thinkin' we're gonna need more than water for this though." She winked and motioned for the waiter.

"We don't need to do this tonight."

"We do." She smiled at me. "It's been a long time coming."

We left the restaurant with full bellies and aching hearts. It was the most therapeutic of dinners, and I felt twenty times lighter than I'd felt in years.

It was too nice of a night to hurry home, and since Laila was watching Jake, Paula and I decided to walk the shops for a little while.

We huddled together in our jackets, enjoying the fall weather, the clear night sky, and even the hum of the occasional car passing along the street. Paula tucked her arm through my elbow as we walked along the sidewalk. She pointed out signs and talked about memories of her childhood and of growing up in this town. I smiled when she recalled bringing Jonah to the town festivals Sunrise Valley was so known for. I saw her memories through the eyes of a mother. Every time Jake experienced something new here, it was like I was experiencing it for the first time too.

Unlit Christmas decorations hung in the trees—we could see the wires along the trunks and the storefronts. In a few weeks, during our town's lighting ceremony, this place would look like something out of a movie. I always went with Jake and Laila to the event, and I couldn't help but wonder if Ian would like to go with us this year.

"My boy would be happy for you, honey. So happy." Paula sighed contentedly, puffs of her breath drifting like tiny clouds in the cool night sky. "He knew he messed up with you, and he regretted it every single day for the rest of his life."

I swallowed the unexpected lump in my throat. "Jonah wasn't a bad person. He just made some bad decisions. He'll always be special to me."

She hummed, nodding. "And if this Ian fella makes you happy and is good to my grandson, then that's all I need to know."

Tears welled in my eyes. "That means a lot coming from you."

She squeezed my arm. "Gonna want to meet him officially though. Soon. I'll cook up some of your favorite dumplings. Have you, him, Laila, and Jake over for dinner one night. How does that sound?"

I smiled, happiness spilling into my chest. "I'd love that."

"How about this—"

"Hey there, ladies."

I blinked, freezing in place along the street. Paula squeezed my arm. Carl stood before us, decked out in his sheriff's getup. He wasn't alone, of course. Ruby stood on one side of him, that blue hair of hers making her look more like a troll than ever. Edna stood on the other side of her grandson, looking just as bratty.

"Good evening, Carl." Always the picture of kindness, Paula let go of my arm and reached for Carl's hand. He didn't hesitate. He grasped her hand and brought it to his lips, but his gaze stayed locked on my face.

I swallowed long and hard, wondering what he was thinking.

"You're looking well, Char." He nodded, taking a step closer and kissing me on the cheek. He smelled like mothballs.

"Thank you." I forced a smile.

"What're y'all doin' out so late without an escort?" Edna looked down her nose at me like always.

"We were just walkin' to our cars. No need to worry, Edna." Paula smiled a polite Southern smile.

"There's lots of reasons to worry," Ruby grumbled. "With the likes of these strange men moving into town as of late, no woman should be left alone on the street." She narrowed her eyes and made point to glance in my direction.

I focused in on her pearls, shiny and white like she'd polished them fifty times a day. The devilish part of me wanted to choke her with those things. I waited for the angel side to balk at the idea, but it stayed quiet.

Paula laid her hand on my forearm and gave it a squeeze, like she knew the awful thoughts I'd been thinking.

"Heard about that new fella you've been running around with." Carl pursed his lips and locked his jaw in disdain.

"If you're indicating that Ian Cleary is a bad man, Carl, then I suggest you look again." I took a breath and squared my shoulders, more than ready to go to war here. I was tired of this crap. Tired of their judgement and of them assuming I was someone I wasn't. They had no right. None of them did.

I raised an eyebrow at Carl. "Ian has a demeanor that surpasses all men in Sunrise Valley."

Edna and Ruby gasped, clutching their hero for dear life.

I looked to them, baring my teeth as I finished. "And the women in this town too."

Carl gaped at me, probably confused by my sudden backbone.

"How dare you speak of us all that way." Edna scowled at me, her old, ugly face twisting up in revulsion.

"And how *dare* you speak of me *and* Ian the way you all do. Do you not know how to be nice? I have a four-year-old with better manners than all of you."

"I show plenty of respect," Ruby said, waving a hand in my direction.

"No, you don't." These women, who claimed to be the epitome of Southern hospitality yet treated me worse than anyone else ever had, brought out the angry Chicago girl in me.

"And that fella you've been takin' up with, he ain't right in the head. It's obvious his crazy has rubbed off on you," Ruby screeched.

"And you, Ruby Pearl, are the rudest woman I know."

"Well I *never*!"

"Ms. Ruby," Carl said, patting her arm. "Let's leave the ladies to go on their way. I need to be getting y'all home so I can get back to the station." He glared at me. "Char, here, obviously doesn't know what's good for her."

"Screw you and the horse you rode in on, Carl. If I never have to see your smarmy face again, it'll be too soon." Ignoring all three of them, I guided Paula around them. I'd had enough drama for one night.

When we were out of earshot, Paula tipped her head back and laughed. "Wow, honey. Look at you go."

Though my lips twitched, I resisted the urge to laugh. "You ain't seen nothing yet."

chapter fifteen
Charlotte

Once I'd made sure Jake was fast asleep in bed, and also had a chance to fill my sister in on my brand-new bravado with the GOLs, I raced to my room, eager to get on the phone with Ian. After throwing on my favorite, threadbare t-shirt, I dialed his number and fell back onto my pillow, a stupid grin on my face as I listened to his ringtone.

He answered on the third round, a sleepy crackle in his voice. "Charlotte," he said by way of hello.

My cheeks ached from grinning so much. "Hey, you. How are things?"

"Hmmm, tired. It's been a long day."

He sounded distracted. Maybe even a little sad. "You wanna talk about it?"

"Nah. I don't want to weigh you down with my problems." He cleared his throat. Papers rustled on his end, and I frowned, wondering again what was up.

"How was your dinner?" he asked.

The adrenaline rush I'd been feeling from earlier started to crash. In its place was a longing for the man on the other end of the line.

"It was nice." I yawned. "Saw Ruby, Edna, and Carl when we were done though. I had a few words with them."

"Are they giving you trouble again?"

I grinned at the grumble in his voice, then shut my eyes to try and imagine the tiny frown lines between his brows. I really needed to get an iPhone so we could FaceTime, especially if he had to go away like this again.

"A bit. But I think you would've been proud of me, especially since I stood up for myself."

"You did?" He chuckled. "What happened?"

I told him everything, leaving no detail untouched.

"Proud of you," he whispered. "I wish I could've been there to see it."

I settled deeper under the covers and pulled them up to my chin. His compliment had me floating.

"How's the finger?" I asked.

"It's wishing you were here to kiss it better."

I rolled my eyes. Ian and his kisses. "Are you keeping it dry?"

"Yep. Wrapping it in plastic wrap when I take a shower."

"Good." I nodded in satisfaction, loving how easy it was to talk to him, even over the phone like this. "What'd you do all day?"

"I had some work stuff to take care of."

"Work stuff?" My heart skipped. "You have another job, or some secret life, in New York?" I was only half joking. I really knew little about this man and his past. At the same time, I'd exposed a lot of myself to him already. "I thought Adler said you were apprenticing at the market for a while?"

He didn't answer right away. That little bit of silence made the hair on my arms rise. "Ian?"

"Yeah, sorry. I mean..." There was another pause, followed by a heavy sigh. "It's not like I planned on working at Adler's Market for the rest of my life."

I flinched. My belly flopped like a fish and fell into my feet.

And there it was. The truth I'd been trying to avoid since I'd met this man. He really wasn't going to be sticking around. His stay in Sunrise Valley was nothing but a reprieve until his broken heart healed.

Did that mean I was just a rebound to him after all? A different kind of woman to heal him until the right one came along, maybe? I'd been second fiddle to someone before, and I wasn't down with playing that role again.

I might've been jumping to conclusions, but there was no denying that my head had been up in the clouds these past two weeks. It had been a pipe dream to think that a man like Ian would be perfectly satisfied working at some small-town market. Though he dressed like everyone else in this town, I could tell he was the type of man meant for a suit job, not t-shirts and vests. Meanwhile, I was meant to stay here, in this small town, working as a waitress, being a single mom, and planting roots.

I sat up and wiped away my tears.

"I miss you, Charlotte."

At his soft admission, all my anger, fear, frustration, and sadness melted away. My heart had officially betrayed my head.

"You do?" I whispered.

"So much it hurts."

I shut my eyes and flopped back down on the pillow. I was such a goner.

"Listen," Ian continued. "I know it's crazy. We've only known each other for a couple for weeks, but God...you're all I think about. You're *in* me, sweetness. Buried so deep I couldn't get you out if I tried. And believe me, I don't want to try."

My tears fell freely this time. My throat squeezed too, making it impossible to say anything back. Deep down, I knew the truth, whether it scared me or not. It didn't matter where Ian was headed, where he'd go, or where we'd wind up when it was all said and done. I was already his.

"I'm dealing with a lot of stuff right now, yet the only thing I want to do is get on a plane and fly back so I can kiss you again."

"Yeah?" My face warmed as memories from the pond burned through my mind. Ian's kisses, his closeness, his reverence...Jonah had never looked at me the way Ian did.

"Did I scare you away?" He gave a nervous chuckle.

"No." I twirled a lock of hair, suddenly feeling fifteen instead of nearly thirty. "The exact opposite actually."

And in that moment, I knew I should get off the phone. The last thing I wanted to do was say something I'd regret in the morning.

"Hey, Charlotte?"

"Yeah?"

He sighed. "I want to fall asleep with you tonight."

I curled up on my side and tucked the phone between

my ear and the pillow. *Yep, a goner for sure.* "I think I want to fall asleep with you too."

That night, I dreamt of a man with red hair, freckles, and golden eyes.

But I also dreamt of the day he left Sunrise Valley for good, a harem of women following him down the one lane highway that led out of town. It was startling. Unexpected. Filled with hidden, indecipherable meanings.

When I woke up in the morning to find that he'd somehow hung up in the middle of the night, I couldn't shake the feeling that something big was about to happen.

Something far worse than a broken heart.

chapter sixteen

Ian

During the entire flight from New York to Atlanta, I was a bundle of energy. The exclusive interview with Stephanie Wilson would head the entertainment section in Sunday's issue, which left me in a quandary.

I could hope Charlotte wouldn't see it, since she didn't seem too involved in social media or entertainment news, and continue my life as Ian Cleary for as long as I could. Or, I could come clean before the article hit social media.

I knew in my heart what I had to do, especially after talking to her the night before. She'd been so brave about confronting the seniors of Sunrise Valley and dealing with her past. She was becoming a new woman, and I hoped I'd had a little something to do with it.

But at the same time, I was lying to her. Hiding in Georgia, hiding in New York, hiding from paparazzi. All I'd ever done was hide. I wanted to be my true self, like Charlotte was becoming hers, more than anything. But there were loose ends that needed tying up.

The thought of telling Charlotte about my true life— and what that could possibly mean for her, her family, and

Sunrise Valley—felt like a weight I couldn't bear anymore. But the moment I stepped off the plane and took my first breath of the heavy Georgia air, I gave myself a reprieve.

Before I told Charlotte anything, I needed to see her, hold her, kiss her—maybe for the last time—because I had no idea how she'd react to the news that I was Tate. Ian Tate. Not a harmless grad student from New York but an in demand actor from Hollywood, with twenty million Twitter followers and an ex with an attitude.

I texted Mom to let her know I'd landed safely and said I had to make a stop before I came home. She offered to have Adler pick me up in Atlanta, but I rented a convertible instead. Since everything in Sunrise Valley was close by, I hadn't taken a ride in a long time. I needed to get some speed, feel the air and the heat to clear my head.

Clear was the last thing I'd call my head though. The entire trip, I had to stop myself from over-gripping the steering wheel as I focused on the one person I ached to see—*Charlotte*—and the one place I needed to be—*home*. Somewhere along the line, I had started to think of Sunrise Valley as my home. The warm, thick air. The creaky porches and nosy neighbors. The smell of peach cobbler in the oven, and the sound of dogs barking at each other up and down the street.

My art deco penthouse in LA felt more like a distant memory. Like a hotel I'd once visited and used to meet my daily needs but that had no heart. Now, my heart was in Georgia, and that was what made it feel like home.

I must have been speeding like a race car driver since I made it to Sunrise Valley in a little less than an hour. As

I turned into the town, I smiled, passing the landmarks that everyone in town knew and used as directional points. Just like everything in Sunrise Valley was "around the corner," nobody took care to learn the street names, except for Main. Charlotte's voice teased my thoughts as I drove by the haunted ranch house, the stable where John Wayne once trained for a movie, and Old Mister Grady's famous farm stand to Main Street, and then across the tracks to Charlotte's street.

As her house came into view, I slowed down and parked on the wrong side of the street. After flinging open the driver's side door, I darted across the road, taking the stairs in one leap, and banged on the screen door. While I waited for her, I looked up at the sky, tapping my foot on the porch, wondering what was taking so long.

I banged again, until the door finally opened.

"What is going on out here with all that banging?" Laila. Holding Jake.

I leaned forward and kissed the little guy on the forehead. "Hey, buddy."

He held out his arms to me and I pulled him into mine. We were growing on each other. How could he not make me smile when he peered at me with those big blue eyes, his face all red from whatever the heck Laila had fed him?

"Where's Charlotte?" I asked, looking at Laila as Jake grabbed my nose.

"Well, hello to you too, Mr. Cleary," Laila huffed.

"I'm sorry. It's just... I'm anxious to see her, you know?"

Laila put a hand on her hip and rolled her eyes. "It's only been a few days. She's been moping around here like you've been gone forever. I finally sent her to Adler's to get us bananas and ice cream so we could make sundaes—"

"Adler's? Great." Without letting her finish, I kissed Jake again and held him out to her. When she took him, I waved goodbye and darted back to my rental.

"You better be nice to her, Cleary!" Laila's voice followed behind me.

"Yeah!" Jake giggled. "Bye, Freckles!"

I snorted at the nickname, then gave them a thumbs-up as I drove away, off to get my girl. The drive to the store was only a few minutes, but it felt like forever. I couldn't wait to look into her eyes, feel her in my arms, tell her...

Tell her what? That I loved her?

Did I love her? Could I love someone I'd just met a couple of weeks ago?

I shook my head to clear it as I pulled into Adler's lot. Just then, Carl drove by in his police cruiser. Glaring at me, he tipped his hat and continued on down the road. I started to get angry thinking about him and his threats, but when I saw Charlotte's dented old Civic with the I Brake for Cake bumper sticker, I chuckled.

The smile stayed on my face as I ran into the store, hurdling a stack of shopping baskets and Adler's potted plant display. The store was quiet and looked empty. Becca leaned against the cashier station, filing her nails and singing along to Barry Manilow playing over the speakers.

She glanced at me when I darted by. "Hey, Red. Whatcha doin' here?"

I scanned the aisles one by one.

"Check the frozen section." Becca gave a knowing laugh.

Right. Ice cream sundaes. I ran to the opposite end of the store, my heart racing at the thought of seeing her.

When I did, I stopped short.

There she was, leaning into the ice cream case, holding the door open with her hip as she examined the cartons. Her hair was down, long and curly. She wore jeans and a simple t-shirt but managed to look beautiful nonetheless.

"Jesus," I whispered.

I could have walked any red carpet with Charlotte in that very outfit and been the envy of the entire world.

I jogged down the empty aisle to her. She must have sensed my movement because she stood up straight and looked through the window of the freezer door. She widened her eyes, and the smile she gave me through the glass door probably could've melted the entire ice cream case if she stood there long enough.

Without a word, she stepped back. I closed the freezer, then grabbed her around the waist. I urged her back until she was flush against the freezer door. She rested her hands on my chest as she studied my face, still wordless. Finally, after too many days apart, I could look into her dark, shining eyes.

And I was home. Where my heart was.

"Charlotte," I whispered low, studying her mouth. And then I kissed her, like we were alone in her bedroom instead of in the frozen food aisle at Adler's Market.

She kissed me back. As she did, she slid her hands from my chest, up over my shoulders, and down my sides to my jeans.

"You're really here. How did I miss you so much?" she murmured into my lips. "It's only been a couple of days."

"Felt like forever." I moved my lips over her jawbone, down to her neck.

She held my head, her fingers tangled in my mess of hair. "Iannnn."

My name was a song from her lips, and I thought she'd make me stop. But in a swift move, she spun me around and pinned me against the freezer instead. She looked deep into my eyes, like she was trying to tell me something without words. Our breathing synced.

"I love how you kiss me," she said finally.

There, in the frozen food aisle, Charlotte seemed more confident, more focused and determined, and I loved it. It's like she'd finally realized how special she was, and that she didn't need to be hiding from the likes of Ruby Pearl. Maybe it took her telling off the seniors to find her courage. Maybe it had something to do with me. Either way, it made me happy that she was feeling her worth.

"I love how you kiss me too. It's all I could think about while we were apart."

"Then we should do more of it," she whispered.

There was nothing I wanted more in the world than Charlotte Dawson, but not without her knowing the truth about me first.

I kissed her again, slower, calmer. I touched her soft cheeks. "I would kiss you all night if you'd let me."

She smiled against my lips, rubbing her nose against the tip of mine. "Want to come over and have sundaes with us?"

"That sounds amazing." But I knew the truth. If I went to Charlotte's tonight, there was a good chance I'd want to spend the night. If that happened, I'd never have the guts to tell her anything about me. And then, when she found out the truth about who I really was, she'd never forgive me. "But I have to get home. Tomorrow?"

She frowned. "Boo."

"I know. I'm sorry." And I was too, especially with her in my arms, her lips so close to mine. "There's...something I have to take care of."

"Fine." She exaggerated her pout. "I can wait until tomorrow. Call me later?"

"Of course."

"I'm glad you're back, Ian." She offered a sad grin. "This all felt...empty without you."

I wasn't sure what felt empty to her. Maybe Sunrise Valley or Adler's Market. Or maybe she meant her life.

One thing was clear. I was falling for her, and Charlotte was falling for Ian Cleary.

I just hoped that she'd fall for Ian Tate too.

Back at home, Mom and Adler sat on the porch in their rocking chairs, with their usual glasses of sweet tea. Their faces lit up as soon as they saw me. Nothing settled me more at the end of a day than walking up the path and seeing them on the porch.

Home.

I sat on the top stair and told them about New York City, the magazine, and my plans to tell Charlotte everything. Then, I reminded them that I had to be back to California to film *Murder 2* by the New Year. They said they'd support whatever I wanted to do.

"You know," Mom said, "the old Orchard Mills Estate is up for sale. Restoring it would be a fun project for you to work on with Adler. There's no law that says you have to be in California all the time."

I shook my head, puzzled as she grinned at me. "Are you saying that because you want me out of your house?"

"You can stay here as long as you'd like." She took a sip of her tea, watching me over the rim of her glass. "I'm saying that because you seem to be growing accustomed to our little town, and maybe some of its residents."

Adler smiled from his rocker. "Becca called us after you left the frozen food aisle. Told us you'd publicly displayed your affection toward Charlotte—"

"That little snitch." But I couldn't help but smile.

"You have real feelings for Charlotte?" Mom asked, cocking her head to one side.

"Yes." I'd never been more certain of anything. "What should I do?"

My stepfather leaned forward, resting his elbows on his knees as he talked. "As far as your identity, you have to do what's right. I think you know what that is because your mama raised you properly."

Mom reached across her chair and squeezed his shoulder. "Adler's right. It's time, Ian. You'll start by inviting her and her family to Thanksgiving dinner."

"Here?" I rubbed the stubble on my chin and tried to recall the date. "Is it Thanksgiving already?"

"Next week," Mom said. "You'll invite her, Jake, and Laila, and then you can tell her what you need to tell her."

"I appreciate that, Mom. I will invite them. But I'm going to have to talk to her sooner since the article comes out on Sunday." I needed to lift that weight off my shoulders as soon as I could.

Thanksgiving was way too far off. Also, I wanted to talk to Charlotte alone, and not on a holiday. That way, it wouldn't ruin the day for her and her family if she decided she didn't want me after all.

My gut twisted at the thought of Charlotte dumping me. I almost curled over from the pain of it. But I couldn't think the worst yet. I had to stay confident.

Mom reached over to squeeze my hand. "Don't worry, baby. She'll think Ian Tate the actor is just as special as Ian Cleary the bag man. As your Hollywood persona, or as your grocery clerk persona, you have the same heart and soul."

I stood and kissed the top of her head. "Thank you."

Then, I went inside, leaving them to enjoy the rest of their tea. As I climbed the stairs to my room, I couldn't help but pray to the Big Guy above that she was right.

chapter seventeen
Charlotte

S arge sat on the counter at Minka's, his booted feet dangling over the edge as he thumbed through a magazine with motorcycles on the front. Mateo was doing dishes at the sink, humming under his breath, while I ate a piece of pecan pie and glanced at the clock.

It was almost closing time. All I wanted to do was go home, hug my son, then crawl into bed and pray that Ian called.

I hadn't heard from him in *two* days, not since he'd texted me after that frozen food make out session. Not wanting to seem clingy, I'd tried to call him just once yesterday, but he'd never answered. Two minutes later though, he'd texted me back to say that he missed me and that we'd talk soon.

Soon had never felt more ominous.

Still, I wasn't going to let myself worry about it. Things between us were new. Which meant—I was fifty percent sure—that it was too early to panic about the little things.

The diner was dead tonight, likely because it was a week from Thanksgiving and everyone was saving their turkey dinner for turkey day. I told Sarge not to take it personally, but from the way his dark eyebrows had bunched together, I didn't think he'd listened.

"So, how's the love life going, Char?"

I looked up from my pie, continuing to chew. Mateo stood in front of me, arms folded, wearing a smug smile.

I swallowed and then took a long drink of lemonade, stalling as I tried to figure out how to answer this question. Coming out as a couple to the people we knew, the town in general, before we'd even figured things out ourselves could get really messy. Still, I couldn't stop myself from smiling.

"What do you know of my love life, Mateo?"

"Word on the street is you and that redhead are hooking up."

I cringed. "Hooking up, huh?" Well, we'd definitely done something with *hooks*.

"Yup." He winked.

"Becca running her mouth again?" I frowned.

Mateo continued grinning but didn't speak, confirming my suspicions.

"Seems like a good guy to me." Sarge's deep voice startled me.

I turned to him, lifting my brows. "Are you giving me love advice, Sarge?"

"Dude, you *do* talk." Mateo jumped up on the counter beside Sarge and clapped him on the back.

"I talk." Sarge shoved Mateo, but not enough to push him away. "Just don't like talking to *you*."

"I'm offended." Mateo settled both hands over his chest, looking anything but offended.

Sarge waved a hand back toward the kitchen. "Go...do something. Leave Charlotte alone."

Mateo rolled his eyes, but he still didn't lose his grin as he jumped down. He started humming under his breath again.

I shook my head and laughed, just as the bell over the door rang.

"We close in five minutes," Sarge barked as he pushed through the kitchen doors, leaving me alone to deal with the newcomer.

I turned to face whoever had come in, readying for damage control. "Sorry about Sarge. He's a little..." I widened my eyes. "Ian?"

He stood in the entryway, a huge smile on his face. His hair was longer than I remembered it being a few days ago. Shaggy red pieces fell in disarray all over his head. Like he'd been running his hands through it for days. He looked adorable...but he also looked like he was carrying the weight of the world on his shoulders.

"Hey, Charlotte."

At his soft words, I raced across the restaurant and jumped him, spider monkey style. This...wasn't me. But he was here, and I'd missed him so freaking much it hurt.

Apparently, we were coming out as a couple tonight after all.

Chuckling low, he wrapped his hands around my waist and held me close, warm and absolutely heaven-sent. He nuzzled his nose against my ear for a moment, then called out over my shoulder toward Sarge and Mateo.

"Don't worry, guys. I'm not here to eat. Just wanting to take my lady home after work."

Tears filled my eyes. The happy kind. I was his lady. He was my man.

"I've been worried about you," I whispered.

The last thing I wanted was to be the needy woman, but I couldn't help myself. I worried. It was what I did.

He leaned back, forcing me to do the same. Our eyes met, and a flutter kicked my heart into overdrive.

"I'm sorry," he said, "I've just been—"

I cut him off with a kiss, not caring where we were or what excuses he had for me. It wasn't deep, just lips to lips, but it held a promise of more to come.

"Ahh, so you do have a secret love life." Mateo chuckled from my right.

Ian stiffened.

Grinning, I cradled my bag man's face between my hands. "Ignore him. He's just jealous because he can't figure out how to get *his* lady."

Mateo snickered to himself but didn't reply—probably because he knew I was right.

Instead of bantering with me, or asking who Mateo's girl was, Ian lost his smile and searched my face, as though he were trying to memorize every inch of me. It sent an unwanted chill up my spine and made me want to hold on to him even tighter too.

"You sure everything's okay?" I asked. "I didn't hear from you yesterday."

"Yeah." He grabbed my right hand, squeezing softly. "Everything's great."

I wasn't sure how I knew it, but I did. Ian was lying to me about something. Something big.

I swallowed hard, but the lump in my throat wouldn't go away. "Are you sure?"

"Yes. I'm sorry for being weird." He released a long breath and then shot me a sweet smile. I knew it wasn't entirely genuine because it didn't reach the corner of his eyes. "I've just been missing my lady." Then he leaned closer and pressed his mouth to my ear. "She's got these phenomenal curves that I kind of want to worship by candlelight."

"She sounds terrible." I bit my bottom lip, fighting a grin.

"Mmm, far from." He pulled back, kissed my nose, and then moved to sit on a stool by the counter. With no hesitation, he tugged me in between his legs. The move was so natural I didn't think anything of it.

Still, his odd behavior lingered in the back of my mind. "Are you sure you're okay?" I traced the line of his jaw, his delicious stubble prickling my fingertip.

He didn't answer right away. Instead, he kissed my wrist, then looked at his hands.

"Did something happen?" I tried again, lowering my voice. "In New York, I mean? We didn't really get to talk at Adler's."

He lifted his chin and met my gaze, fear and sadness battling for control. "Charlotte. I..."

My stomach twisted. "You what?"

He squeezed his eyes shut and blew out a heavy breath. "I wasn't in New York for business."

My palms grew sweaty, and I pulled back from between his thighs. "Oh."

Sarge and Mateo were no longer in earshot of us, but that didn't mean I wanted to have this conversation—whatever it was—with them around. "Maybe we should wait until I'm off before talking."

He ran a hand through his hair and nodded toward the door. "Can we go for a drive after your shift?"

I pursed my lips for a moment before answering. "Sure. But I have my car. We'll have to drop it off at my place beforehand." I crossed my arms, needing to prepare myself, to put up a wall if need be. This was what happened when I opened my heart. When I let someone in that wasn't my son or sister. "Look, Ian, if there's something going on, just tell me—"

"I'll explain when you get off, I promise." He stood and held my face between his hands, stroking my chin with both thumbs.

"Okay," I whispered. But nothing was okay anymore.

During the ride back to my house, my hands trembled around the wheel. Ian drove a respectful distance from my bumper, but it still felt like he was in my car, whispering words of betrayal.

Or maybe that was the memory of Jonah...

"I'm so sorry, Charlotte. I'm so, so sorry," he'd said.

My throat burned, and tears stung my eyes. But I refused to think that this situation was similar. Ian was different. The *situation* was different.

Outside my house, I parked in the driveway and took a deep breath. Ian pulled up next to me. I held a finger in the air, asking him for a minute. Jake stayed with Paula every Thursday night, which gave Laila some free time to go hang with friends. From the looks of things, she wasn't home, but I still felt like I should check in.

I pulled my phone from my purse and hit Laila's name on the screen. She answered on the first ring. "Char? Everything okay?"

I smiled at the sound of her voice, suddenly desperate to see her. She'd tell me I was overreacting, but if things went wrong, she'd hug me close when the tears inevitably fell.

"Yeah, yeah." I sniffled. "Fine." I leaned back against my seat and swallowed. "I, uh, just wanted to let you know I'll be a bit late. Ian wants to talk, and well..."

"Well, what?"

"I dunno. He's being strange." I peeked at him in his truck. He'd draped his arms over the wheel and pressed his forehead against them. I swallowed hard and looked away.

"Anyway, where are you?" I asked.

"Langston. An old friend from high school called and asked me to meet her for dinner. She's in town with her stepbrother. They're visiting her mom and his dad. I'd much rather be home with you, of course. But apparently, I have to actually socialize sometimes."

"What a tragedy." I laughed, despite my sudden need to cry. "Want me to make up an excuse for you? You can tell them your cat died or something."

"Nah. I'll just have to suck it up. He's big into photography. Might pick his brain." She paused. "You sure you're okay?"

I shook my head. Thankfully she couldn't see me. "I'm fine. We'll talk tomorrow, okay?"

"Alright. I love you, Char."

"I love you too." Breathing deeply, I slipped my phone into my purse before unlocking the door and sliding out. Ian still hadn't moved from his position, not even when I opened his pickup door and sat inside.

"You okay?" I touched his arm, and he finally turned to face me.

"Hey, sweetness." His eyes were so sad. "Still up for a ride?"

The air was thick with unspoken questions—his and mine. I nodded, my chest squeezing. And though I wanted to ask against what was wrong, I was suddenly too scared to speak.

Ian blew out a shaky breath and sat back. But instead of putting the truck in reverse like I'd assumed, he remained parked. He leaned over and opened the compartment between us. Slowly, he pulled out what looked to be some trashy, celeb magazine and settled it on my lap.

I frowned at him, then looked at the cover. It was the same tabloid I'd read the first day I'd met him at the market.

My hands shook when I picked it up. "What's this?"

"The truth." He pointed to the face of the celebrity, his hands shaking too. "I'm not Ian Cleary, Charlotte. I'm this guy." He patted the flimsy pages, his Adam's apple bobbing. "I'm Ian Tate."

chapter eighteen

Ian

Charlotte stared at me, then the magazine. I cringed, saying a quick prayer that she wouldn't be disappointed, that she wouldn't hate me for lying or push her way out of the pickup. The seconds felt like hours as I waited, tapping my thumbs on my thigh, forcing myself not to start explaining. The magazine spoke for itself.

The day after I returned home from New York, I received a courier package, sent overnight by Stephanie Wilson. The *A-OK! Magazine* proof copy was what I'd expected. Sure, they'd kept the pictures of me with my red-headed, chubby Southern look, but they'd coupled it, of course, with a side by side picture of Hollywood's famous "Tate." Luckily, Stephanie Wilson hadn't mentioned my whereabouts, like we'd agreed. The article mostly described my relationship with Brittany and how I'd felt after being dumped at the altar. It was embarrassing and vulnerable but otherwise harmless to the folks of Sunrise Valley.

After perusing the article, Charlotte looked from the magazine back to me. And then, she did the last thing I expected.

She burst out laughing.

Waving the magazine at me, she stuttered between laughs. "Are...you...*kidding* me?"

"Um..." Did she not believe me? Is that why she was laughing?

She glanced at me, her dark eyes darting across my face. She touched the light on the ceiling of the pickup and looked back at the side by side, Hollywood Tate/Georgia Ian photos in the magazine. "But he's got dark hair. And... his eyes aren't your eyes, and he has no freckles. And..."

She stopped talking. Stopped giggling. And there it was. The realization.

"Oh God." She held her breath and slowly shook her head. "The jawline..." She looked up at me again, batting her lashes. "You're...this guy?"

I cringed. "I—"

"What in the name of Christmas are you doing here? With me?" Her voice quaked, with a mixture of confusion and shock.

I could see her mind wandering while she scanned the pictures in the tabloid. My hands shook as I leaned over the console to hold her face, tilting her chin so that she'd meet my gaze.

This was my moment to convince her that I was still the same person. "I'm here, with you, because this is where I'm meant to be."

Her eyes started to water. She opened and closed her mouth. "But you lied to me—"

"No!" Panic set in, desperation too. "Please, give me a chance to explain?"

Slowly, she shook her head and pulled my hands from her face. She dropped her gaze back to her lap as she played with the bottom corner of her Minka's uniform shirt. "Why do I let this happen? Why do the men I lo... Just... Why? I'm such a fool." She glanced out the window. "You must think I'm so *stupid*."

My heart beat faster. "I don't think that at all. I think you're beautiful, and smart, and the most amazing woman I've ever met. Please, sweetness—"

She covered her mouth, her brows furrowed. "Don't call me that. Not now."

I took her hand off her mouth and held it to my heart. "Mary is my mother. Adler, my stepdad. I needed to get away from California—"

"You told me you were left at the altar, Ian. That you were at NYU. But I never..." She stared out the windshield this time, lost in her thoughts, lost in my betrayal.

"I was left at the altar. It's all in the article." I pointed at the dumb magazine. "Everything I've told you—well, not everything—but everything about Brittany is true. I swear, Charlotte. I hated lying to you about who I was. But I was...scared."

"Of me?" She huffed out a breath. "You—Mr. Hollywood—were scared of me?"

"No." I ran a hand through my hair and paused to find my words. "I wasn't scared of you. I was scared of losing you."

Charlotte raised an eyebrow, like she didn't believe me. I reached for her hands, but she pulled them away.

I sighed. "I...I know how strong you've been. You lost your husband, you stood up to the old ladies for me and for you. You have honor and pride. Here I was hiding out in a damn grocery story from what? Fame? My career? I'm a big baby when you compare my life to what you've been through."

She blinked slowly, her expression softening a bit. "So why are you telling me this now? Does this have to do with your trip to New York?"

"This magazine, with this article, is coming out on Sunday. It's a stupid tabloid. I'm telling you now because—"

"Because you knew you were going to get caught." She curled her lip. "That's why you're telling me, isn't it?"

"No. I've wanted to tell you since the first time we went out. Since the Fall Fest. And now, especially, because I'm..." I took in her profile, her furrowed brows and her beautiful, pursed lips. "Charlotte, I'm falling in love with you."

Then she started laughing again.

I waited for her to settle down, but she didn't. Instead, she grabbed the magazine, folded it in her hands, and whacked me on the knee. "Ah, this is just great. Freaking *splendid*." Then she started laughing, so hard that she started to cry.

"Do you mind telling me what's so funny?"

She huffed a long breath and turned to face me, throwing her hands up in the air. "You're Ian Tate—Hollywood's Golden Boy, according to this magazine." She snorted, but this time, no laughter followed. "You are, in no way, *falling* for me. You date models and actresses, and...and I'm just a single mom and a waitress."

"Yeah, you are. And you're also the most amazing person I've ever met. You... You're everything to me, Char." I squeezed her hand, the one I still held against my chest, the one I couldn't bear to let go of. "You have to believe me, please."

"Why?" Tears welled in her eyes, and a knot formed in my throat. But I needed to let her talk. "Why should I believe you when all you've done is lie to me? This entire time, Ian. I don't understand."

"Because it's the truth." I wiped her wet cheek, thankful she still let me touch her. That had to be a good sign. "We have something special here, can't you feel it?"

After a long pause, she squinted at me. "Wait. Didn't you win, like, an Academy Award or something?"

I shrugged. "None of that matters to me. All I want is for you to give me a chance, as Ian Tate." I tried my mother's line. "I'm the same person, Char, with the same heart that beats only for you."

She dropped the magazine and slipped her purse over her shoulder. "I don't know. I...I need time. To process all of this."

It was the best response I could hope for, given the position I'd put her in. I let out a long breath, wishing she could hear my heart cracking into pieces for having lied to her. Especially knowing what she'd been through with Jonah.

If she needed space, of course I'd give it. "I'm not going anywhere. I'll wait for you however long you need."

Still, I knew we were on the clock. I had to be back to work on *Murder 2* at the start of the new year. But that was one bomb I wouldn't be dropping for a while.

When she moved to get out of the truck, I held her hand for a moment longer. She turned to me, her sad eyes breaking my heart even more.

"Um, I'm not sure if this is appropriate, given our conversation, but Adler and Mary...Mom...wanted me to invite you to Thanksgiving dinner. Jake and Laila too." I smiled weakly. "I'd love if you'd all join us. I won't put any pressure on you, if you're not ready..."

She shook her head. "Please thank them for me, but I'll have to decline."

I nodded, unable to talk over the painful lump in my throat. I gulped instead and whispered, "I understand."

She sighed and stepped out of the truck. Only, she didn't leave. Instead, she stood there, staring back at me, a little lost.

"I'm really sorry, Charlotte," I said again. "Please don't give up on me."

On us.

With one final look my way, she turned and walked toward her house, leaving me in pieces that I didn't want to put together without her.

As expected, the magazine story broke on Sunday. Even though Charlotte already knew the truth about me, I still hated it. I was trending on all social media outlets, and each time I saw the #BrokenHeartedTate hashtag, it felt like a kick in the shins. The truth was, my heart was fine, but I was missing the brunette with the coffee-colored, sparkling eyes.

I couldn't help but wonder if Charlotte had read the article. I hated thinking that she would learn about my past relationship, a relationship I now knew was wrong for many reasons. I wasn't brokenhearted like *A-OK! Magazine* made me out to be. But whenever I texted her, begging her to call, she didn't bother to return my messages.

Adler had done me the favor of removing all copies of *A-OK* from the supermarket. Besides the online version, and the social media links, the only other place in town where someone could find a hard copy of the article was the library. After the longest Monday in history—working four double shifts in a row to keep myself busy and hiding in the stockroom from the Thanksgiving crowd—Tuesday finally arrived. Charlotte's *official* shopping day.

I woke up earlier than usual at the thought that I might see her. I got to the store before it opened, with a little spring in my step and a smidgen of hope that maybe she'd made her decision. But as the hours passed, my hope dwindled. At quarter to five, the end of my shift, I finally saw her car pull into the parking lot.

More than anything, I wanted to run out and greet her, kiss her lips, twirl her in a hug. But when the door of the Civic opened, Laila got out.

I walked toward the registers, making my way to the entrance of the store, right past a swoony-looking Becca.

She'd been off on Monday, and I'd been avoiding her all day since my shift started. "Red! Why didn't you tell me you're—"

"Not now," I said, holding up a hand to stop her questions. Leave it to Becca to know the truth when nobody else in the town did. At least, not as far as I knew.

"You have to tell me everything," she called after me.

As soon as Laila entered the store, our gazes collided. She glared at me with quiet rage. After she grabbed her cart, she beelined it my way. Her driving skills were even worse than her sister's. She sideswiped a display of Thanksgiving themed paper products, but even that didn't stop her.

"You!" She curled her lip. "You're Ian—"

"Shh!" I waved my hands at her. "Don't say it."

"You." She held up her phone and flashed the magazine article at me. "Oh. My. God. How could you do this?"

I flashed a hand at Becca. "Taking five."

"Sure thing, Red. Or should I say, *Tate*?"

Ignoring Becca, I waved for Laila to follow me. "This way." I led her through the store to the stockroom. She clipped my heels with the front of the cart twice before we made it.

I spun and grabbed the cart, leaning over the empty basket, my hands sweating as I gripped the metal. "Where's Charlotte?"

Laila crossed her arms. "She didn't want to see you, so she sent me to the store today."

I ran a hand through my hair and squeezed my eyes shut. That was exactly what I did *not* want to hear.

"But I have no clue what I'm doing here." Laila dropped the mocking tone. "Where the heck are the roll ups? And do y'all sell marshmallow fluff, or does she stop somewhere else for that?"

"This is what you want to talk about? Marshmallow fluff?" I raised my eyebrows, then shook my head. "Tell me about your sister. Why isn't she returning my messages or calls?"

Laila pushed the cart toward me, jamming it into my thighs. "Why do you think? You're a freakin' superstar and you didn't tell her?" She looked me up and down. "You really let yourself go, huh?"

I couldn't argue. "It's all this Southern cooking."

"And the hair. You know, gingers are in. You should totally keep it natural. You just need a haircut." She reached over the cart to ruffle my head, but I moved back.

I wiggled the cart from side to side to get her attention. "Focus. Tell me what to do about your sister."

"Why?" She raised her eyebrows. "So, you can win her back and then leave her for Hollywood? Where do you see this going, *Tate*?"

I shushed her and glanced over my shoulder to make sure no one had overheard. "Please don't call me that here. I'm trying to keep the town, and everyone in it, off the radar. The magazine promised me they wouldn't reveal where I am as long as I did that article." I pointed at her phone. "Some photographer spied on me and got a picture of me and Charlotte together."

Laila's eyes grew wide. "A photographer?"

"You haven't met any rogue photographers wandering around Sunrise Valley, have you?"

Laila took a strand of hair and rolled it between her fingers. "Uh, no. It's just that, you know, I'm a photographer too... I've come across a few in my day."

I remembered the photos around their house. "You have actual talent. You aren't some scumbag who stalks people for a bounty."

She smiled, but it didn't reach her eyes. "I appreciate that. But everyone has to eat, right? Maybe...the photographer...had to feed his family or something."

"His? How do you know it's a he?"

She glanced around the stockroom as she waved her hands. "Just guessing." She looked back at me. "I can't believe you're Tate. You realize I have about ten thousand questions for you, right? Charlotte's not into the celebrity scene, but I am. First question—"

"Not now, Laila. Seriously, what should I do?"

She tipped her head to one side. "You really are smitten with my sister, huh?"

That was an understatement. "Did she tell you that Adler and my mom invited you all over for Thanksgiving?"

"She did. And I'm sorry she declined. But I'm also not surprised since neither one of us have celebrated Thanksgiving in years."

I jerked my head back in surprise. "Really?"

"Yep. Even when Jonah was alive, she still didn't go overboard. Usually I came to visit, and we ate pizza. Then once he passed, we continued the tradition with Jonah's mom."

"So, what, no big family meals? Turkey? Pumpkin pie?"

"Are you judging us?" She put her hands on her hips.

"No!" I held my hands up in defense. Laila would likely have a conniption if I made one wrong move or said the wrong thing. And since she was my only "in" with Charlotte, I needed to be careful with how I worded things. "Just curious, that's all."

"Well, when you grow up poor and have an unreliable mom who gambled and drank, especially on holidays, you tend to make adjustments." She looked down at her hands. "Besides, she and I both suck at cooking anything other than frozen meals. And even when Jonah's mom tried to teach us, we still struggled. It was always just easier to order out."

"Hmm." I nodded, my mind running with ideas.

Outside the stockroom door, Adler stood close by, juggling sweet potatoes for a little boy and his mom. The kid laughed and clapped, and a bulb flickered on in my head. "But Char isn't completely against traditional dinners, right? You guys just don't know how to cook them?"

"I guess you could say that." She pursed her lips and searched my face, suspicious. "Spit out whatever the heck your thinking already. I don't have time for this."

I hesitated for another second, then blew out a long breath. "Will you help me with something?"

She grabbed the handle of the shopping cart. "I won't betray my sister—"

"I would never ask you to. But I need someone on the inside." She squinted, and I flashed her my superstar grin. "I'll answer all your Hollywood questions if you help me."

She narrowed her eyes even more before she nodded. "You've got a deal, Tate."

Two days later, at five o'clock on Thanksgiving morning, I loaded the pickup truck with the food Mom, Adler, and I had cooked for Charlotte and her family. Laila knew we were coming and had promised she'd unlock the back door for us.

Mom and I brought the feast to the house, sneaking in the trays of food one by one and lining them up on Charlotte's counters in silence. Mom had even crafted a centerpiece for their dining room table and a special quilted turkey placemat for Jake, monogrammed with his name. Laila met us downstairs and helped us set the table, without making too much noise.

As we were putting dessert in the fridge, we heard footsteps from the second floor. I waved my arms around, indicating for Mom to follow me out, but we didn't make it. Laila tried to block Charlotte's view of us as she bounded down the stairs.

"What is that delicious smell?" Charlotte's voice sounded like an angel's, and goosebumps covered my arm. It'd been too long since I'd heard it.

I froze in place, waiting to see her, ignoring my mom as she tugged on my shirt from behind.

Charlotte stopped at the bottom of the stairs. She looked at her sister, then the dining room table, Mom, and then finally me. Her Georgia Bulldogs nightshirt wasn't quite long enough, and I glanced down at her bare legs. When my gaze met hers, she rubbed her eyes, then opened them again.

"What is going on here?" she asked.

Jake toddled down the stairs behind her and then ran to me. He lifted his arms. "Freckles!"

With a glance at Charlotte, who didn't seem to mind, I picked him up and held him against my hip.

"Breakfast," he said, pointing at the table.

I hoisted him higher on my hip and gave him a little squeeze. "It's dinner actually. For later. For you, and Aunt Laila, and Mommy." I glanced at Charlotte, unsure if she'd be happy or upset. "My mom and I made it for you with stuff from Adler's Market."

Charlotte circled the table, then brushed past me to get to the kitchen.

Mom yelled out behind me. "I'm going to go wait in the truck. You take your time, Ian. And thank you, Laila, for all your help."

I couldn't take my eyes off of Charlotte, the curls brushing her pink cheeks and her wide, innocent eyes most of all. Mom and Laila's words muffled like background music as I got caught in her spell.

A minute later, Charlotte looked up from the display of food, tears in her eyes. "Y...you did this? For me?" She looked around at all the foil covered trays again, lips trembling.

I watched her, missing the lemony scent of her curls against my nose, the touch of her skin under my fingertips. I missed *her*. The stories she told, her infectious smile...

Nothing made me feel as right as I felt around this woman. Not a single thing.

"Well, for you, and Jake, and Laila." My voice shook from nerves, and I held Jake tighter. "You can throw it in the oven later. I mean, if you want..." I let my voice trail off before I went into full babble mode or made her feel sad.

"Are you and the McDow...your parents...joining us?" she asked.

I shook my head. "No. This is for you. I know you asked for time and space, and I want to honor that. But I wanted to do something nice too. I hope you don't think I over-stepped—"

"No." She took the two steps closer, and my heartbeat sped up as I watched her. Jake reached out his arms, and she took him from me.

Tears filled her eyes, and for a split second, I thought I'd screwed up royally. Then she reached out with her free hand and touched my shoulder. "This is the sweetest thing anyone's ever done for me and my family. Thank you."

I sighed. More than anything, I wanted to wrap my arms around her and Jake, kiss her on the temple at least, but I refrained. Instead, I cleared my throat, giving her the distance she needed.

"I'm glad you think so. And I hope you don't mind that I gave you a little piece of my tradition." Because I couldn't help myself, I wiped her tears away.

"Maybe it could be..." She licked her lips, hesitating. "...a new tradition. I mean, if you do all the cooking, of course." She laughed a little through her tears as she looked around at the fully-occupied kitchen counters.

I smiled, and at the same time, hope filled my chest "If you'd let me be near you every year on Thanksgiving, I'd do this and anything else you want."

Charlotte studied me with those big, brown eyes. Jake wiggled out of her arms and ran away, leaving the two of us face-to-face and alone.

She rubbed her eyes. "I don't know how I'll ever thank you. Or the McDowells."

"You don't have to. You thank us by accepting and enjoying." Before I said or did something to ruin the moment, I leaned in and kissed her on the top of her head.

"I miss you," I whispered. "I'm sorry about everything."

Without waiting for her to reply, I spun on my heels and darted out the back door, praying she'd let me back into her life.

Because without her, mine had lost all of its luster.

chapter nineteen

Charlotte

J ust reply, dummy." Laila tugged at the sleeve of my sweater. Jake sat next to me on the couch, bouncing his foot on my lap while I attempted to tie his shoe for the fifth time.

We were getting ready to head out for the annual town square Christmas lighting. No matter the issues I was having in my personal life, I refused to let it deter our family traditions.

"I'm sure he's changed his mind. I mean, I didn't answer his text. He's likely got other plans anyhow."

"Sis, it's Sunrise Valley on a Sunday night, three days after Thanksgiving. Where else is he gonna be?" She huffed and pulled her knees to her chest. "He asked you to meet him there. So, meet him!"

"Mommy?" Jake crawled onto my lap after finally letting me tie his laces.

"Yeah, baby?"

"Is Freckles goin' with us to see the trees?"

My throat clogged at his question. Tears welled in my eyes at the same time. My baby was already attached, and

he'd barely spent any time with the man. Out of everything, that scared me the most. If I accepted Ian for who
he really was, then I'd be willingly setting my son up to
suffer another loss if it didn't work out. And I'd be expos-
ing him to a world I wasn't sure *I* wanted to be a part of.

Before I could open my mouth, my phone buzzed with
an incoming text. I pulled it out, trying to figure out an
answer to my son's question. Ian's named popped up on
the screen.

**I'm heading out to the tree lighting now. Will I see
you there?**

Laila put her chin on my shoulder. "It's a siiiign."

I rolled my eyes, trying to form a text that was suitable.
One that didn't scream, "I miss you like crazy. I don't care
that you lied. I'm totally not a pathetic loser who replays
every moment we've ever spent together in my head at
night before I go to sleep."

"Cut him some slack, Char." Laila squeezed my arm.
"He can't help who he is."

I huffed. "You're just enamored by his celebrity status."

"Not gonna lie. My inner fangirl is squealing over the
fact that I now know Hollywood's biggest star, but that's
not the reason I like the guy." She nudged my shoulder
with her own. "He cares about you."

"If he cared so much, then why did he lie about who
he is?"

"Technically, he didn't lie." She chewed on her bottom
lip, not even the least bit convincing.

"What do you call it then?"

She hesitated, eying Jake, then squinting up at me. "Withholding vital information?"

"Same difference."

Ian *had* lied, for the sake of his own anonymity, and he *had* come clean about it. He also seemed to genuinely regret it. But that didn't make this any easier for me to sort through. Especially since I already had some major trust issues thanks to Jonah.

Then again, I'd caught Jonah red-handed in his affair, but Ian had come clean before everything had fallen apart. There was a difference between the two, though the effect was the same in the end.

Or was it?

Had my heart ever ached this bad with Jonah?

No. It hadn't.

I'd been hurt, yes. And I'd been sad about the loss of my marriage. But in the end, it was a different kind of sadness. Not the soul-wrenching kind. More the fear of losing the only sense of normalcy I'd had in my life up until that point. The fear of losing my home, the picture-perfect life I'd always imagined having when I grew up.

Laila laid her head on my shoulder. "Maybe we should just stay home and watch *Murder in the White House* again?" She lifted her eyebrows and wiggling them up and down at me.

"Don't even go there." When I pinched her side, Jake giggled.

"I can't help myself." She tossed herself back on the couch in dramatic fashion, her long hair spreading over the armrest and trailing to the floor. She waved a hand over her face, a stupid smile on her lips. "The man is shirtless in sooo many scenes, you can't blame me for wanting to watch it again and again. Those abs of his are ridiculous." She sat up on her elbows, eyes widening. "Tell me you've seen him shirtless in person. Puh-leeease tell me they're not photoshopped."

I tossed a pillow at her head, not needing the reminder. When I shut my eyes at night, all I could see was a dark-haired, blue-eyed hottie with a chiseled body, who happened to have the same perfect lips and cheekbones as the man who'd broken my heart. Hollywood Tate really *was* the spitting image of Sunrise Valley Ian, at least to me. And though I'd yet to see him shirtless, I'm pretty sure that the body on the screen was the same body I'd touched.

Ian was still just Ian to me. He was the man who'd bagged my groceries, witnessed me at my worst, and kissed me at my best. He was my freckle-faced, golden-eyed redhead, the man I was falling in love with—trustworthy or not.

"Go on and get your jacket, Jake." I patted his cheek. "We don't wanna miss the chance to see Santa." His blue eyes grew wide with excitement as he galloped toward his room.

Once he left, I covered my face. "I don't know if I can do this, Lai. I mean, what if he leaves in the end? What if Jake gets attached more than he already is? What if he realizes I'm not who he wants after all? I can't put myself or my son through that."

"You stop that right now, Charlotte Renee." Laila sat up and tugged my hands from my face. "You're a freaking catch. Absolute perfection. And if Mr. Hot Shot Hollywood Tate can't see that, then he's not worth it."

"You're my sister. You have to say that."

"I say it because it's true."

My cheeks heated. I *hated* compliments. They made me feel all gross inside.

"Can you imagine what his life has been like?" Laila asked. "Brittany leaving him, the constant limelight after the fact..." She frowned. "The poor guy just wanted some anonymity, for himself *and* this town. He wanted to nurse his broken heart at home, with his family. But if the paparazzi had exposed his whereabouts, it would have been awful for Sunrise Valley. He was trying to protect himself and all of us." She took a breath. "But I'm confident in saying this next thing, Char..."

"What's that?" I frowned.

"Ian didn't know what you two would become when you met. He didn't set out to hurt you." She squeezed my shoulder. "It's just an unfortunate case of the wrong time, right girl."

I pursed my lips. Was it that way for me too? The wrong time, right guy?

"All I'm saying is, you should give him a break."

I looked at the now black phone screen, hating that I didn't know what to say. Ian was trying to make things right, especially with that delicious Thanksgiving meal. Yet I hadn't bothered to text him more than four words in three days.

"He did end up telling you the truth too. Remember that," Laila said, obviously Team Ian.

"He did."

"And he apologized. Like, a million times."

I nodded.

"Charlotte?" Laila grabbed my hands again. "Just answer me one thing."

I lifted my head and looked at her. "What's that?"

"Are you in love with him?"

I bit my bottom lip to stop myself from blurting out yes.

"I…I don't *know* him. It's too soon for love."

"You do know him. Just think about it." She squeezed my hands tighter. "You know him for who he really is. Not the Hollywood, Academy Award-winning superstar. Not the blue-eyed, dark-haired man with the runaway ex. You know him as the sweetheart who'd do just about anything for you and who didn't go running when you made a fool of yourself countless of times." She winked.

I opened my mouth to defend myself just as Jake came into the room—wearing his jacket, a sweater beneath that, and nothing else but his underwear.

"Jake." I stood and put a hand on my hip. "Where are your pants?"

The doorbell rang.

Laila snort-laughed. "I'll let you handle the pant-less wonder. I'll get the door." She left the room, still laughing.

"I'm hot." Jake crossed his arms, a huge pout on his lips.

"You *have* to wear pants out in public." I pinched the bridge of my nose and sighed.

"But I don't wanna wear pants."

"That's not a choice. Now, go upstairs and grab your jeans before I—"

"Hey, Char?" Laila called out from behind.

"What?" I huffed, trying to rein in my patience.

"You, um..." She bit her bottom lip, like she was trying not to smile. "You've got a visitor."

Frowning, I turned to see who it was. My cheeks flamed the second I spotted Ian standing next to my very smug looking sister.

"See, Mommy. Freckles isn't wearing pants." Jake pointed.

I glanced down at Ian's cargo khakis. When I lifted my gaze and our eyes met, he grinned.

Well then. This should be interesting...

Ian sat in the back seat with Jake, teaching him how to play rock, paper, scissors while Laila peppered him with a million questions about acting and Hollywood—something I couldn't care less about.

To my chagrin, Laila had invited Ian to ride with us to the tree lighting, and because I hadn't wanted to be rude, I'd agreed. Having him in my car, riding with my family, both terrified and thrilled me.

"So, you seriously know Sebastian Montgomery?" Laila turned in her seat, a stupid, starstruck grin on her face as we pulled into the lot across from the town square.

"Yeah, he played my brother in—"

"*Blue Street City*? Oh my *God*. You were the long-lost brother he'd been searching for. I remember now!"

She clapped her hands and bounced in her seat—a total freaking traitor.

"He's a good buddy of mine. Hasn't let Hollywood touch him like a lot of the guys."

"And he's only twenty-three, right?" She wiggled her brows. "You should invite him here. Introduce us."

Ian laughed and then turned back to Jake. "Oh man! You beat me again."

I watched them in the rearview mirror, hearts likely dancing in my eyes. There was something irresistible about a man who was good with kids.

"Hey, I think I see Tonya and her boy." Laila pointed out the windshield. "Jake loves him. How about I take him over, and you guys can find us in a bit?"

I squinted out the window, trying to make out faces, but everything in the square looked blurry from this far away. Before I could tell my sister to stop doing what I knew she was doing, she was out the door and scooping Jake up onto her back.

Once Ian and I were alone, neither of us made a move to get out of the car. Or speak. The air in the car was so thick we could cut it. Thankfully, he broke the uncomfortable silence first—though his voice cracked with obvious nerves.

"I've never been to a tree lighting before."

"It's a tradition in Sunrise." I dropped my gaze to my lap. "Since moving here, I've never missed one."

When he touched my shoulder, I blinked and glanced at him in the rearview mirror.

"Thanks for taking me, Charlotte," he whispered. "I know it was kind of a bold move for me to just show up like that, but Mom and Adler..." He shook his head, cheeks growing pink under the interior lights.

"What about them?"

He sighed and ran a hand over his mouth. I heard his stubble scratch against his palm. I'm pretty sure that was my new favorite sound. Heat built up inside me, and all I could envision were those delicious whiskers brushing against my cheeks, my throat too.

"They left me. I told them I just wanted to see if you were okay, check in because you haven't...you know...texted or called. Then the second I got to your door, they pulled away from the curb."

Despite everything, I couldn't help but grin. "They're sneaky."

Ian leaned forward and placed a hand on my cheek, encouraging me to face him. "And *you're* amazing."

I shut my eyes, relishing his touch and his sweet words, both loving them and hating them all at once. I'd missed this—I'd missed *him*. But where did we go from there? He had a life far from Georgia, and I couldn't exactly upend my own life to be with him in California, especially when I had roots in this town.

"Ian..." I spoke his name like a plea. The tug-me-closer but let-me-go kind.

He pulled his hand away and opened his door. A few moments later, he opened mine and offered his hand.

"Come on." He smiled sadly. "We've got Christmas lights to see."

We selected a prime spot for viewing the upcoming show. After the lights turned on, there'd be a firework display over the town square, which tended to draw the biggest crowd. I couldn't wait to enjoy this special tradition, especially with Ian joining us.

"Mama." Jake tugged at my pant leg.

"Yeah, baby?" I pulled his hat down over his ears. A slight breeze had turned the night air chilly. At least he'd put on pants—at Ian's suggestion.

"I'm thirsty." He pointed at the hot chocolate stand nearby.

Margie Lincoln, one of the only decent older ladies in town, always ran it. Her grandchildren and great-grandchildren served fresh kettle corn in the stand next to hers. My stomach grumbled at the sight, reminding me that I hadn't eaten much all day.

"Three hot chocolates, coming right up." I looked at Laila, but she'd buried her head in her phone. She'd been talking to someone a lot lately, and I wondered if it was a guy—though I didn't ask.

"What about Freckles?" Jake pointed behind me, grinning.

I didn't want to look any more than I already had in the last half hour. Apparently, Ian had grown quite a fan club with the ladies, and other than Becca, I was pretty sure nobody knew who he was. One of the only perks of living in a tiny town with one market. I could only imagine what they'd say if they all found out his true identity.

Becca, and her friends who'd come into town from college, had been monopolizing Ian's attention since we'd arrived—hovering, giggling, smiling...flirting. They were all young, with perfect bodies, graceful in ways I was not. I didn't wanna be jealous. But I was.

Part of me wondered if that was what it would be like if Ian and I were actually together. Gaggles of women throwing themselves at him constantly. As Ian Cleary, he was still charismatic and drew a crowd. Ian *Tate* would no doubt cause chaos.

I stood, determined not to let this spoil our night. "Ian doesn't need hot chocolate." I curled my nose. "But we sure do, don't we?"

Jake nodded and swung his legs back and forth in excitement.

"Lai." I nudged her in the shin with the toe of my shoe. "Who are you texting with that's so important right now?"

She grumbled at me and shielded her phone from my view. "Just a guy. He caught some feels, and now he won't leave me alone. Total creeper." She stuffed her phone into the front pocket of her hoodie.

"Creeper, creeper." Jake sang the word and danced around.

When I looked back at the hot chocolate stand, I cringed. Ruby stood close by, chatting with Margie. *Lovely.* I'd known she'd be here tonight, but I wished I could get just a little peace every once in a while.

"Watch him, would ya?" I said to Laila, motioning to Jake. I'd suddenly grown impatient. Agitated.

Laila nodded and dropped her attitude. She made a goofy face at Jake, and he laughed.

I made my way to the line, money out and ready so I didn't have to stand there any longer than necessary. There was no telling what Ruby would say if she noticed me.

Luckily, for once, she didn't.

A few minutes later, I paid for our hot chocolate and then walked over to the small candy station filled with peppermints and marshmallows. I grabbed a cup holder, thankful that I didn't have to carry all the drinks in my hands and risk spilling hot cocoa all over my white sweater.

"And there she is."

I stiffened. I knew it had been too good to be true.

Slowly, I turned to face her. "Hi, Ruby." I nodded. "Good to see you again."

She tsked and shook her head. "Such a shame."

I'd started to reply—more to excuse myself—when Edna walked up beside Ruby, her wrinkled face twisted in an angry frown. The hair on the back of my neck stood on end as I stared at the two women.

"*You.*" Edna jabbed a finger at me. It hit the cardboard carrier, and bits of hot chocolate dripped over the side.

Feeling trapped, I took a few steps back. My thigh hit the table of toppings. I glanced over the GOLs shoulders, looking for Laila and Jake, even Ian, but I didn't see any of them anymore.

Okay then. This was all me tonight. That's exactly how it should be anyway. I'd stood up to these women once before, and I *would* do it again.

I cleared my throat and lifted my chin. "Good evening to you too, Edna."

"Don't you play coy, honey." Ruby stepped forward and clicked the end of her tongue.

"I'm not sure what you're talking about. But if you'll excuse me, I need to get to my son before—" I moved to walk around them, but they block my path.

"You're an absolute disgrace." Edna folded her arms. The red reindeer on her sweater practically glared at me. "First, you run my Annabelle out of town, and now you're traipsing around like a hussy? Did you really think we wouldn't find out?"

"Excuse me?" I jerked my head back, confused.

"You're a homewrecking tramp. How could you do that to Jonah? How could you do that to this poor Brittany girl?" Ruby dropped a magazine on top of my carrier. I jumped, causing the hot liquid to splash against my sweater. Tears—from the heat of the hot chocolate and from my own embarrassment—burned my eyes.

"Charlotte?" Someone touched me softly on the shoulder, but I couldn't bear to face Margie. Instead, through my tears, I caught sight of the photo...

Me, with my face buried against Ian's shirt, on the front of the magazine.

The headline read:

**SWAMPY SECRETS?
THE LOWDOWN ON TATE'S
SOUTHERN LOVER.**

Words like "affair" and "cheating" jumped out from the article, but none of it made sense. Ian wasn't cheating with me. He and his fiancée had broken up. She'd left *him* at the altar.

Apparently, *A-OK! Magazine* had printed a "special holiday issue," and Ian and I were the top story. When I saw my full name in print and read about myself as a "miserable widow" and "single mom" who was nothing but a "gold digging homewrecker," I had to choke down the rising bile.

"Someone from the library gave this to Carl when she saw that Sunrise Valley was mentioned. Did you know about this fella and his Hollywood status all along?" Ruby asked. "Because if you did, and you chose not to kick him to the curb, then you've not only ruined Jonah's good name but our town's good name too."

I looked up, my vision blurry. This time, through the tears, I saw him—the man who'd rocked and ruined my world. He touched Becca's arm to excuse himself, but he kept his eyes focused on me.

Cheers rang out around me as someone lit the lights. The entire town transformed into an instant Christmas dream. Seconds later, when the fireworks began to erupt, Edna and Ruby took their leave, muttering under their breaths about me being a tramp again.

I couldn't move, let alone speak. My chest ached as I tried to breathe. And my throat...God, did it burn when I tried to swallow. It was like someone had pushed razor-blades into my mouth and forced me to swallow them.

More tears fell, fast and out of control. I wanted to wipe them away, but I couldn't because I still held the hot chocolate. Its sticky liquid soaked through my sweater, burning my skin.

Margie called my name a second time. She took the tray out of my hands, set it on the table, and offered me a paper towel. I was so numb that I wasn't even sure what she was saying, though I knew it had to be kind.

Ian made his way over. Panic filled his eyes when he spotted the magazine on top of the cup carrier. I knew right then that he had no idea the pictures were being printed.

Still. It was too late.

The damage had been done.

chapter twenty

Ian

When Charlotte's face grew paler than the moon, I excused myself from Becca's group to go to her. Charlotte held a copy of the newest edition of *A-OK! Magazine*, and even from my position a few yards away, I could see the photo of us at the swamp.

The photo that Stephanie Wilson and Oz said wouldn't be printed.

Last week's article, the *only* article we'd agreed to, was supposed to be the end of this. Our deal was our deal, and I was learning to live with it. But this new article in the so-called "holiday edition" was an incredible breach of our agreement. If it weren't for the smug looks on the old ladies' faces as they marched toward me, and the terror on Charlotte's as I marched toward her, I would have called my lawyer right then and demanded she file a lawsuit. And my second call would have been to Stephanie to flip out on her for reneging on our deal.

But first thing first.

The old ladies followed me to Charlotte and stopped, looking at me from a few feet away with a mixture of wonder and disgust.

I held out my hand to Charlotte. "Can I see that, please?"

She looked down at the paper, trembling so badly it almost stopped my heart. In one fluid movement, I took it and tossed it into the trash can.

I pointed at the ladies, one by one, and warned, "You. Leave. Charlotte. Alone."

Then, a little too roughly, I grabbed Charlotte's hand and dragged her back to the car. On my way, I whistled and waved for Laila and Jake. They ran to catch up with us.

At the car, I held out my hand. "Keys."

Charlotte tipped her head back and met my gaze. The sight almost made me soften, but my heart raced and my temper flared. I was mad at everyone—the magazine, the people of Sunrise Valley. Mostly, I was mad at myself for not protecting Charlotte.

"Ian, please. Don't be upset. I know it's not your fault," she whispered. "It just took me by surprise is all."

Upset was an understatement. "Keys. Please." I made my voice a little softer this time.

Charlotte pulled the keys from her pocket, handed them to me, and then wiped away her tears. Neither of us spoke another word as I opened the passenger door and pointed for her to get in. When Laila and Jake reached us, I opened the back door for them.

"What's going on?" Laila asked, her gaze darting between Char and me. "Why were the GOLs mobbing you two?"

"I'll explain later," I said. "I'm afraid I created a mess by trying to hide my identity."

I drove to Charlotte's house without speaking. After Laila's attempts to make small talk failed, the car fell silent, except for the sound of Jake's deep breathing as he snored from his booster seat.

When I pulled up to the curb in front of their house, Charlotte reached for the door handle.

"Not you." I grabbed her hand in a desperate attempt not to lose her. "Stay with me."

Laila got the hint. "Don't worry, sis. I got Jake." In a matter of seconds, she lifted him out of his booster seat and leaned into the passenger side window, kissing Charlotte goodbye. Then she looked past her sister to me. "Lighten up there, Freckles. They were going to find out sooner or later."

I knew she was right, but I'd wanted my identity to come out on my terms. So far, I'd done an awful job of controlling the narrative. I gritted my teeth as the image of the GOLs chastising Charlotte flashed through my mind. How they'd waved that article around, outing me in the middle of a public, holiday event. How they'd said that my life would shame not only them and their little town but also Charlotte's memory of her husband. They displayed none of the politeness the South was famous for. Instead, they were complete savages.

Once Laila and Jake were safely inside, I sped off.

"Where are we going?" Charlotte asked, her voice soft.

I didn't answer. I wasn't calm enough yet. Even though my silence might have been scaring her, I was afraid I'd start spewing cuss words and freak her out even more.

Three minutes later, I pulled into Adler's Market. The parking lot was dark and empty. Only Mr. Forgery's broken-down trailer, which had been there for fifteen years according to the folklore, sat in the lot. I parked Charlotte's Civic, pocketed the keys, darted out of the car, and walked around to the passenger side. I opened the door and guided her to the store.

The place was closed, but I had a key. I unlocked the door and hit the code on the alarm. Without turning on the lights, I marched to the magazine rack next to Becca's cash register.

No copies of any holiday edition of *A-OK! Magazine*. Must not have made it to the rack yet.

Charlotte's hand started to sweat in mine, but when she tried to take it away, I kept my grip and guided her to Adler's office.

"What are you doing, Ian?" she asked. "Can you take me home please?"

Still reeling, I shook my head. "No."

The office was lit by a small nightlight. I guided Charlotte inside and looked at the boxes on the floor. When I found the one with the return address from *A-OK! Magazine*, I ripped it open and saw the latest edition. Embarrassed, I suddenly hated everything about my fame that had culminated in that ridiculous **SWAMPY SECRETS** headline.

In Hollywood, I'd never been one to care much about the paparazzi. I'd see my photos around and shrug. This taunted me though. I'd never felt so exposed, vulnerable, and embarrassed.

I lifted half the copies and carried them into the hall-way, Charlotte on my heels.

"Ian. Stop."

I didn't though. I tossed half of the supply into the re-cycle bin, then went back to the office for the rest. But as I grabbed them out of the box and stood, ready to march them out of the trash where they belonged, Charlotte held my arm.

She looked beautifully sad in the glow of the night-light. Her watery eyes reflected the soft light even more. "Please, stop."

My anger washed away as a tear spilled onto her cheek. I wiped it away with my thumb, then drew her into a hug.

"I'm so sorry," I said into her hair. "I never meant for this to happen."

She moved away, eyes downcast as she ran a finger over the copies of *A-OK*! "Are you upset about the article or because of what Ruby said? Or because...you're ashamed of me?"

I jerked my head back. "Ashamed?" She pressed her lips together and nodded, as if I could actually be ashamed to be with her.

I shook my head. "No, Char. I'm not ashamed. But those ladies—"

"I've been dealing with them for years." She waved a hand at me. "You don't have to save me."

I grabbed her hand. "But I want to help you. You shouldn't have to do this alone."

She narrowed her eyes. "I've been doing better with that lately. It's just...there's a history here."

Her bottom lip quivered like she might burst into tears. It nearly broke me. I understood that she couldn't stand up to them the way I could because she was Jonah's widow. The man had been no saint, but she hadn't wanted to tarnish his reputation by telling them all the truth. I could respect her for that, as much as I wish they all knew that their hero had been so flawed. But I was glad she was starting to realize how special and worthy she was, how much better she was than those old ninnies.

I softened my grip on her hand and rubbed her palm with my thumb. "It's fine to protect your history, but there's a future too. And if I'm going to live here and be with you, I'm going to stand up for your honor, and Jake's too. I'm not going to let them walk all over the woman I love."

She blinked. "You just said a lot of things that I'm not sure you mean."

I silently rewound my words, feeling my face got hot.

Yep. I'd really dropped the L bomb.

My shoulders sagged. I'd just revealed a lot of my plans for us, and probably not in the most romantic, leading man kind of way. Hating myself, I took a deep breath, looked around the office, and came up with a plan.

I let go of her hand, maneuvered around Adler's desk, and wheeled his big, black leather office chair around to her.

"Your chariot," I said, holding out my hand.

She raised an eyebrow. "I'm afraid you've lost your mind."

Huffing, I pointed at the chair. "It's this or a shopping cart." I quirked a brow, waiting. "Sit. Please."

247

After a few tentative steps, Charlotte plopped onto the chair.

I rolled her out of the office.

She gripped the arm rest and lifted her feet. "What in the heck are you doing?"

"Hush up." I grinned at the phrase I'd heard more than once during my time in Georgia.

I pushed her to the liquor aisle and spun the chair. She squealed, her eyes wide with amusement.

Squatting in front of her, I pointed to the vodka shelf. "This, right here, is where I first saw you."

She nibbled on her bottom lip.

"You know what I thought?" I asked.

"Hmm?" She rolled her eyes. "What kind of woman frequents the liquor aisle on a Sunday morning before you're even allowed to buy liquor?"

I smirked. "I didn't care about your drinking habits. I was nervous because you were gorgeous. The first woman who'd ever made me want to do bad things in a grocery store." She gasped, and even in the dim light of the store, I could see she was blushing. But I couldn't stop now. "It's also where I first got a look at that sweet smile of yours."

She laughed. "And then I saw you again at Becca's register, where I crashed into the DVD rack."

"You did. And I was smitten."

"That makes no sense. You're..." She cringed, waving a hand at me. "*You*. You won an Academy Award!"

"Yeah, yeah," I said. "You're way prettier than that stupid statue."

She gaped at me, her brows knitted. I winked at her and spun her around. As I pushed her through the empty, dark aisles, she lifted her legs like before and laughed, gripping the armrests even tighter. When we passed the little refrigerator where Adler kept the fresh cut flowers, I opened it and pulled out a daisy.

"For you." I held it out to her.

"Thank you." Her voice cracked, and I smiled to myself, happy that the romantic leading man role I'd been studying for years had finally come in handy.

Then I spun her again, taking off at full speed to the canned goods section.

"Are we going to the produce aisle?" She grinned, teasing me. "I heard there was a pineapple there you used to date."

"Har har," I said. "And in my defense, the pineapple was super cute."

"Now I have to compete with a pineapple?" She looked up at me with bright eyes. How she managed to be so cute and stunning at the same time was a mystery for the ages.

"You don't have to compete with anyone." When we got to Aisle Four, I swung her around to face me and pointed to the overstocked canned vegetables behind her. "This is where you first flirted with me."

She held the daisy to her nose. "Ian Cleary, you are something else." I smiled when she used my Georgia name.

She snickered. "I was so shaken up that I ripped Laila's skirt and then ran away."

"You were adorable." I took her hand and kissed it.

249

She laughed again and dropped her head back this time. I took the driver's position once more and sped away, pushing her to the frozen food aisle next.

"Here." I said, spinning her around. The glow of the frozen cases hummed softly and lit her from behind. "This is where I realized that all I'd ever need in life were your kisses."

She tapped her lips with one finger, sparing me a sideways glance that was half sweet and half mischievous. When I squatted in front of her, she pointed the daisy behind me.

"It was actually over there, in the ice cream case. You tried to ravage me."

"I did?" I feigned innocence.

She touched my face. Her eyes were so warm, so full of energy, that I finally understood what it meant to see into someone's soul. My heart sped faster, like it might explode from the soft touch of her palm on my scruff.

"You did. I didn't mind."

I held her hand against my cheek and leaned into it. "Everywhere I go, Charlotte. Everything I do in this town. Every moment I've spent here has been for you. Because before you, Sunrise Valley used to be a place where I come to cool off. But since I met you..." I took her hands in mine. "... it's been so much more."

She searched my face, her eyes both watery and wonderous. "What are you saying?"

"I want to stay in Sunrise Valley with you." I cleared my throat. "I want to be a part of your life, and Jake and Laila's too. I want to love you, hold you, and protect you."

She slouched, her shoulders drooping. "But your life is in Hollywood. And I can't go to California."

I kissed her finger. "My life is here. With you."

She met my gaze again, tears forming in the corners of her eyes. "Aren't you afraid?"

"Of what?" I didn't tell her that I was only afraid when I was in Hollywood. Here in Georgia, I hadn't been afraid of anything, except losing her.

"What if you rearrange your life, if *we* rearrange our lives, and then..." She hesitated, twisting her hands together. "I don't know..."

"It doesn't work out?" I gulped, unable to imagine that scenario, but I knew from firsthand experience that not every relationship ended happily.

She nodded. "What if you get bored? Of here. And...me."

"I love you, sweetness." I leaned close to her, nose-to-nose, and trailed my finger down her neck, over her shoulder. "There's no way that my life with you could ever be boring."

When she smiled, my heart sped up.

"There's only one thing I need from you first," I said.

"What's that?" she whispered.

"I need you to tell me that you want me to stay." My voice shook with the statement.

She stood up, and for a split second, I was afraid she'd walk out. But then she grinned and pointed to the chair. "Sit, Freckles."

"But you're the one—"

"Now." She pushed me backward.

I fell into the chair. To my absolute delight, she sat on my lap. Her hair fell over her shoulders as she looked down at me, and I smelled her lemony scent. Of their own accord, my hands went around her waist. She tangled her fingers in my hair and turned my face so hers. She didn't look scared, nervous, or curious anymore. She didn't even look cute. She looked...gorgeous.

When she leaned down and kissed me, I felt like a dorky teenager making out with the hot cheerleader. My head spun as my body came alive, like I was suddenly living a dream. It wasn't like how she'd kissed me at the swamp. This kiss clearly wasn't meant to be the end of a date, but the beginning of something more.

Then, in the middle of the frozen food section in my stepfather's supermarket, Charlotte Dawson squeezed her arms around me, took my face in her hands, and said, "I love you too, Ian."

chapter twenty-one

Ian

Istayed with Charlotte that night, on the couch, falling asleep with her head against my chest once more. If I could have planted myself there forever, I would have. It was what home should feel like. Like the fairytale of having a wife who loved me, living a life full of laughter and togetherness, showing each other our love, and then falling asleep in each other's arms.

I'd had a lot of things in my life. But I'd never had that.

As the morning sun peeked through the living room curtains, Charlotte rested her head against me while she slept. My phone vibrated from the coffee table, reminding me that life continued outside of these walls. Slowly, I rolled Char off my chest, knelt on the floor next to her, and settled her head against a throw pillow. I sat beside her, my gaze never leaving her sweet face as I grabbed my phone. When I saw Fink's ugly mug on the screen, I wished I never would've looked at my cell.

Pre-production for Murder 2 starting day after Xmas. Get to LA.

"No," I whispered, pinching the bridge of my nose.

Christmas was only two weeks away, and then I'd have to leave. My heart ached with the thought, until an idea popped into my head.

Maybe Charlotte and Jake would come with me. When I wasn't shooting, I could show them the lay of the land, take them on tours, to amusement parks, and to kid places. Then we could crash at my place and have dinner together every night. I'd bring on my driver, send a bodyguard their way when I couldn't be with them. I'd make sure they were both safe and taken care of when I couldn't be the one to do it.

Excitement lurched into my chest, so much so that I had to wake Charlotte. Tell her my idea. Maybe Laila could come too. Even though she was nosy, she was still pretty cool.

Still on my knees, I turned to look at Char, smiling as I brushed the hair off her cheek while she slept. When she stirred, I kissed her forehead, her nose, then her lips.

"Morning, sweetness."

She opened her chocolate brown eyes and flashed a bright smile. "You're really here?" She moved toward the back of the couch and patted the space next to her. "I thought I was dreaming."

"Nowhere else I'd rather be." I snuggled next to her and lined our bodies up on the sofa. The fit was tight, but we made it work. I rested my head next to hers on the small, square pillow.

"Come to LA with me for Christmas. You, Jake, and Laila. Filming for *Murder 2* starts the day after, but we'll make it work."

It had to work. I didn't see any other way around it. I needed Charlotte with me. Everyday. All day. Any hours I could spare. I loved her too much not to have her by my side anymore.

She bit her lip, no longer making eye contact. "Wow, I mean...that's so nice of you to offer, but, um, I'm not sure if I'm quite ready to face your career yet." She laughed, but it wasn't real.

I frowned and touched her chin, lifting it to meet her gaze again. My stomach somersaulted at the thought of leaving her behind, but I wouldn't push, no matter how much I ached.

"You really have to go back so soon?" She searched my face.

I swallowed hard, then nodded. "I thought I'd be able to stay until the New Year, but my agent just texted me."

"No, no. It's fine." She took a deep breath and then put on a brave face. "If this is going to work between us, then we have to deal with it, right?"

"Yeah." I grinned, but God, it hurt to do so. "After *Murder 2*, I'm not under contract for anything. I'm all yours. I promise."

"Ian Tate..." She paused. I hated that she'd used my Hollywood name. "You are an actor. I would never keep you from that."

"But I'm not just an actor. I'm an actor in love with you, and you're here." My throat swelled up with emotion.

Then I cleared it, determined to be strong like her. "After the shoot and the media release events, I'm coming back to Sunrise Valley, and I'm never leaving again." I settled my forehead against hers and shut my eyes.

A few minutes passed before she dropped a new bomb on me. One I hadn't even thought about. One that didn't really matter, as long as I was there with her.

"What will you do then, career wise? If you're not acting, that is. Sunrise Valley isn't exactly known for its theatres."

I kissed her cheek and spoke against her skin. "I have enough money saved that I could be a grocery store clerk at Adler's Market for the rest of my life, and we'd still be comfortable." I wasn't sure if Charlotte realized I was a millionaire. "But the next year is going to be rough. I have to be in LA, New York, and overseas. There will be a press junket, talk shows, tours..." I took a breath. "Will you travel the world with me?"

I knew she wouldn't. She couldn't. But I had to ask.

She pulled back and smiled, a whole lot of sadness in her eyes. "Jake starts preschool in January, and Laila needs me around. There's Sarge and the diner too... I'm rooted here, Ian. I can't go traveling with you."

"It's okay though, right? Tell me it's okay..." I cupped her face between my hands, holding her there, needing the reassurance. "You'll wait for me to wrap up this film? You'll be here when I can fly back—even if only for a night—to be with you, like this?"

She sat up, bringing me with her, and stared at me with her tired eyes. They held the only promise I'd ever want from her. "I'll wait a year, two years, however long it takes for us to be together because I love you. And that's what you do when you love someone." She paused and took in a deep breath before she continued. "But you *will* go back to Los Angeles and do your movie things, Ian." Her bottom lip quivered, and her eyes filled with tears.

My stomach dipped. I moved in closer again, squeezing her to my chest. "What's wrong, beautiful?"

"It's just..." She covered her face. "I'm really going to miss you."

I shut my eyes and blew out a shaky breath. "I'm going to miss you too. But Christmas is two weeks away. We still have time together. Last night, this morning... God, Charlotte, this isn't goodbye."

She looked down at her lap, face red. Her words weren't so convincing though. "I know."

I took her chin between my thumb and my index finger and forced her to look at me. "Hey. I love you. I mean it, and I'll keep trying to prove it to you until you believe me. I know it's early in the story for us, but...you're my forever, Charlotte Dawson."

chapter twenty-two
Charlotte

Either there were magic feathers in my shoes this afternoon or it was proof that falling in love did wonders for a woman. The second I popped up off that couch and kissed Ian goodbye before he headed to Adler's, I felt lighter than I had in years.

When it was just the two of us, in our shared little bubble, I could believe that this thing between us was real and right. That all of my previous doubts about making it as a couple, when our lives were obviously so different, could be washed away with those three little words I'd never tire of him saying.

"You look like a woman in love."

At the sound of my sister's voice, I turned to find her at the at the top of the basement stairs, hands on her knees. She was a mess. With her red eyes, wild hair, and pale cheeks, my normally put together baby sister looked worse than I'd ever seen her.

"And you look like death warmed over." I set my late morning coffee down and felt her forehead. "You've got a fever, Lai."

"Yep." She groaned. "Kill me now. Put me out of my misery."

I dropped my hand and folded my arms. "When'd you get home? I thought you were staying in Atlanta all night."

She walked to the counter and poured herself a cup of coffee.

"Hey." I followed. "What's going on?"

"Nothing is going on." She huffed, took a drink, then gagged and spit it back in the sink. Then she groaned again, flopping her upper body across the countertop. "I think this is the end for me. When coffee tastes bad, what else is there to live for?"

"Go back to bed." I frowned. "Sleep."

She rolled her eyes. "I'm fine. Just need to rehydrate or something."

Ever since she was little, if I'd been the one taking care of her instead of our mom, Laila would get cranky and continuously deny that she was anything but okay.

"No. You're not *fine*. You need some meds for that fever is what—"

"Charlotte. Seriously." Laila faced me and propped her hip against the counter. "Stop with the mothering. I'm a grown woman and can handle myself without your constant hovering, alright?"

I flinched. Laila had only ever spoken to me like that when she was a teenager—and usually when something major was bugging her.

"Sorry." I stepped back, losing some of that magic I'd felt earlier. It was hard to be happy when my baby sister wasn't. We'd always been a team.

"Don't be sorry." Laila coughed into her elbow. "I just had a bad night, and I don't have time to be sick. I've got a huge wedding gig in Atlanta coming up this weekend. You know those brides pay top dollar for good photos. I can't afford to miss it."

"But—"

"No buts." She put her hand up in front of my face. "If you really want to help me, could you go to Adler's and grab me some cold meds? Before I up and die right here on the kitchen floor?"

"Sure." I nodded. "I can do that."

"Thank you." She dipped her chin and blew out a breath. An unusual silence sliced the air between us. Until her phone buzzed inside her pocket.

I watched her take it out and scowl. She cursed.

"Are you sure you're..." I stopped myself from asking her the question I wasn't supposed to. I loved my sister so much, but I had to give her space. I also knew that when Laila was sick, everything around her seemed to fall apart.

The parking lot at Adler's Market was full for a Monday morning. Nearly every space was taken. I frowned, hoping it wouldn't take too long. As much as I would have loved to stay an extra few minutes and flirt with my bag man—rather, my *award-winning, famously hot actor boyfriend*—I knew I was cutting it close already. I was due to get Jake from Paula's in twenty minutes. But I had to see

Ian just once more today—to prove to myself that what had happened yesterday, last night, was real.

Before I made it to the front door, a police car pulled up along the curb, followed by a stretch limo. I recognized the back of Carl's head as he got out and approached the limo door, but I quickly skirted into the side door of the store with my magical, floating feet, not wanting to risk seeing him.

Sometimes, but not often, he had to escort the occasional politician through town. Or he *chose* to do it, to look important. Whether he'd admit it or not, Carl thrived on being Sunrise Valley's biggest superhero now that Jonah was dead.

Inside, there was only one checkout lane open from what I could tell. Becca ran it, of course—the poor girl never seemed to get a day off. I didn't catch sight of Ian, sadly. Maybe he was in the back, hanging out with the produce again? At that thought, I all but skipped to the pharmaceuticals.

Over the speakers, the Spice Girls played, singing of having it all, then letting go. A fast-paced, breakup song—something I didn't hear all that often anymore. It would seem that Adler had let Becca choose the tunes on Mondays. I could get down with shopping on Mondays if it meant I got to hear nineties jams blaring through the speakers.

After picking out some meds for Laila, I grabbed a box of premade brownie mix, along with a can of her favorite soup. But before I could make it down the last aisle, two handsome men in suits caught my eye. The limo people must have needed to stop for something.

Curious, I watched the suits part and caught sight of a blonde from behind. A blonde who just so happened to be standing dangerously close to my boyfriend.

My stomach twisted at the sight, and nerves caused my heart to flutter. Still, I managed to scoot behind a low shelf of Cheez-Its to watch. I'd become a complete and utter creep, but I didn't see any other options. Other than ripping the extensions right out of her hair—they *were* extensions—which would definitely draw attention to me.

"Baby..."

"I love..."

"Actor..."

Her soft, pleading words floated through the air. All of them incredibly sad. I swallowed hard, trying to give the situation the benefit of the doubt, but Jonah's betrayal flashed through my mind—like snapshots I'd never be able to delete, no matter how many times I tried to rip them from my memories.

The backseat of Jonah's car, Annabelle's head dipped back, his face hovered over hers while his moans echoed into the dark night.

I remember thinking to myself that I didn't want to wake the neighbors—that's why I hadn't knocked on the window or even opened the back door of his car. It would've been rude of me to ruin the neighbors' sleep, even though my life was on the verge of falling apart right there in my garage. Still, I'd turned on the flashlight of my cell phone and pointed it through the window to see what

I'd already known was there. And to this day, I would never forget when Jonah met my gaze, his eyes wide through the glass, or the way his lips had moved as he mouthed my name in a desperate plea.

That was the moment I'd stopped trusting men. Stopped trusting my heart, most of all. Until now. Until *Ian*.

Tears filled my eyes, but I tried to stop them from falling. I shuddered too, torn over what I was seeing versus what my heart wanted me to feel. Ian wouldn't do this to me. He wouldn't intentionally hurt me like Jonah had. He *knew* how it felt to be betrayed like that, so he could never do that to me.

"The girl in the fishing picture was no one, Brittany." Ian's soft voice pierced my soul.

My breath caught.

No one. Brittany.

Oh God.

I placed a hand over the top of my stomach, but the twisting intensified. Still, I couldn't walk away. Not yet.

"It didn't look like nothing to me." The woman placed her hand on Ian's chest and stepped forward until their bodies pressed together.

Without backing away, Ian gave a nonchalant shrug. "It was nothing. I swear."

My world rocked off its axis right then, taking my equilibrium with it. I took one step back, then two. My elbows hit a shelf of bread, and the plastic crinkled behind me.

I shook my head to try to rid my mind of the awful things Ian had said and the awful things Jonah had done, which melded together into one heartbreaking blob.

Brittany pressed her lips to his and pulled him closer.

I gasped as I watched in horror.

Ian didn't step away.

Ian. Did. Nothing.

"No." I covered my mouth and turned away to hide my sob. Loaves of bread fell to the floor, four in total. Out of the corner of my eye, I caught sight of one of the suits. He lifted his glasses to study me, emotionless. He had no idea what I'd seen.

Or who I was.

I wouldn't apologize for spying. Not ever. Because that was *my* boyfriend, kissing *another* woman. Right there in front of me. And I deserved to *know* the truth—to *see* the truth with my own eyes.

Shaking my head to try and clear it, I began a death march down the aisle. My hand shook as I grabbed a can of frosting. Then I picked up a pan I didn't need to buy but suddenly had to have. I put the frosting, some brownie mix, and Laila's meds in the deep tin. Grabbing sprinkles, I slammed them and a bag of marshmallows into the pan as well.

Why not? Just why the heck not?

And Jell-O too. Jake liked Jell-O. I would make him Jell-O. We'd do it together once we got home. When real life was back. When it was nothing but me, my son, and my sister, all of us living a content life—not a single moment of grief available to eat away at us anymore.

At me.

Once my pan was full and my tears were dried, I lifted my head and walked with purpose toward the front registers, turning off my emotions. Rebooting myself.

Maybe what I'd just seen, what I'd heard, every moment I'd experienced since Ian walked into my life was all
some sort of tragic fantasy. Bitter, tragic fantasy. Maybe
I was so pathetically lonely that I'd imagined all of our
moments together. And maybe once I hit the end of the
line, Ian would be there, a stranger again bagging my groceries—a dream in my head that only I could experience.

Life had been just fine the way it was pre-Ian Tate. Why
hadn't I just let it go? This was what happened when I let
people in. They hurt me. Fool me once, shame on you.
Fool me twice, shame on me. That was the old saying and
now the sad truth about my life.

Running out of the store wasn't an option this time. It
was too cliché. My sister was sick and I needed to buy her
meds. And then I would leave and go pick up my son, like
nothing else mattered but my family. Because it didn't.

I stood in line, still shaking, and slammed my items on
the conveyor belt with more force than was appropriate.
I laughed under my breath too, not feeling the least bit
humorous as I thought of all the rumors that would go
around if anyone witnessed me in that moment.

Holding onto the edge of the checkout for support, I
waited my turn. For all that it was worth, I managed to
keep my eyes dry, though they occasionally blurred out of
focus. I felt dizziness and couldn't catch my breath.

"Morning." Becca smiled as she greeted me.

I didn't say anything back, but I managed a small nod.
She looked at me funny. Her mouth moved and her eyes
narrowed into slits, but I couldn't make out her words.

Didn't want to either. Instead, I nodded, grabbed the receipt, and then proceeded to bag my own groceries.

I was numb. Officially so.

I shouldered my bags and turned around. That ridiculous DVD stand stood in my way, mocking me. In my mind, I shoved it with both hands, then stomped all over the scattered mess with my feet.

I took my time walking out, thinking that Ian would show. The selfish, lonely, needy part of me that had fallen in love with him prayed he would suddenly jump in front of me, hold me, dip me, and then kiss me like one of the old Hollywood movie shorts. The black and white kind.

But he never did. Which proved that my life wasn't a movie after all.

Instead, as I walked out the front door, I caught sight of Edna and Carl, whispering near the limo like a couple of middle-school-aged brats.

"Hey, Char." Carl greeted me first. He took his hat off and pressed it to his chest. For a split second I thought maybe he was the type of man I should be with. He wouldn't leave me and Jake. He wouldn't *kiss ex-girlfriends* right there in front of me. But then I shuddered at the thought. *No way.* I'd rather be single forever than be with him.

I swallowed hard. I would hear Ian out...if he bothered to tell me at all. If he didn't, then I'd know the truth, that we were just not meant to be.

Edna turned to me. But instead of her normal, witchy greeting, she looked on me with pity. That was almost worse than her hatred.

chapter twenty-three

Ian

There was nothing more surreal to me than Brittany standing in the middle of the produce aisle, dressed in her tight pink pants and matching stilettos, telling me she still loved me.

"But Britt. I. Don't. Love. You. How many times do I have to say it?" I hated myself for ever thinking she'd been what I wanted, and then I thanked God that she'd walked out on me. Today, her declaration of love, her begging me to forgive her, made my skin crawl.

She took a step toward me. I flinched when she traced a finger down my arm. "That's okay, baby," she purred. "It was never really about *love*, right? Daddy has a role he wants you to take—"

"I'm not taking any more roles. After *Murder*, I'm done with Hollywood."

There. I'd said it. She needed to get the hint and leave before someone got wind of what was going on and told Charlotte. Or worse, that photographer showed up again.

Brittany laughed. "What do you mean *you're done*?"

I looked past her and happened to glance at the pineapples. I couldn't wait to get to Charlotte. Everything about Brittany being here, in *our* market, felt wrong. I inched my way toward the door, hoping to get her out as soon as possible. "After *Murder 2* wraps, I'm not signing any more contracts. At least for a while. I'm staying here."

Brittany shook her head and jutted a hip. "What are you going to do here, besides catch malaria from all the bugs?"

When I heard a gasp in the next aisle, I cringed. The entire senior population was probably huddled together, listening to our conversation. I glared at Brittany.

"You need to leave. Now."

Rolling her eyes, she switched her weight to the other hip, ignoring my request. "You have a degree in musical arts and, gee, guess what? You're an actor. You don't belong in this town. You belong in California."

She wasn't wrong, but I knew I couldn't explain it either. Charlotte aside, there was no way for me to convey to Brittany the wonders of Sunrise Valley. How could I describe the senior population's love-hate relationship with the younger generation? The way everyone sat on their porches at night, drinking sweet tea. Sarge's Thursday night Thanksgivings. How could I describe that, in this town, everyone cared about each other like family, even while they gossiped about each other at the market?

I met Brittany's stare. "You don't have to worry about me and what I'm going to do. You lost that privilege when you left me at the altar and hooked up with my best friend."

"Oh, Tate, come on." Brittany rolled her eyes again. Fink had told me that she'd called off her engagement with Russ. Still, the relationship had been so quick that I hadn't even gotten the chance to tell them off.

She waved her hand dismissively. "Russ and I didn't last. I got it out of my system, and now I know I'm ready to be with you. We're a team." She stood tall and ran her hands down the front of her pants, like she was flicking off dirt. "Now when can I expect you back?"

"I'm not coming back, Brit. Not to you. Not to Hollywood."

She crossed her arms, studying me. "Who is she?"

I jolted back. "Who?"

"It has to be that woman who's got you staying here. The one from the magazine? Let me guess. A lonely, pathetic Southern girl who makes you pies and takes you to church on Sunday."

I gritted my teeth. I did *not* want Brittany to bother Charlotte. She didn't deserve to be pulled into Hollywood drama, and frankly, I didn't want to share her with my old life. Although I wasn't a fan of lying—even to Brittany, who was the master of it—I knew I had to protect Charlotte. To protect Sunrise Valley.

So, I gulped down my nerves and tried to muster my acting skills. "She's nobody."

Brittany glared at me, raising a perfectly threaded brow. "It didn't look like nothing to me when she was all over you at that swamp place. What does she need? Money? Fame? We can take care of her..."

I shrugged, hoping to throw her off with my sweetness. "Really. It was nothing."

She grabbed my shirt and pulled me to her. "Of course it was nothing."

When her lips met mine, I froze. They were cold, and it felt like kissing a stone. I wasn't into it, but the surreal nature of the whole scene made me pause. When I came back to life and realized what was happening, I jerked away, hating that her lips had found mine so soon after I'd told Charlotte that she was the only one for me.

"Now I definitely know there's a woman." She shook her head a third time. "You're a mess, Tate."

Feeling nauseous about what I'd done and about the woman standing before me, I took her by the arm and led her through the storage room, out the back of the store. Her goons followed us. "Time for you to leave."

Brittany laughed, like everything was a big joke. "Calm down, Tate—"

"Don't tell me what to do." I leaned into her ear. "And don't *ever* kiss me again."

She grimaced as I let go of her, giving her arm a shake. "Get yourself together. I'll be in touch."

I gave her a dismissive wave, knowing that she'd get over the idea of us once she realized I was serious about leaving Hollywood. She didn't have real feelings for me. Probably never did. As soon as her father set her up with the next up-and-coming, fresh-faced actor, all would be well in her world again, and I'd be nothing but a line in her Wiki page under "Formerly Dated."

When Brittany's entourage drove off, I tapped out a text to Charlotte and looked around the lot. Carl's police car had stayed behind, but otherwise, the coast looked clear.

Until a car drove by.

A little Civic with an I Brake for Cake bumper sticker.

"Oh God." I reentered the store, rushing through the aisles toward the register. "No, no, no." The universe couldn't be that cruel.

Becca ran to meet me by the front door. She put her hands on her knees as she tried to catch her breath. "Charlotte...just left...upset... I tried to stop her..."

I squeezed my eyes shut and let out a loud groan. "Did she see Brittany?"

She nodded. "Think so."

After thanking Becca, I ran to the storage room, grabbed my keys from my locker, and sprinted to Adler's truck. I slammed it into reverse, and was about to tear away in pursuit of Charlotte, when flashing lights blinked behind me.

That freaking sheriff. I continued to drive out of the lot as I watched in the rearview mirror, unsure how to handle the situation. He turned off his lights, so I figured he didn't want to pull me over, but he kept following me.

"Yeah, yeah, jerk," I muttered under my breath. "I know you don't like me. Everyone knows who I am now, but I still made the donation to the Rotary Club."

Even when I slowed down to make sure he had no reason to pull me over, he continued to creep along behind me.

The speed limits in Sunrise Valley were painfully low. Every local road had a fifteen mile per hour limit, which, in the truck, felt like crawling. I could probably walk faster. But with Sheriff Carl on my tail, the last thing I needed was him slowing me down even more with some ridiculous traffic stop.

I had to get to Charlotte. Make sure she understood what she may have seen at the store. I needed to explain that I'd finally gotten the closure I needed with Brittany.

I pulled up to the house and parked at the curb. Sheriff Carl parked across the street and stared me down as I jumped out of the truck. It took everything in me not to run over there and tell him to mind his own business. But I was on a mission.

I took the porch steps two at a time. Flinging open the screen, I banged on the wooden door.

Finally, it opened, but it wasn't Charlotte who answered. It was Laila. At least, I thought it was Laila. The woman held a tissue over her nose. Her red eyes watered, and she scowled at me in a way I'd never seen before.

"Go away." She coughed as she tried to shut the door on me.

I stepped between the doorframe and the door, stopping her. It hurt like crazy when she jammed the thing against my foot, but I wasn't going to let her push me away. "I need to speak to Charlotte."

"She doesn't want to speak to you. Go back to where you came from, *Tate*." Laila rammed the door against my foot again.

I winced. That hurt almost as much as what she'd said—that Charlotte didn't want to talk to me.

"Please. I need to explain. I don't know what she saw, but whatever it was, it wasn't—"

"Wasn't what, Ian?" A sweet voice replaced Laila's sick, raspy one.

The door creaked open, and there she was—my sweetness. But her face was red too, and not from whatever germ Laila had caught. "Wasn't that you kissing your ex? Wasn't that you calling our relationship nothing?"

I stiffened. She'd heard everything. "Char, listen. Please. Brittany kissed *me*. I had no idea she was coming. I had no idea she would do that. She saw the article—"

Charlotte held a hand up. "Laila's right. You need to leave."

My stomach twisted. "No. I'm not leaving until you hear me out. I *love* you, Charlotte. Everything you saw and heard today can be explained."

She wiped away a tear. "I'm sure it can be. And you know what? I do believe you. But that's not the point." She leaned against the door. Laila stood behind her, arms crossed, waiting to pounce.

Charlotte sighed. "Seeing you with her, it reminded me. You're Ian Tate. A movie star. And I'm a small-town waitress with nothing to offer someone who's won acting awards and who's used to getting everything he wants, no matter the cost."

"Charlotte, that's not me. I—"

"Let me finish," she said, her tone resolved, like she'd made her decision a long time ago. "You don't belong here with me. This is like some little Southern fantasy you're living out. You think you love me, but you're just

273

fascinated by how different this life is from the one you're used to. That's all."

"Don't say that. Please. I *am* fascinated by you. Every day." I reached out to touch her cheek. "But this is so much more than that."

She squirmed away and shook her head. "You're also fascinated by the small town, the people, the community here. I was just a...a distraction."

"Sweetness—"

"Don't call me that."

"Okay." I held up my hand. "I'm sorry. It's just that you're wrong. Me wanting to be here *is* about you. If you don't believe me, then come to Hollywood with me. I want you anywhere, everywhere. *You're* my fascination, my everything, not Sunrise Valley."

She shut her eyes. "Don't, Ian. Please."

"I do love this place. But I love *you* most of all. And whether you want to be here, or Hollywood, or Siberia, I want to be with you."

This time, when I reached out, she let me touch her cheek. "I'm sorry that you saw that, and I'm sorry that I didn't insist Brittany leave the moment she stepped into the store. I shouldn't have indulged her. But everything about my relationship with her was wrong, and today just solidified that for me. I love you," I whispered. "Please let me in."

Her face softened, and she reopened her eyes too. Whether she meant to or not, she opened the door a little wider. I was about to step inside when footsteps behind me drew her attention. She looked over my shoulder and frowned.

"Everything all right here, Char?" Sheriff Carl's Southern drawl was extra annoying tonight. "Mr. *Cleary*—or should I say *Tate*—isn't giving you any trouble, is he now?"

I clenched my fists but resisted turning around and punching the smug look off of his face. It would do nothing but land me in jail, and I needed to be here, with Charlotte.

"Everything's fine," I said through gritted teeth.

He took another step closer. "I wasn't asking you." I cringed as his nasty breath brushed my neck.

Charlotte nodded, her face emotionless. "It's okay, Carl. Ian was just leaving."

My heart ached, and I wanted to clutch it through my shirt. "Please, Charlotte."

"You heard the lady," Carl muttered. "Need an escort to your truck, Hollywood?"

I took a deep breath, squeezed my fists, and closed my eyes, doing my best to ignore the nickname. "We're fine, *Sheriff.*" Then I opened my eyes and looked at my beautiful Charlotte again. "Please..."

She took a step back and started to close the door on me. "Goodnight, Ian. Good luck in California."

The sadness in her voice, and then the click of the door, shattered me into a million pieces. Pieces I wasn't sure I'd ever be able to put back together without her.

chapter twenty-four

Charlotte

As much as I'd always loved Christmas, I could've done without it this year.

For Jake's sake, I pushed through my heartache and pretended like everything was perfect. But later, when I hit the shower before bed, I'd allow the tears to fall.

Paula stepped up next to me at the kitchen counter and bumped my shoulder with hers. She picked up a plate and helped me load the rest of our post-Christmas dinner dishes into the dishwasher. I could barely hold my eyes open, and I wanted to crawl into bed and cry myself to sleep. I hated how Ian had ruined this day for me.

More so, I hated myself for letting him.

"You look tired, honey." Paula frowned.

"I'll take that as a compliment."

"Come on now." She closed the dishwasher and grabbed a rag from the drawer. "Let me finish up here. You go rest. Sit with Jake and watch movies."

I laid my head on her shoulder, beyond thankful she was there. Normally, she spent a few days with her sister in Florida during the holidays, and Lai and I usually asked

Sarge to cook and cater dinner. After what had happened though, my sweet mother-in-law had stepped up and offered to do the cooking. She'd said she just wasn't in the mood to travel—though I knew she'd stayed for me. Like Laila, she had to have seen how off I'd been over the last few weeks. Since Ian had left, everything felt so mundane. Boring. Lonely, most of all.

It'd been two weeks since I'd ended things with him... and exactly four days since he'd taken off for California. Between my lack of sleep over that, and Jake's incessant need to sleep in my bed, I was running on empty.

Ian had heeded my words and stayed away, though nothing about it felt right. I'd been so angry that day on the porch. My judgement had clouded everything to the point where I'd seen nothing but red. I hadn't been able to see straight, let alone think though his apology. And with Carl there, interjecting himself every minute, I definitely hadn't been myself.

Now I'd do anything to hear Ian out.

Maybe I'd call or text him tonight. Tell him I was finally ready to talk. Then again, his mom and Adler had flown to California to spend the holidays with him. Did I really want to disrupt them? And what about Brittany? What if she was there? What if he'd gone back to her after all? At the same time, what right did I have to be jealous?

I was the idiot who'd pushed him away in the first place.

"Have you spoken to Ian since he left?" Paula asked out of the blue.

I stared at her red Rudolph apron with the glowing nose. "No. Not real sure if I want to either."

Liar. I wanted to talk to him so much it hurt.

"She's a hot mess, Paula." Laila swooped into the kitchen, Jake's Darth Vader mask covering her face and a lightsaber in her hand. "It's making me miserable."

I snorted a laugh at my sister's ridiculous getup, ignored her words, and turned to look for my boy. When I saw him roll in, I grinned, forgetting for a second that I was miserable. In one hand, he held his own lightsaber. In the other, he carried a flat box, wrapped neatly in red paper with a checkered ribbon.

"I'm gonna get you, Auntie Lai." He bent over and dived for her.

Quickly, I wrapped my arm around him, stopping him in place. "Whoa, slow down there, Luke Skywalker." I lifted him up, grinning as I poked his belly. His lightsaber fell to the floor with a crack, and Laila swooped it up, holding it over her head.

"Victory is mine!" She shouted at the ceiling.

Jake laughed, rattling the box he held.

"Where'd you get this?" I bopped the top with my knuckles.

"Freckles gave it to me."

"Freckles?" I swallowed hard, thinking I'd misheard him. "As in Ian?"

He nodded. "I forgot to give it to you this morning. Sorry, Mommy."

I kissed the top of his head, exhaling an unsteady breath. "It's fine, baby. No worries." Pulling back, I glanced at my mother-in-law and Laila. They both averted their gazes, choosing to look at the package instead of me.

Swallowing a lump in my throat, I set Jake down, walked to the kitchen table, and took a seat.

"You gonna open it?" Jake bounced up and down on his toes. "Ian said it's special."

My stomach dipped, and my eyes welled with tears. I knew I needed to keep it together, but the fact that Ian had left me something—with my son, for that matter—pushed all my emotions into overdrive and made it hard to breathe, let alone get words out.

"Yes. But later. Maybe after you get your jammies on?"

"No, open it nooow." Jake pressed his hands together and started bouncing in place again.

"Come on now, Char. Don't leave us hanging." Laila winked, then smiled knowingly at Paula. My mother-in-law nodded right back, a smug smile on her face. I knew a conspiracy when I saw one, and these three were definitely plotting something.

"Did you all know about this?" I looked between the three of them.

Paula held up both hands.

I lifted my brows and locked gazes with Laila, who was most definitely being obtuse. She stared up at the ceiling, whistling the quietest whistle ever.

"Laila," I said. "I swear to God, if you know what's in here and there's a chance that it's gonna break my heart even more, then I will *never* forgive you for not telling me what it is."

She scoffed and looked at me again. "Don't worry. You'll only hate me for a few minutes."

I glanced at my son, the only honest one in the bunch, it seemed. He'd finally stopped bouncing and was now sitting on the floor, his face flushed with exhaustion and excitement.

"Pleeease open it!"

"You three are so freaking terrible." I sighed, undid the bow, and then ripped the paper, struggling to keep my shaky hands in check. Underneath the paper was a white box, one that would have fit a shirt.

The longer I stared down at the lid, the more my hands began to shake. Whatever was in there would serve as nothing more than a reminder of all the things I'd pushed away. Ian, our chance together...if there ever actually had been one. No matter what anyone thought, I knew it was too late. Not just because I'd made him leave but because he'd likely realized that we weren't right together after all.

"Go on now," Paula said. I studied Laila, who waved me on, her eyes narrowed in annoyance.

Slowly, I set aside the tissue paper, and my breath caught at what was there. An *A-OK! Magazine*—the dreaded, awful tabloid that had started our descent in the first place. But the more I examined the front cover over, the more my throat began to burn.

The picture on the front was Ian. *My* Ian. Not Hollywood's version. Not the award-winning actor or the man who was once going to marry another woman. It was the red-haired, hazel-eyed, freckle-faced bag man I'd fallen in love with.

"Look at the date." Laila sat on the chair beside me and pointed at the month.

I blinked away my surprise and glanced at it. January of next year.

"I...I don't understand. It hasn't even been published yet."

"I think he wanted you to see it before anyone else got their grubby hands on it," Paula said. "Now, go on and read it."

I sighed again and began reading.

IAN TATE: I'M TIRED OF HIDING.

Tired of hiding? As in, tired of hiding out as Ian Cleary?

Anger rose inside of me, and I nearly tossed the magazine across the room. But then my little man pushed my hand away and turned the crisp pages. "Look! More pictures of Freckles."

I narrowed my eyes as I studied the photos. Sure enough, there were several pictures of him, all around Sunrise Valley. A booth at the diner with a turkey dinner in front of his face. Him in the frozen food aisle at Adler's Market, leaning next to the ice cream case, wearing a baseball hat. But the one picture that got to me the most was of him standing in front of the produce section at Adler's, holding one lone pineapple in his hands. He wasn't smiling though. He looked so...sad.

"Dang it, Ian," I whispered. Tears blurred my vision as I scanned the article. Even though I felt like I was spinning—moments from falling off the chair—I found lines written there in black and white that nearly melted my soul.

Love of my life.

Forever girl.

Finding my place in the arms of the sweetest woman I'll ever know.

With a finger, I traced one line in particular, one that caused my bottom lip to tremble.

Hollywood's had me long enough.

"Mommy, look!"

I lifted my chin just in time for Jake to point to something else in the box. With an excited grin on his adorable face, he pulled out an envelope.

"What's this?" I took the second present from his tiny hands. Slowly, I unpeeled the seal and found a Post-it Note and a voucher. On the little square piece of yellow paper, Ian had written three words. *Please visit me.*

Then I read the voucher. It was a plane ticket. To LA. For tomorrow.

"Wh...what?" I jumped from my chair and dropped the ticket to the floor like it might burst into flames. A plane ticket that left *tomorrow*? For *me*?

I shook my head at my sister. "Laila, no. I can't—"

She held up her hands. "Sorry. Sarge has already agreed to let you have the time off."

"I'm not leaving Jake. Or you." I focused on Paula. "I... hate flying."

She lifted her hands in a what-do-you-mean kind of way and smiled.

God, though...I *did* want to go. From the depths of my soul, that's *all* I wanted. Not tomorrow but right now. I wanted to go that very second—which was definitely *not* the responsible, logical thing to do. A person did not just take random vacations like this.

Laila scooped up the discarded paper, shoving that and the Post-it against my chest. "You're going. End of story."

I lifted my chin. "I'm not."

"Oh, you are." Paula stood beside my sister. "Even if we have to sedate you to get you on that plane. You *will* be in the Atlanta airport tomorrow, and you *will* be going to get your man. Because, honey, you deserve every single bit of happiness that awaits you."

Tears rolled down my cheeks. "But I'm scared."

Laila cocked her head to one side and started to speak, but Jake beat her to it. "Mommy, you're not scared." He tugged on my pant leg. I sniffled and pulled him up into my arms. "You're the bravest lady I know." His words undid me.

I shut my eyes, inhaling the scent of his shampoo, trying to keep myself from breaking down. He wrapped his little arms wrapped around my neck, charging me like a battery, giving me the strength and power to do everything in life.

I'd never thought of myself as brave. But the fact that my son believed I was made me feel like, maybe, I was doing something right in my life. But to leave it all behind for a dream, even temporarily... Could I do that? Not just to myself, but to my boy? My family?

It wasn't like I'd be gone forever.

In the end, it might also mean bringing something into my life that would affect them all—change their worlds as much as it would change mine. Aside from Ian breaking my heart, *that's* what scared me the most.

Was I ready for that? Was I capable of picking up the shattered pieces of myself *and* my family if we all got broken in the end?

Yeah. I think I am.

I blew out a breath, slow and steady before I spoke. "Laila?"

"Yeah?" She pressed her hands together, holding them beneath her chin like she was praying.

"I think I'm gonna need to borrow your suitcase."

chapter twenty-five

Charlotte

I stood outside the LAX airport, bouncing on the ends of my boots and looking left to right. Taxis galore lined up along the curb, but every time I started toward one, another supermodel looking lady, or some buffoon in a suit, would inevitably beat me to it. In the six years I'd been away from Chicago, I'd forgotten how the whole hail a taxi thing worked.

That just added to my already crap-tastic adventures in traveling.

After bad weather delayed my flight—which included a huge amount of turbulence that made me spill wine on my sundress—I'd landed in LA sans my sanity and my sister's luggage. Somehow, between Atlanta and LAX. my sister's suitcase—with all my stuff—had gone missing.

Still, I tried to focus on the positives. Like the fact that I was currently in the same city as Ian again. It was time to find him. Apologize profusely. And maybe—hopefully—kiss the absolute heck out of his freckled face and full lips.

Now, if I could just get my taxi skills back.

Chin high, I channeled my inner Laila and approached a cab driver with a mustache. He was tall and skinny, with pale, gaunt cheek. A cigarette hung from his mouth as he leaned against the hood of his taxi.

"Excuse me, sir. Are you on duty?

He lifted his shaggy brows, looked me over—my stained sundress, my crusty brown boots, and my dark, unruly curls—then stubbed out his cigarette beneath his shoe. "Where ya headed?"

I spouted off the name of Ian's studio. Since I hadn't actually called Ian to let him know I was coming, I was kind of lost when it came to finding his home. My sister, thanks to her PI skills when it came to stalking celebrities, knew exactly where his film was being produced, so she had suggested I head there. With security and all that stuff, getting inside the place would be a whole other issue. But I had to try, dang it. I had to make it seem like I was worthy of being in his world.

"Got any luggage?" The man opened the back door for me.

I clicked my tongue, narrowed my eyes, and slid into my seat. "No, actually. I don't."

He stared at the stain in the middle of my dress again, then shrugged. *Jerk.* "Alright then. Let's get you where you need to be."

Twenty-five minutes later, we got stuck in traffic along some major freeway. My stomach twisted with nausea, from both nerves and the fact that the cab smelled like BO. Part of me wanted to get on out of the cab and walk whatever distance was left.

But then my phone pinged, thankfully stopping me from making another idiot mistake. I smile to see Laila's face, something familiar in this unfamiliar place.

Assuming you made it in one piece?

I shook my head. "Hardly." **Will call you soon. Love you. Give Jake a kiss for me.**

Go get your man. <3

Who would've thought that this was where my life would end up? Thoughts of Jonah ran through my head just then. His laugh, mostly, how it always cheered me up, even when we both knew our marriage was over. He'd constantly told me I was a little crazy, in the best possible way. I'd never really understood what he'd meant until now. Because I'd most definitely shown my crazy by flying across the country to declare my love to an actor who, for some reason, seemed to love me.

Traffic eased up on the highway, and before I knew it, we'd exited onto a main street downtown.

"How much longer do we have, you think?" I asked the driver as I glanced at the time on my cell phone. It was close to three.

According to Laila's stalking abilities, Ian was scheduled to be shooting until five. That meant I had two more hours to make my way—somehow—into the studio.

"We're here," he said, pointing to a long row of buildings up ahead. A black cast iron gate, maybe ten feet tall, surrounded it. My heart thudded even louder in my ears. Seeing the sign for Rose Hill Studios made this all the more real...not to mention terrifying.

"They've got heavy security up front. Most fans tend to linger along the west side of the gates. You want me to drop you off there?"

Crap. I'd have to hang with the *fans*? How'd I not think of that? "Sure, that's fine."

Knowing it'd be a long shot, I typed up a text to Ian, quick and simple.

I'm here at your studio. Right now. Can you come outside the gates and meet me?

This could go a lot of different ways though. One, in my favor—he'd rush through the gates and sweep me up into his arms, spinning me in a circle. It would be a fitting Hollywood romance since we were, in fact, on the set of a movie. But more realistically, he'd either respond with something less dramatic or tell me to go home because he'd changed his mind. Or, most likely of all, he wouldn't even have his cell phone on him.

"God, help me, please." I dropped my head back against the seat, angry at myself for not figuring this all out beforehand. Maybe it'd be best if I just counted my losses and left.

The driver slung his arm over the passenger seat. "You getting out sometime today or not, lady?"

"Oh, um..." I hadn't realized we'd stopped until he spoke. "I..."

I peered down at my phone screen again and saw that my text sat unsent. For some reason, Edna's pitying glance outside Adler's Market, the day Brittany had come to town, flashed through my mind. Then I thought of Ruby, all her teasing and taunting. I imagined her there beside me, calling me a foolish girl.

For once though, the GOLs and their terrible attitudes only spurred me on. In fact, right there in that moment, all I wanted to do was dial *them* all up instead of Ian. Tell them the truth—about me and Ian and our love. Then spoil their fantasies about their town hero, Jonah, and what he'd really put me through.

Still. What good would that do? Paula already felt guilty and pained enough about her son's choices. I didn't want those old women going after her like they did me.

In the end, I deleted my text to Ian and decided to go full-on fate mode. If he saw me, it was meant to be. If he didn't, so be it.

I handed a fifty-dollar bill to the driver and bumbled out of the taxi. "Keep the change."

The man chuckled and said good luck, but *luck* wasn't what I needed right now.

After taking a deep, steadying breath, I walked to the man working the security booth. "Excuse me, sir?"

"Can I help you?" He set aside his newspaper and straightened his hat. He was a good-looking older guy who reminded me of Adler, but with a few more years on him.

With my most charming smile, I batted my lashes and put what little Southern manners I'd garnered over the last few years to work. "I'm looking for a Mr. Ian Tate."

The man laughed. "And so is every other woman in America."

He pointed a thumb toward a crowd of women next to the booth. From young to old, they all stood along the fence, fingers through the black metal, eyes wide, posters and signs held high.

"Oh." I bit my lip, refusing to give up. If I had to push the Southern charm even more to make it happen, so be it. "You see, sir, I'm his girlfriend." I pulled the magazine out of my purse with a shaking hand and set it under the glass for the gentleman to see. "Page seventeen. Read up."

He pushed his glasses onto the bridge of his nose and glanced down at it.

"Turn the page, you'll see. He talks all about me." I grinned.

He quirked a brow. "You a stalker or something?"

"No, sir." I winked. "Just a lady in love."

He tapped the front cover, then shoved it my way. "What'd you say your name was again?"

I lifted my chin. "I didn't say. But if you'd really like to know, it's Charlotte Dawson."

He folded his arms and quirked his hairy brow.

I pointed to his radio. "Why don't you call someone. Tell Ian I'm here."

"Afraid I can't do that, miss." He reached for the walkie-talkie in his pocket.

"And why not?"

"Because you're not allowed on set."

I stiffened, then narrowed my eyes when he brought the walkie to his mouth. He said something into it, but I couldn't hear it over the thundering in my ears.

"How can I not be allowed in when Ian Clear—*Tate*—is my *boyfriend*?"

He jabbed a finger at me. "Don't try and pull this on me, lady. You came in last week, throwing that same line my way. I know who you are. Now do yourself a favor and leave. Otherwise, I'm gonna call the cops."

My jaw dropped. I pressed a hand over my chest, willing my heart to slow. "With all due respect, I was in Sunrise Valley, Georgia just a week ago, sir, waiting tables. I remember because Turkey Thursday was dead, and Sarge was complaining about Mateo..."

Great. And now I'm rambling. "Whatever. Never mind." I shook my head. "I assure you, I'm not the person you think I am, and when Ian finds out you wouldn't let me in, he won't be happy."

An older woman stepped up beside me, her eyes flitting between me and the gentlemen. "Excuse me but are you an actress?" she asked me.

I shook my head and studied her wrinkled face, tensing the longer she stared at me. She was about Ruby's age, but her eyes were much kinder. "No, I'm not."

Her shoulders fell. "Oh. See, my granddaughter over there *swears* she's seen you before."

I smiled at her granddaughter, who regarded me with wide eyes and a hand over her mouth.

"I've never acted a day in my life. Well, except for the time I played a mouse in my sixth grade Cinderella play. I think it's because I'm so short and all. That's why I got the part. Not for the skills, trust me."

She smiled, nodded once, and then looked at the security man, whose lips were set in a hard line. "Don't mind Jimmy here." The woman took my arm. "He's a prickly old thing." Then she winked at Jimmy.

"I'm not old." He pointed a finger at the woman.

"You're retired, aren't you?" The woman let go of my arm and nodded at her granddaughter.

"Just because I'm retired doesn't mean I'm old, damn it. How many times do I have to tell you this, Rita?"

The granddaughter approached me and took my arm, just like her grandmother had. She tugged me back a few feet, still grinning, leaving Jimmy and Rita to go at it.

"I can't believe it's really you!" the girl squealed. She was young, no older than Laila.

My face heated. "Um, I'm sorry?"

"*You're* the mystery brunette from the magazine. The love of Tate's life." She pointed at my feet. "I'd know those boots anywhere."

I cleared my throat, glancing at Jimmy and Rita once more. "Oh. Well, um, hi."

"You two are *so* cute together. Way better than he was with Brittany. That girl..." She tsked and shook her head. "..was trouble. I heard she was actually cheating on him with Russ, his BFF, and OMG, you *don't* cheat on Tate. I mean, he's *the* perfect specimen of a man. Top-notch, Grade A perfection. I think I like him even more with the red hair and freckles too."

"I'm gonna have to agree with you on that." I laughed.

"Anyways, I'm getting off track. Follow me." The girl's eyes filled with mirth as she pulled me around the crowd of fans. A few of them threw glares our way, while others glanced with disinterest.

"So, there was a lady here a couple of days ago, posing as Tate's new fiancée. Jimmy wound up calling Ian out to verify things because she *claimed* to be you. Then when Tate got outside..." She dropped her head back dramatically, fanning her face. "...and saw it wasn't you after all. He lost it on Jimmy. My grandma and I witnessed the whole thing."

I could only imagine the things Ian had said to him.

"Seeing Tate like that... It *broke* us. Me, and my grams, and my aunts too. There's no faking that kinda sadness, ya know?" She puckered her lips into a frown. "We're his biggest fans, by the way. I run the Tate Fan Club, and these lovely ladies..." We stopped in front of two other women who were middle aged with black hair. Twins, I guessed. "...are my aunts. They're just as obsessed with Tate as me and Grams are."

"It *is* her." The one on the left said, wiping something—a tear?—from under her eyes. She moved forward, arms outstretched.

"Do *not* hug the fiancée, Aunt Lily." The girl wagged a finger in warning.

"I'm not Ian's fiancée," I said.

The girl winked. "Oh, but you will be."

"He declared it as a fact in front of *everyone* that day," the other twin said. "It was so utterly romantic..." She held her clasped palms to her chin and sighed.

Emotions clogged my throat, and my eyes welled with tears. "He, um... He said that?"

293

The young girl nodded quickly. "He did. Which is exactly why we *have* to get you inside." She paused. "I'm Shay, by the way. Short for Shayla."

I looked at Shay, relaxing despite the circumstances. I didn't know her, but I liked her already. "I'm Charlotte. It's nice to meet you"

"I know who you are." She scoffed. "Now, let's get you to your man."

"How?" I blinked away the tears and held my shoulders back and my head high. "This place is built like Fort Knox."

Shay tucked her arm through mine again, then nodded toward another security booth a few feet away. "Kind of helps that my boyfriend is *also* a guard here. He'll get you inside, no worries."

My heart leapt into my throat. Talk about Fate having a hand in my life. *Jeez*. "Why are you doing this for me?"

In all my life, nobody had ever really gone out of their way to help me. Especially strangers. Maybe California had done something sweet to the souls of its residents.

"I'm a romantic. I love to see happy endings unfold, and I love it even more if I get to help make it happen, especially with my favorite actor."

A few minutes later, I sat in a golf cart with Shay's security guard boyfriend. She'd taken his spot in his booth, which sat on the least busy side of the property. She'd slipped on a pair of dark sunglasses and tucked her blonde hair up into her boyfriend's hat. I had to wonder if they'd done something like this before.

The boyfriend, whose name was Spike, didn't question my identity when I offered it. With his California blond hair and bright blue eyes, he was the epitome of a surfer boy, without a care in the world.

He stopped in front of the furthest building on our right, about a half mile inside the gates. "You're gonna wanna go in there." He handed me a set of keys. "Use these. But I need them back."

I frowned. "This is illegal. You could lose your job."

"Probably." He curled one side of his mouth into a lazy smile. "But what Shay says goes in my world."

To be the center of someone's universe like that, to the point where they'd risk their job and stability, wasn't something I was familiar with.

There again, wasn't Ian willing to do the same for me?

Yes. He was. Which is why I was here, willing to get arrested just so I could see him again.

"Up until now, I've never done anything illegal. Except for this one time when I was in high school. Me and my sister, Laila, were protesting..." His eyes glazed over at my babbling. "Never mind." I sighed, trying to rein in my nerves.

Spike jingled the keys in front of my face and winked. "No worries. If you are who you say you are, Tate will keep you safe."

"Thank you." I nodded and lifted my hand, watching as he set the keys in my palm.

"Now, when you get inside, you'll hit the utility closet first thing on the right. Go in there; it's open. You'll climb the shelves to the top, then push through a vent in the ceiling. You're small enough that you'll fit—"

"A vent?" I blinked. "You want me to climb into a vent."

He nodded and furrowed his brows. "Yeah. I mean, you can't just walk right in the front door. There's no access pass around your neck. I'm a miracle worker on my good days, but even I can't do that for you. "

I covered my eyes. "Sweet Jesus…"

"Huh?"

"Nothing." I waved a hand and stood, heart pounding in my ears. "Door, utility room, vent, then what?"

"Crawl through the ducts. But you're gonna wanna be careful cause of the rats."

"*Rats*?" My knees weakened. I gripped the side of the cart for support. "Maybe I'd be better off waiting out front with Shay."

"Won't work." He scowled at something around the building. "Tate always leaves through a secret door in the back of the lot so he won't see you."

Tate. Everyone seemed to call him that. Was that what he went by here? Did he prefer that name over Ian? Since I knew him as Ian Cleary—my bag man, the man who seduced pineapples for the sake of seducing me—it wasn't something I could wrap my head around.

"Okay." I straightened out my wine-stained dress and hiked my purse up onto my shoulder. After zipping it up to keep the magazine safe, I nodded at Spike and told him thanks again before walking down the alley toward my destiny.

"Hey," he called to my back.

"Yeah?" I spun around, thankful for my new friends who believed in happily ever after.

"Good luck."

"Thank you." I smiled through my nerves and then took a deep breath. "I'm gonna need it."

chapter twenty-six

Ian

The makeup artist, Mara, patted some foundation on my face, making sure my freckles were covered for the last take of the afternoon. My scene was dialogue heavy, a lot of close ups and emotion. Mara wasn't happy that I'd been in the Georgia sun without sunscreen for the past couple of months. Made her job harder, she'd said, while swiping a makeup brush over my nose. As I reassured her that the special effects group would CG the rest of the freckles out, I thought about Jake and his nickname for me.

Every night for the past week, I'd been running home after the shoot and washing the makeup off. I wished I could wash the dye out of my hair too, but that would take a few weeks to come out on its own. I felt like a stranger to myself—in a fancy suit, with blue eyes and dark hair. I didn't know Tate anymore.

Being in Hollywood felt weird. During my short time in Georgia, I'd suddenly become an outsider in California. Tate felt weighed down by the pressures of a celebrity life. I missed my parents. The seniors at the supermarket. Becca and her gossip. The peach cobblers and Sarge's turkey dinner. Even more so, I missed the lightness of Ian Cleary.

But most of all, I missed Charlotte.

By now, she should have gotten my gift. The plane tickets were for today, and had she used them, she would've called to let me know. But she never did.

"Are you okay, Tate?" Mara asked, smoothing my makeup with a sponge thing. "I know it's been a long day. But you're almost done."

People scurried around us, checking the lighting on the Oval Office set, fixing props. The director spoke to the prop guy while glaring at me over the guy's shoulder and tapping on the face of his Rolex. I knew Mara was right—we were almost done. But the day had sucked, and I wasn't sure I could pull off this final scene.

"Thanks, Mara. I'm good."

She grinned and teared up. "You know my name."

"Of course I do." She'd done my makeup on the original movie too. She'd been sweet, had even brought coffee when she'd run out for some.

Mara swallowed hard, and her bottom lip quivered. "It's just...you've never talked to me before."

"I haven't?"

Mara shook her head.

How could I have not talked to someone who'd had her hands on my face all day? Who'd been kind enough to think of me and provide me with caffeine? Now that I'd had a little space from the place, it was clear to me that I'd been a jerk when I was working my way through Hollywood. Here, this poor woman had spent twelve-hour days on set with me, and this was the first time I'd spoken her name?

"I'm sorry." I gulped down my embarrassment over my past behavior. "I was a jerk. I wish I'd been nicer."

She patted my shoulder. "You're not nearly as bad as some of the people I've worked with. And if I may say..."

"Go on."

"You seem a lot...*different*...now than you did in the first movie." She waved her brushes around like she was searching for the right words. "*Realer* or something."

I grinned. *Realer*. Yes, I was "realer" since I'd been away. "I feel realer. Thanks for noticing."

"Five minutes, Tate!" someone yelled from the set.

I acknowledged the voice with an arm wave and inched closer to Mara. "Can I tell you a secret?"

She widened her eyes and nodded.

I knew she'd probably seen the magazine with the pics of me and Charlotte, but I told her anyway. Soon enough, when the next *A-OK!* issue released, everyone would read my version of how I'd met my soulmate in a small town in Georgia.

But at the moment, I wanted to tell Mara about Charlotte. To put the words out there in the universe. "I met a woman. She's amazing. Taught me how to slow down and enjoy life a little."

Mara gasped. "That's wonderful! Is this the woman from the magazine? The one you yelled at poor, old Jimmy at the security booth about the other day?"

I'd felt awful after that incident. "I apologized for that." And I'd had Fink send Jimmy weekend passes, with hotel accommodations, to Disneyland for him, his wife, and his grandkids.

The director leaned over Mara's shoulder. "You ready, Tate?"

"One second," I said. When he left, I looked back at Mara. "Her name's Charlotte."

Saying it out loud conjured up all the images of her that I'd kept filed in my mind and replayed over and over like a movie reel. Charlotte in her leather skirt. Charlotte at the Fall Festival. Charlotte on Thanksgiving. Charlotte telling me she loved me.

Suddenly, something behind me drew Mara's attention. Someone yelled. A crash made my ears ring, and I cringed, knowing that whatever had happened behind me couldn't have been good.

"Oh my God," Mara said.

"I'm okay," the soft feminine voice replied.

I furrowed my brow. That sounded an awful lot like...

I spun around and found her on all fours, surrounded by dust and plaster. The cameraman bent down next to her, helping her to her feet. As he did, she reached for the camera, likely to balance herself, and it came tumbling to the ground. Everyone groaned.

Charlotte. *My* Charlotte. And even though she was covered in dust and her cheeks were bright red, even though she sat in a pile of shattered camera parts, she looked like a damn angel.

"Char?" I ran to her, Mara on my heels. "Are you all right?"

She stood and wiped the front of her dress. Then, she looked up.

I blinked a couple times to make sure I wasn't dreaming. That I hadn't conjured her up in my mind simply by telling Mara about her seconds before. But when she smiled at me, and my blood started to pulse through my body again, I knew it was her.

Charlotte looked adorably frazzled. Her hair was down over her shoulders, and she wore a white sweater dress that had a streak of red across the middle. Her legs were bare, ending in her cowboy boots, which seemed to have been tinted the same color as her dress. Knowing Charlotte, there was a story behind that stain. I couldn't wait to hear it.

I took a step closer and gazed at her, looking for injuries and happily finding none. "Sweetness? Are you okay?"

Everyone stared, rooted in place, myself included. I held her elbows to steady her, and so she couldn't run away.

But she stood up straighter and lifted her chin. "Oh, me? I'm fine. I'm sorry about the camera." She cringed. "And the ceiling."

Holy crap, it really was her. Or some crazy version of her that had fallen through the ceiling.

My two worlds crashed together. "You're here? In LA?"

She nodded and sniffled. "I missed you."

"I missed you too." I pulled her into a hug. "Is there a reason you came through the ceiling?"

More of the crew and actors gathered around, seemingly forgetting we were in the middle of a movie set. A lot of interesting things happened on set in Hollywood, but a woman falling from the sky, breaking a hundred thousand dollar camera in the process, was a first for all of us in the *Murder* franchise. Everyone stared at us.

Even the director circled, scowling at Charlotte, both amused and confused. "How'd you fall onto a movie set, young lady? Somebody call security!"

I scowled back at him. "No security needed."

Charlotte looked around at all the faces and started to ramble, her cheeks flushed a bright red. "I fell through the set because, apparently, Ian was mean to the security guard a few days back when someone who claimed to be me showed up, and well, the man didn't believe me when I told him that I was... I mean... I showed him the article and all, but he..."

I took her hands to steady her. "He didn't know you are the love of my life?"

"Aww," Mara whispered behind me.

Charlotte pulled her hand away and smacked my arm. "Why were you being mean to the poor security guard?"

"Ow." I rubbed the spot.

"I said the same thing." Mara sang over my shoulder.

I threw a grimace at her, then turned back to Char. "I apologized to him. I was out of my mind missing you."

The director planted himself next to us and crossed his arms. "How'd you end up in my ceiling, Miss..."

"Dawson," I answered for her.

The crew murmured around us. "Hey!" and "Is she the one from the magazine?" floated through the air, but I didn't care.

She turned to the director. "Oh, um, like I said, Jimmy outside stopped me at security." Charlotte pointed behind her. "But I kind of found my way into the storage room and, you know, crawled through the duct work—"

"You did *what*?" I grabbed her hands again. "Why didn't you call me? I could have gotten you inside."

"I tried, but I was afraid you wouldn't want me here. And, by the way, you'd better watch your tone with me, mister..." She looked me up and down, lips twitching. "Mister...*Suave Man*."

Random chuckles sounded from the crew. She was so charming, without even trying.

"As I was saying..." She grinned at me, and I could've sworn cartoon hearts circled my head like a halo. "I'm afraid I ruined my dress and my sweater. Why is it so cold on planes? Does that help them fly? I needed the wine to keep warm, so I asked the flight attendant for some. And like an idiot, I got red." She swiped her arms down, presenting the stains on her dress. "And of course, we hit turbulence because I think we may have flown through a blizzard." She took a breath, looked around, then kept going. "Obviously, I spilled the wine, which was really frustrating because I didn't have a carry-on. I only wore white because Jake...um, that's my son...covered the colored laundry in silly string and made a mess out of the dryer—"

"Char." I could have sat there and listened to her ramble for days, but I knew the crew wanted to get home to their families at some point. "I'm so happy you're here."

She took a deep breath. "Me too. Anyway, I don't have any other clothes. So, excuse my appearance."

"You didn't pack a bag?" Mara asked.

Charlotte cringed. "I did. But it's lost somewhere flying the world without me. I didn't want to waste time tracking it down, so I just ran to a taxi." She stopped and looked at me. "To get here. To Ian."

I stood up straighter as she locked eyes with me. My smile was so big it hurt my cheeks, but I didn't care.

"So...here I am." She breathed, searching my face.

"Here you are." I chuckled.

"Hey, uh, Tate?" Someone cleared their throat behind me. "You wanna tell us who this is or what?"

I shoved a hand through my hair. "Excuse my rudeness. This is Charlotte Dawson, of Sunrise Valley, Georgia. I love her. She's my life. I'm hoping someday she'll be my wife."

Everyone around me ohhed and ahhed.

Charlotte teared up again, and she took a step closer. "Does that mean you can forgive me? I've done a lot of dumb things in my life, Ian Cleary. But the dumbest thing I ever did was to let you walk away."

The group waited, and all eyes turned to me. I opened my mouth to answer, but Mara stepped between us. "Why'd you push him away?" she asked Charlotte.

Charlotte moved around her, taking my hands in hers. "Because I thought I couldn't handle..." She waved an arm around the studio. "This. I got scared." She looked up at me with her big brown eyes. "Like I said. Dumbest thing I've ever done."

More ohhs and ahhs.

The cameraman murmured, "And crawling through the HVAC system probably wasn't so smart either."

I glared at him. He took my cue and scurried away.

After placing my hands on her shoulders, I dipped my chin so that Charlotte and I were eye to eye. "I'm sorry about what you saw in the market that day. I'm sorry that you thought my heart wasn't true. But from the moment I met you, you've been the only one."

She touched my face. At the feel of her skin against mine, I let out a long breath. "Maybe we can start over?"

She shook her head. "No."

My palms started to sweat. I wiped them on the suit jacket. "No?"

She moved even closer, so we were toe-to-toe, and kept her gaze locked with mine. "I wouldn't want to start over if it means that our time together up until now disappears. I've loved every moment I've spent with you. I love *you*, Ian. Cleary. Tate. Mister Suave Man. Freckles." She looked over my suit and then scanned the set of the Oval Office. "Mr. President."

Mara nudged me in the shoulder. "Maybe you should kiss her," she whispered.

I looked back at Charlotte and smiled. "Can I?"

Her lips twitched, and her face grew even redder. Still, her sass came through like always. "You think I flew all the way to California just to hold hands?"

With that, I couldn't wait any longer. I leaned down and kissed her warm, sweet lips. My world lit up again, and everything felt instantly right.

The crowd around us clapped and cheered.

When we pulled away, I whispered in her ear, "I'm anxious to get you alone."

She nodded, grinned, and then reached up and tousled my perfectly coiffed hair. "I like your red hair better."

I sighed, loving the feel of her fingers on my scalp. "Me too," I said, as the hair stylist appeared at my side and tsked.

I couldn't wait to get back to being Ian Cleary. Red. Freckles. To feeling her fingers in my hair all the time, every day.

When my publicist managed to wedge herself between us, mumbling to Charlotte about a casual, impromptu appearance at a restaurant with me, I knew I had to save her from the madness. The quicker I got this done, the quicker I could get to Charlotte.

"Okay, okay," I yelled to the crowd. "Enough. Don't we have a movie to shoot? Can we get someone to clean up the floor? Someone head outside and stop Jimmy from calling the police, please. Get Fink on the phone about the cost of the camera. I'll pay for a new one."

Everyone stood staring. I clapped hard to pull them out of their trance. "Let's go, people. I have to take my lady shopping. Let's wrap this up!"

Finally, the crew came to life and everyone scattered. I looked back to Charlotte, who giggled, hiding her smile behind her hand. "You're bossy in Hollywood."

"Just want to get through this so I can concentrate on you." I wrapped her in my arms.

She looked up at me as she tugged me closer. "I'm sorry I caused such a ruckus."

"Are you kidding me?" I wiped a spot of dust off of her cheek. "I can't believe you did all this for me. That you're here, in my arms." I bent to kiss her lips again, this time with promises of more to come.

"Quit it," Mara teased. "I know I told you to kiss her, but if you want to wrap this up tonight, I need to redo your makeup." She turned to Charlotte and extended her hand. "I'm Mara. You have the most beautiful eyelashes I've ever seen. Are they natural?"

"All mine. Nice to meet you, Mara," Charlotte answered.

I pulled Charlotte to my side, not wanting to separate from her. "Will you stay and watch?"

"There's nowhere else I'd rather be."

I led her to one of the canvas-style director's chairs and held her hand as she hopped up. Then I kissed her fingers. "Thank you for coming."

She pushed her hair back over her shoulder. "Your gift. The magazine... I loved it. You don't have to, you know. You don't have to give this all up. We can make it work—"

"I wouldn't be giving anything up, sweetness. I'd be gaining a whole lot. You, Jake, and Laila. There's nothing I wouldn't do for you."

Someone called my name again. I kissed Charlotte on the tip of her nose and started to walk away.

She squeezed my hand, pulling me back. I turned around and met her gaze. "I love you," she whispered.

I sighed at the sound of her words, like the lovesick idiot I was. "Love you too."

The only thing that stopped me from planting another kiss on those sweet lips was Mara, who was already dragging me away.

"I like your girlfriend," she said.

"I do too." I smiled at Charlotte, and then Mara, and practically skipped into the Oval Office to finish up filming my last Hollywood movie.

My future had never felt so bright.

epilogue

Charlotte
one year later

Take that—"

I gasped and put my hands over Jake's ears, a second too late. With my eyes narrowed, I zeroed in on my boyfriend, who leaned against the wall across the room. He was talking to Mateo, grinning about something, but his gaze never seemed to stray far from my face throughout the evening.

He winked at me. That heated stare of his glistened with mirth under the low lights of the Sunrise Valley Senior Center. Mateo shook his head, going on and on about something. But Ian was in full on Hollywood Charm Mode, melting me into a gooey puddle. So much so that I forgot I was letting my five-year-old boy watch an R-rated movie.

We'd decided to watch *Murder in the White House* to prep for the sequel's release next month. Over the past few months, Ian had been in and out of Sunrise for the tour junket, and in three weeks, we'd be making our red-carpet debut together. I was nervous—actually terrified—but at the same time, I loved the idea of being on the arm of the dark-haired, blue-eyed actor in the lead role of this very movie.

As far as Ian was concerned, that version of himself was long gone. I, on the other hand, knew better. He could take the superstar out of the limelight, sure, but not the limelight out of the superstar. Which is exactly why I didn't intend to let him quit acting completely.

My freckle-faced bag man currently worked two jobs, though he claimed he didn't need either of them to keep us financially afloat for the rest of our days. A part-time manager at Adler's Market, mainly to help out his stepdad, and a part-time actor at the Atlanta Horizon Theatre. I'd kept my job at the diner part-time because I loved it, so I worked every Turkey Thursday and on Monday evenings.

Ian often said I'd made all of his dreams come true—being with me, in Sunrise, acting small and living large. And though it was still hard for me to wrap my head around most days, I was trying.

"Mommy?" Jake leaned back in my lap and pressed his mouth to my ear. "Is the movie done yet?"

"Almost, honey. Just a few more minutes."

He bounced off my lap, stumbling across the room toward Ian. He'd been back and forth between us for the past two hours, bored out of his mind. Part of me wished I would've just left him with Paula, but Ian had insisted that she come too, which was strange to me.

Rows of chairs were set up in the room, each of them filled with the town's seniors, including the GOLs. Edna, Margie, Betty, and, of course, Ruby all sat up front, gasping with every punch and cheering with every hurdle the President had to overcome on the screen.

This was their night really. Ian had built this place for them. Though they definitely hadn't taken to Ian being in town at first, they'd sure as heck taken to Tate—the altruistic, wonderful actor who'd given them this very center to do all their gossiping in.

It was the least he could do, Ian had said, after claiming he'd stirred up enough drama in this town to last a lifetime. And thanks to a very nice settlement from *A-OK! Magazine*, whom he'd taken to court for their original article, Ian hadn't even had to delve into his own money to bring the building to life.

Every day there would be someone here to run events for the seniors. Movie Fridays, like today, and Gardening Tuesdays too. We hadn't figured out all the details quite yet, but I knew I'd be teaching a painting class every Sunday afternoon after church. Not only would I be getting to do what I loved, and had almost given up on, but it was also the perfect opportunity for the GOLs to come in and treat me with respect. Something they'd recently become accustomed to. I was pretty sure they only did it because of Ian, but it didn't matter. If they ever treated me the way they once had again, I had the power to take them down this time.

The people in the center erupted into cheers when the credits began to roll. The best part about it was that my once upon a time worst enemies were on their feet, cheering the loudest.

"Ugh, these ladies are gonna make me go deaf." Laila groaned and stuck a finger in her ear, shaking it.

"They can't help it." I giggled.

Over the past year, I'd witnessed my sister run through a gamut of gentlemen to get over her musician ex, only to stop at a man named Xavier. He was an actor too, who worked with Ian in Atlanta. A nice guy with a nice family, someone good for my sister. That was all I wanted for her in the end. To find someone to love her like Ian did me. She deserved happiness more than anyone.

Her phone buzzed. She tugged it out of her pocket, and her shoulders slumped at whoever was calling. Instead of answering, she ignored the call, mumbling something not too nice under her breath.

"You okay?" I touched her elbow.

She nodded, but her smile looked forced. "Never been better."

Before I could question her further, a loud whistle sounded at the front of the room. I looked up to find Ian standing in front of the crowd, with Jake propped up on his shoulders.

At the sight of my two favorite boys together, my eyes welled up with tears. I was pretty sure there'd never been a more amazing view.

"I'd just like to thank everyone for coming tonight." Ian cleared his throat, looking oddly nervous as he set Jake on the floor beside him and tugged at the neck of his Polo shirt. "I, um, have something I'd like to say, if you'd give me the chance."

"Go on now," Ruby said, piping in first. "We're listening."

Ian nodded and ran a hand through his shaggy, red hair. It was almost orange under the light tonight. And I loved it so much.

He bent over to whisper something in my boy's ear, and Jake nodded excitedly. I frowned.

"What's he doing?" Laila asked, sitting back on the folding chair.

"No clue."

Ian stood taller, cracking his neck from side to side. Then, he looked directly at me again. "Charlotte? Can you come up here and help me with this?"

I nodded slowly and stood.

The crowd was hushed as they watched me. I passed Adler and Ian's mom, Paula too, giving them all a nervous smile before maneuvering my way through the aisles. The next set of eyes I saw as I reached the front were Ruby's—blue and filled with knowledge, and a little bit of self-satisfaction.

I wasn't sure if I'd ever learn to like her, but now that she considered Ian her newest, most favorite town hero, I'd deal with her. I nodded a hello.

"Hey," I whispered to Ian.

"Hi." He smiled, took my hands, and then brought them to his lips for a gentle kiss. "Thanks for coming up here."

"What's going on?" I bit my lip and shuffled my feet.

"Just a second, okay?" He peered over my shoulder, his eyes widening a bit. I turned to look too, but he settled a hand on my cheek, holding me hostage with his gaze.

"I love you, Charlotte," he said.

"I love you too." I smiled and squeezed his hand.

"Good. Because I'm pretty sure I'll never be able to live this down if you don't hear me and Jake out."

My stomach dropped. This time, when I looked down, I found my son standing next to me, holding a sign on his head. His gap-toothed smile lit up as he watched me from beneath it. On the white poster board—decorated with pineapple stickers—were four simple words.

Will you marry Ian?

"Charlotte. I know I'm not your first love..." Ian dropped to his knees in front of me. I blinked back tears. "But would you do me the honor of letting me be your last?"

I covered my mouth. Ian grinned wider than I'd ever seen him, and in turn, butterflies swooped around my stomach.

This was happening.

This was really and truly happening.

"Say yes, Mommy." Jake bounced up and down, his sign rattling against my thigh.

I looked his way, then back at Ian once more. He now held a black box with a stunning ring inside.

"So, what do you say, sweetness?" Ian searched my face, giving me everything I didn't think I'd ever find again in life. "Will you be my wife?"

Ian
four months later

Charlotte floated through the registers, with a huge grin on her face and a daisy bouquet in her hands, as the music played over the speakers at Adler's Market. Jake, in a suit that matched mine, held the pale green silk of her long dress as she laughed and talked with the residents of Sunrise Valley, the guests at our wedding.

Becca and Mateo had taken care of the decorations, and they'd done a first-class job of it. Every aisle was decorated with the spring theme Charlotte had suggested. They'd cleared out the tables in the coffee shop, which served as our dance floor, and lined small cocktail tables down the frozen food aisle. Sarge served his famous turkey dinners, and Ms. Margie, one of my favorite seniors in town, made our dessert—pineapple upside-down cake. I had to admit, it had all come together nicely.

When Charlotte told me she wanted to get married at the market, I'd started laughing.

"What's so funny?" she'd asked from her spot next to me on her sofa.

I'd scrunched my nose, like she was crazy. "We can't get married in a supermarket."

"Well, why not? That's where we fell in love."

She was right, and she wasn't. I may have first fallen for her at Adler's, but every day I spent with her, in and out of the market, just made me love her more.

I'd rubbed my chin, thinking, as she waited for my answer. "I guess that's as good a place as any."

"Then it's settled!" She'd clapped and called her sister, who'd been on a date with her boyfriend. "He's on board," she'd said.

Laila's squeals of excitement had carried through the room.

I'd stood and walked to Charlotte as she ended the call, wrapping my arms around her from behind. "I don't care where we get married. You know that. But are you sure you don't want something fancier? A castle in Italy? A tent on a beach? A rooftop hotel in Atlanta?"

She'd spun in my arms and pouted. "Do any of those things sound like me?" she'd asked. "All I need is you, Jake, and my sister, but you know this town will go nuts if they don't get a piece of the cake themselves."

I'd lifted a brow. "This town? Are we inviting everyone?"

She'd nodded. "As crazy as they all are, they're our family, and I want them to witness the best day of our lives." She'd stood on tiptoe and kissed me. "I can't wait to be your wife."

Now, here at Adler's Market, I twisted the ring on my finger, already used to the feel of it, and smiled at my bride. When she waved from across the room, my cheeks grew hot. I wondered if I'd ever get used to the feeling. I felt the same warmth of love, right to my bones, every time I remembered she was mine and I was hers.

"Ian Tate. Married in the produce aisle of a supermarket. Who would have guessed?" Fink glanced at me sideways, his champagne glass full to the rim. "You know that mercenary freelance photographer who took the magazine pictures is here, right?"

I put one hand into the pocket of my slacks. "Oz? He can take all the pictures he wants as far as I'm concerned. All of my secrets are out."

"Well, as a present to you and the lovely Charlotte, I convinced him to donate half the money he makes off the pictures of your wedding to the Sunrise Valley local library."

I turned to him, not sure if he was joking. His tight smile proved he wasn't. "Thanks, man," I said. "I know I'm kind of screwing you by leaving the business."

"Nah." He waved his free hand at me. "I've got people lining up for my services since I've repped you. I should be thanking you. I'm actually thinking of signing Spike there." He pointed to Spike and Shay, dancing in the coffee shop.

Charlotte had insisted I fly them out for the wedding. "They're fans," she'd said. I'd recognized Spike from working around the production lot and Shay as my fan club president. And I'd do anything to please Char.

One of the townspeople who'd volunteered to be a server today walked by with a tray of glasses. I took one, thanked her, and held it up to Fink.

"To new beginnings," I said.

He clinked his glass with mine. "To new beginnings. I'm going to miss you in LA"

"I'll miss you too." I grinned over my glass as I took a sip.

Fink chuckled. "Liar."

He had me there. I wouldn't miss LA, and I could always keep in touch with Fink. He'd be busy with new clients, and I'd be busy here—with Charlotte and, hopefully, a little team of Dawson-Tate babies someday.

A pair of arms wrapped around my waist. Charlotte had snuck up behind me. Her warm breath gave off a faint hint of champagne.

Fink winked at me and took my glass. "And that's my cue. Spend some time with your lovely wife."

"Thank you, Mr. Fink." She kissed my neck as Fink walked away. "What are you thinking about, Freckles?"

I turned to face her. "Having babies with you."

A deep blush crawled from her chest, over her strapless dress, up her neck, and to her cheeks. "Oh. How many are you talking?"

I wrapped her in my arms and looked up at the ceiling. "Five."

She gasped. "Five? Are you out of your mind? Where exactly are we going to put five babies?"

Wiggling out of her grasp, I took her hand. "Funny you should ask..."

She furrowed her brow as I pulled her toward the exit. "Ian! Where are we going?"

"Out."

"But it's our wedding! What about Jake?"

"No worries. Everyone's in on the plan but you." I waved to Adler, and he nodded. Then I pulled my phone out and texted Laila that my surprise was in motion.

The long, white stretch limo sat right where I'd planned. Carl, dressed in his sheriff's getup, balanced his police motorcycle between his legs—right in front of the limo, ready to give us an escort.

Charlotte froze when she saw the limo. "What the..."

"Your chariot."

"But—"

"No worries. Jake's taken care of. Trust me, okay?" I held out my hand.

Charlotte looked at me, her big, brown eyes reflecting a glint from the late afternoon sun. A strand of her hair, tired of being held up in a twist, fell down her cheek. She pushed it over her ear with her delicate hand. I marveled at her beauty. I'd remember this, my wedding day, forever.

The driver had come to open the door for us. I gave Carl a thumbs-up sign as we climbed into the limo. She leaned forward and talked through the screen. "Where are you taking us, sir?"

"No, no, no," I said. "No cheating. It's a surprise." I shut the privacy screen and scooted closer to her. Finally, I had her full attention. I ran a finger over the silky skirt, from her hip to her knee. "This is the first I've gotten you alone all day. Wanna make out, wife?"

She nodded. "Yes I do, husband." And she kissed me. Hard. "Maybe we could just go home?"

I laughed against her lips. "Yeah, sweetness. Let's do that. Let's go home."

We kissed until the driver stopped the limo and opened the door for us. I hadn't been nervous all day—not when we'd said our vows, not when we'd danced our first dance as husband and wife, not when the townspeople had offered their congratulations as they accepted me as the second husband of their town hero's widow. But at that moment, as I stepped out of the limo, my hands shook and my palms started sweating.

I held Charlotte's hand and helped her step out. She mumbled about being dressed up and her heels hurting, but I couldn't talk. I just waited.

She looked up at the house. "Um, Ian? Why are we at the old Orchard Mills Estate?"

The large, white mansion sat on a hill of green. A line of tall oaks spread the length of the dirt road to the house. I held her hand and started walking down the path, under the shade of the trees. "I heard you liked this place."

She smiled, pushing that strand of hair back again. "I do. I remember seeing this place the first time Jonah drove me through Sunrise Valley. It hasn't been occupied in years though."

I grinned and glanced at her sideways. "There are enough bedrooms for five kids. And Jake. Laila, too, if she's interested."

She stopped walking.

I held my breath.

"What do you mean?" she asked.

I inhaled deeply, then spurted it all out in one breath. "I bought it for us, for our family. There's a back house that Laila can have. A pool for Jake. A huge kitchen. There's even a gardener's shed that I sort of had turned into an art studio for you. I don't know..." I ran my hand through my hair. "I thought maybe you'd like the idea..."

I braved a glance at her face. Her eyes were shiny with tears. I knew it had been a risky move—buying a home together should have been a joint project. I should have known that a huge place like this wouldn't be her style. "If you hate it, we can stay at your place—"

"I love it." One of those tears fell and her voice shook.

I reached to wipe it. "You...do? Are you sure?"

"Sweet Jesus, Ian! Of course I love it!"

Then she shook off her heels and ran down the path. I chased her, laughing, until we got to the house. Panting, we ran up the steps and stood on the porch, in front of the big red front door.

Charlotte turned to me, catching her breath. "It's really ours?"

I nodded, the knot in my chest loosening the longer I looked at her smiling face. She seemed happy. That was all I ever wanted to do—make her happy. "I closed on it a couple of months ago. I had to make the realtor promise to keep it a secret—gave her some hush money."

I didn't tell Charlotte that I had paid her a double finder's fee to keep me anonymous and had bribed Laila with the promise of a trip to Hollywood to stay silent. Mom had said that word of the sale was out around the Sunrise Valley Seniors' Facebook page, and there'd been speculation that I'd bought it. Apparently, Charlotte had no idea, and that was the only thing I cared about.

"But it's not ours yet. Not until we make it ours. There's a lot of remodeling going on, but it's waiting for your input for final touches. I hung some of your painting too." I was anxious to show her the paintings that Laila and I had dug out of storage. They gave the place life and color. "Want to see inside?"

Charlotte gazed over the front grounds, turning to look from one side of the property to the other, until she'd spun in a complete circle. "Not yet. Can we stand here for a minute? Watch the sunset together?"

The request was simple and beautiful, just like her. A husband and wife, partners for life, enjoying the first sunset of the rest of their days together.

"I like that idea." I took her hands in mine and pulled her to me for a kiss.

"Ian?" she murmured between kisses.

"Hmm?"

"You're my dream come true." She rested her head against my chest.

I held her, there, on the front porch that would be the site of so many things in our future, while the sky turned pink and orange. I imagined bringing Jake there for the first time. Hosting Adler and Mom for some sweet tea. Carrying in our first baby. Jumping over Jake's bicycle, which would undoubtedly be left on the stairs. Maybe someday Laila would get married on the grounds, or Jake, or any one of our future kids.

"And you're mine, sweetness. I can't wait to start our life together."

Later, when the sun set over the horizon, I lifted her into my arms and carried her over the threshold.

We never made it back to Adler's Market that night for the rest of our wedding reception, but we had a lot of fun checking out the rooms of our new house. Every smile she flashed me, every time she touched me, my life's purpose grew clearer.

Charlotte had become a part of me. A part of my heart. A part of my soul. And now, my entire future.

THE END

acknowledgements
Heather Van Fleet

Without Jessica, Heather would definitely not be here writing this dedication. Ian and Charlotte's story was meant to be Heather and Jess' since the idea first hit, and there's no one Heather would rather have in her corner, co-writing wise. Jessica is the best friend a girl could as for, and though they live hundreds of miles apart, they are forever going to be attached at the virtual hip.

A special shout out and thank you to Heather's husband and three daughters. They are her backbone, and she loves them to the moon and back.

Jessica Calla

Jessica would like to thank Heather, first and foremost, for being a swooning klutz at the grocery store and coming up with the idea for *Love in the Aisles* (also for being a great friend and mentor, a wonderful co-writer and commiserator, and an all-around awesome person!).

As always, Jessica is thankful for the time and dedication of her readers, the support and advice of her author friends, and for all lovers of romance!

A special thank you is reserved for Tenacious Books Publishing, for believing in Ian and Charlotte's story, and to Erin Rhew, the most amazing editor ever.

Most of all, Jessica is grateful she has a wonderful family in her corner, rooting for her and inspiring her to follow her dreams.

about the authors

Heather Van Fleet

Heather Van Fleet is a stay-at-home-mom turned book boyfriend connoisseur. She's married to her high school sweetheart, a mom to three girls, and in her spare time you can find her with her head buried in her Kindle, guzzling down copious amounts of coffee.

Heather graduated from Black Hawk College in 2003 and currently writes Adult contemporary romance. She is published through Sourcebooks Casablanca with her Reckless Hearts series and Bookouture with her Red Dragon series.

Jessica Calla

Jessica Calla is a New Adult and Contemporary romance author who moonlights during the day as an attorney. If she's not writing, lawyering, or parenting, you'll most likely find her at the movies, scrolling through her Twitter feed, or gulping down various forms of caffeine (sometimes all three at once).

Jessica is a member of the Women's Fiction Writers Association. She's volunteered as a mentor in the PitchWars contest for unpublished works, and loves helping out the writing community any way she can. A Jersey girl through and through, Jessica resides in the central part of the state with her husband, two sons, and dog.

One of our favorite things about being writers is building relationships with readers.
We occasionally send out newsletters with details on new releases, information on how to become part of our advanced reader team, as well as subscriber-only material.

If you sign up for the mailing list, you'll get a Tenacious Books Starter kit which includes a free, award-winning novel.

You can get your **free** book by scanning the above QR code with your smartphone.

Alternately, you can register at:
http://www.TenaciousBooksPublishing.com/News-letter-SignUp.html

Thank you for being a
Tenacious Books Reader!

www.TenaciousBooksPublishing.com